YOUR BROTHER'S BLOOD

YOUR BROTHER'S BLOOD

David Towsey

Jo Fletcher

New York • London

JF

Jo Fletcher Books
An imprint of Quercus
New York • London

ISBN 978-1-62365-659-1

Library of Congress Control Number: 2015950131

Distributed in the United States and Canada by
Hachette Book Group
1290 Avenue of the Americas
New York, NY 10104

Manufactured in the United States

10 9 8 7 6 5 4 3 2 1

www.quercus.com

For my family

Patterns are most pleasing to the senses. Man is a creature of pattern; he understands them, seeks them everywhere, longs for them even when he dreams. They occur naturally and are thought to be beautiful. In literature, a narrative pattern gives a reader a sense of self-importance—he or she is sharp-witted and astute for finding and understanding it. In music, the repetition of notes speaks inherently to the primitive nature of the tribal self.

I argue that every action—be it day by day or century by century—follows this preoccupation with patterns.

At one time, humanity lost a great deal of its intellectual power and dominance over the world. Some historians place this event eight hundred years ago, others only seven hundred, more suggest closer to a thousand. I mean no offence to any historian present when I say: that argument is irrelevant.

At one time, there were tools, devices, and mechaniks everywhere. They influenced every element of life, and even death. Science was the shining spear humanity thrust into the dark. But this light would only last so long. This period of history, of the pattern, we refer to as the Automated Age.

Debate continues over the cause of Automated Man's fall from scientific grace. War would be an obvious cause. Regardless of man's level of sophistication, time has proved him to be an aggressive creature. We can only imagine what kind of weapons would have been at his disposal.

Perhaps man outgrew this world and journeyed to the stars? Leaving nothing but scraps—both human and otherwise—behind. Abandoned by science, those remaining lived as best they could, resulting in the societies of today. A neat and possibly even correct theory.

Yet, despite finding no obvious flaw in this hypothesis, my personal preference leans towards another explanation:

The resources that fuelled man's domination ran out.

For all his subtleties, he was finite. It is the pattern of humanity: like the moon, their influence waxes and wanes. Mechaniks, magic, the power to fly, are all hollow trinkets; nothing can escape the pattern.

Before I take my seat, and allow a mind no doubt superior to my own to take the floor, I will venture one more point. Throughout my argument, I have deliberately used the words "man" and "humanity." Brothers and sisters, this is because patterns are the realm of man. We Walkin', whose origin is just as inexplicable as the disappearance of Automated Man, are infinite; and thus beyond this concept.

—transcribed from *Time to Walk*, an open forum
in the Black Mountain Common Consensus of
Winters 2917—Councilman Cirr speaking

BOOK 1

1 : 1

Pastor Gray scorched the church and the congregation. He was the noonday sun burning down on pale and ready skin. Behind him was the altar, covered in plain cloth, and the whitewashed walls. His hair was a tangle of red knots; as a married man, he was allowed to let it grow. The Pastor's marital beard was just as striking. It covered the sides of his face, his chin, and his upper lip in fiery curls.

Mary McDermott played with her two fat braids. She'd gotten up early before church and her mother had cut her hair. It was so long it had almost reached her waist. She didn't mind, but Sarah said she'd soon be sitting on it and that would be strange. She watched the bent, old scissors in the mirror. Sarah had brought water from the well and filled a clay bowl. Mary washed her face first and then watched as long, shiny black hairs covered the top, wriggling like croaker spawn.

"We will begin today with a reading from Proverbs—Wisdom and the Foolish," Pastor Gray said, his voice shaking the eaves.

Mary's family were sitting all along the bench, her mother next to her. She could see the two thick braids of Auntie Hannah, then Peter, Samuel, and finally Grandma and Grandpa.

"Tuck your shirt in, Samuel," Grandma hissed.

Her big uncle fumbled at his shirt. His fat fingers struggled to get the white cotton into his trousers. His shirt looked itchy.

"'Forsake the foolish, and live; and go in the way of understanding. Give instruction to the *wise* man, and he will be yet wiser.'" The Pastor paused, adjusting his black cassock. Mary imagined it would be a very hot and uncomfortable thing to wear.

"Teach just a *man*, and he will increase in learning. The fear of the *Lord* is the beginning of wisdom, and the knowledge of the Holy is understanding.

"But he knoweth not that the dead are there; and are in the depths of hell:

"'Murderers. Deceivers. Those who act in defiance of the Good Lord. Hell is their home; a fiery and torturous embrace.'"

Something tickled Mary's nose. It was dusty in the church; she could smell it. She squeezed her nostrils together with her fingers. Now would be a bad time to sneeze.

"Damnation awaits the bearer of any arm. So we ask forgiveness. Forgiveness for those we sent to war."

Grandma had her eyes closed and was mouthing a prayer. Everyone else stared down at their laps.

"For those we sacrificed for our own safety: Jared Peekman," the Pastor said. "For those we lost from our own flock: Daniel Harris. For those we shall remember for ever: Thomas McDermott."

Her mother raised a hand to her mouth.

"'For by me thy days shall be multiplied, and the years of your life increased.' Amen."

The congregation called "Amen." The Good Book closed like a peal of thunder.

The soldier woke coughing. His throat was on fire. Dry and spluttering, his body lurched. There was no air, only ash.

The coughing stopped. His eyes felt gritty. Blinking was an effort; he could feel sand scratching his eyelids.

He tried to move, but nothing happened. He was lying down. Darkness surrounded him. He couldn't hear anything, not even the sound of his own breathing. His mouth was dusty and tasteless.

Pain raced across his forehead and he cried out. A thousand fingers pressed behind his eyes. A pool of white washed across the darkness, like oil thrown onto water. He began to panic. The white was blinding. He screamed, not a word, but a childhood fear.

"Learning. What is it we mean by learning?" The Pastor threw his arms wide.

Mary knew the answer, but didn't want to speak up. She didn't like the idea of the whole church looking at her.

"Is it numbers and letters?" the Pastor asked.

Mary wished it was. She liked letters.

"And what is wisdom? Or knowledge? Is it how to plough a field, or knit a hat? The Good Book says the fear of the Lord, the fear I say, is the beginning of wisdom. Open yourselves to the fear, and what follows is his *love*."

Mary listened to the words. They did make a kind of sense. She was always afraid of the Lord; of someone watching her.

"We meddled. We poked and searched and then we ate from the tree. Fearless. The Good Lord saw our lack of fear and punished us as only He could."

Mary had questions, many questions. But, like the other people in the church, she ignored them. She couldn't help but watch and listen only to the Pastor.

"He took it away. He took away the only thing mankind had. He took away paradise."

The congregation was silent. Nobody fidgeted on the hard wooden benches. Nobody coughed or cleared their throat.

"This," our Barkley taught, "was the First Fall. Exiled from paradise. Lost to walk a harsh world. But, we did not learn."

"Again we forgot our fear, children, we forgot our fear. Once more we *meddled*." The Pastor stepped in front of the altar, the Good Book thrust at the roof. Mary licked her lips. They felt so dry.

"A thousand years ago we *poked* and *searched*. And once more He took away paradise," the Pastor cried. His words crashed around the eaves of the church and back down onto the congregation.

Women gasped, the men grumbled. The Pastor grimaced as he waited for quiet.

"So clever. So much learning; the people of the past. Mechaniks. Magical items of all kinds and shapes. Our ancestors ate again from that forbidden tree of knowledge."

"The punishment was the same and we live with it *today*; here in Barkley, in Pierre County and all over the world. The gates of heaven are closed to the kin of those damned souls. They are left to walk the earth; abominations; foul creatures of the night. Twisted husks: they fester instead of finding eternal joy."

The white faded, lurking at the edge of his eyes as unshed tears. He adjusted to the dark. The pain became a numb ache. He couldn't remember where he was, or who he was. His head felt woollen.

Something tickled against his hand. A carri-clicky crawled onto his chest, its feelers frantically swaying. He looked at it, and it looked at him. Carri-clickys were never alone. There would be hundreds. He tried to move his hand, swat it away. Nothing. The clicky circled, a mocking dance, and then found a gap in his uniform. The bulge in his shirt moved down his chest. Its feelers stroked his skin.

Why can't I move my hand? he thought. This is my hand. This is my hand.

He screamed silently.

The bulge disappeared.

It'd been near his bellybutton. Then, gone. He couldn't feel it anywhere. He couldn't see it.

Click. Click-click-click.

The sound echoed and crashed. His ears were going to burst. The insect was still there.

There was a twinge. Not painful, more like a stitch in his side, where he'd lost sight of the clicky.

Click. Another twinge, this time harder.

The insect was inside him.

His body suddenly tensed. Cramps rippled across his back, along his arms and down his legs. His toes curled. He bit down, his jaw locked. Then, like an overstretched rope, the tension broke and he felt the weight of his limbs again.

He clawed away his shirt. A hole three inches wide, edged by dull red skin, gaped up at him. Layers of his insides: purple and yellow and red—colours drained but still vivid. The carri-clicky emerged and didn't move as he slowly picked it up. He thought about squashing it, but put it down instead. He didn't see the insect go.

With a tentative finger he explored the wound. It didn't hurt or sting. It felt spongy, like overripe fruit. He pulled his shirt back down.

He tried his legs. They moved, but something was in the way. There was ground beneath him; he rubbed the warm dirt between his fingers. Whatever was above him, it was soft. He pulled and pushed. He wriggled and squirmed.

Something shifted.

A face fell from the dark.

Its nose stopped just before his. Its mouth hung slack. From the eyes up it had no skin, just dirty bone.

Flailing, he pushed as hard as he could. He felt scraps of cloth and bone. The face dropped away and he sat up. More bodies tumbled above. Layer upon layer sought to drown him, to drag him under. Panic shook him. He climbed, tearing through the corpses.

A mist of rain touched his parched skin and he sucked hard at life. It was too sweet—he almost choked. The sky was a brilliant grey.

For a moment he lived, there in a pit of the dead.

"Will *you* walk with the dead?" The Pastor pointed at Mrs. Turner in the second row. Her face lost all colour; she shook her head.

"And you!" Pastor Gray turned to the bench in front of Mary and glared at Mr. Gregory. "A father in this community. Will your family feel the taint of *your* blood? Does Satan spill from your loins?"

"The Good Lord, no!" Mr. Gregory shouted, standing up.

The Pastor rushed forward.

"Do you carry the evil of the past?"

Mary was warm in the rays of the Pastor's fury.

"The Good Lord, no!" Mr. Gregory cried again.

"Will you burn on a pyre to save your soul?"

"The Good Lord, yes!"

"And well you would," the Pastor said. His voice cooled, like a smithy's iron put into water. Mary felt as if she'd been dropped into the same bucket.

Pastor Gray looked across the congregation.

"In His infinite wisdom—as the Good Book says—He found forgiveness for our sins. We found our fear again, and we found the Lord's love there. We burn on a pyre, as His son taught us after the resurrection; we burn for our sins and the sins of our ancestors. We will find paradise in His forgiveness."

"Hallelujah," the congregation cried.

1 : 2

He was standing waist-high in burnt bodies. Earth walls surrounded him, covered in jagged marks left by spades. They had dug deep.

Smoke and ash hovered like a fog of dust motes, caught by the light rain. Some flames were still burning, licking at cotton uniforms. They lit the night like candles. He could see an arm, blackened bone, reaching. He wanted to retch, but nothing came. There was a little give underneath his feet, like recently turned topsoil. But it was a body.

The reek of wet ashes and burnt flesh was sweet and thick. He could taste the men left here. They'd smelt of sweat and piss and life. Now, charcoal and damp cloth.

The army called it a "pyre pit."

He'd dug a few; watched as nameless uniforms were tumbled on top of one another. It was quick, it was dirty and it was necessary. Burn them so they don't Walk. There were no words from the Good Book, no urns for the ashes. Wood was laid down first and last. Everything was done as fast as possible and without supervision. No sergeant would watch his soldiers burn. Men chose latrines over digging a pit.

His forefinger was bare bone, skinless and scorched, edges rounding to a light brown. He flexed it and watched his knuckle joints roll. The tip of the finger looked as if he could just pull it off. The urge was undeniable, but the bone didn't move. He felt nothing as he pulled at it. The skin that still clung to his palm was black. He pressed his bony finger against it. His hand felt the touch of the finger, but the finger felt nothing. It was as if someone else were touching him. Despite his uncovered bones, despite the singed and scarred skin, there was no pain.

The corpse beneath him shifted. He had to get away from the other soldiers. They were dead. He was dead, but now he Walked. His head swam, his stomach knotted. He wanted to vomit, to rid himself of the bile and whatever was inside him that had caused this. He would climb out of the pit and then find a place to end the abomination he had become. The Good Lord would guide him.

He struggled over sodden remains. Recognisable features—a nose, a foot, a whole face—floated to the ashy surface, like meat in a stew, and then sank again. His hands and knees pressed down on men he'd stood, fought, and drunk with. He tried to focus on the brown wall.

He climbed using the indentations left by the army's shovels and was out moments later.

He stood on solid ground. His legs wobbled, as if he'd been on a river boat for a season. The wet grass was slick, the soil muddy, but it was solid.

"Hello?" he croaked. It didn't sound like his voice. He couldn't see anyone; no soldiers or other survivors.

He hunkered down, his head between his legs. He wasn't breathing. In a panic, he gulped hard, forcing air into his lungs. He didn't breathe out, but the air hissed as it escaped from holes in his chest. He could still smell the pit and the lighter night air, but he didn't breathe in again. He collapsed, face-down on the ground.

"Hello."

A little girl was sitting beside him. He must have blacked out; she wasn't there before. She dangled her feet over the edge of the pit.

"My name's Typh, what's yours?" Her voice was light and high, but it crackled over the words, like autumn leaves. Her hair frayed in the breeze, across pale cheeks. She was staring down at the bodies.

His name. What *was* his name? It was important, but he'd lost it there, amongst the hundreds of uniforms. Or had it been burnt, the only part of him caught by the flames? In the army he was just another body, but before—

He remembered his wife. His mother. His father. They all mouthed one word.

"Thomas," he said, coughing. The faces faded away.

She was wearing a cream cotton shirt with the buttons undone. It was a boy's shirt. He could see rose spots on her belly. She picked up a big book and put it carefully on her lap.

"T-h-o-m-a-s," she said, marking it on a page with some kind of stick. She turned to face him, her eyes red and sunken. She looked ill, as though she hadn't seen the sun in a month and hadn't slept either.

"Where are you from?" she said.

He opened his mouth, trying to shape the words. But instead, he coughed again. Ash and dust shot out of him with every dry wrench, like grey puffs swept up from a wood floor. His body shook. He rolled away from the girl, covering his mouth. He expected blood to coat his fingers and his insides to spill out onto the grass.

But there wasn't any pain. Not from his throat, not from his skinless hands, not from the hole that ran through him. Just spasm after spasm.

Minutes, hours, weeks might have passed as he lay there. Finally, the coughing stopped.

He turned back to Typh. She hadn't moved, hadn't even flinched when he'd started coughing. She'd sat silent and still as he choked, a small smile on her faded lips.

"Where are you from?" she said again.

"Bark . . . ley," he scraped from his throat.

"Barkley? A lad from Barkley in an army pit?" It was a man's voice, deep. Thomas looked away from the smiling girl.

An old man stood in front of him. He was wearing a robe that whipped about in the wind. His skin was blotchy and yellowed. Deep lines criss-crossed his cheeks. Like the girl, he didn't look well.

Thomas scrambled onto his knees. The child made another note in her book.

"Do not be afraid. We won't hurt you," said the old man. "Welcome back."

"He's not far from home," Typh said.

"I can't go home." He closed his eyes and pressed his hands against his head. "I'm . . . evil." The word sounded childish and simple.

"You don't say?" the old man said with a grin: yellow mushroom pegs lining a cave.

"His name's Tho-*mas*."

"Good, solid Bible name that."

"How old were you, Tho-*mas*?" Typh said.

Were. That was how he had to think of himself, how others would see him. If he let them.

"Wh-why should I tell you?" he stammered. "Who are you people?"

He stood up. Typh stared up at him, her small nose carving through the moonlight. She didn't look anything like Mary, but he saw his daughter's face. He closed his eyes. Typh should be in braids, playing chase and threading flowers, not sitting on the edge of a pyre pit asking questions of the dead.

"My name is Cirr," the old man said. "We're the ones with answers. You're little more than a child, taking his first steps, uttering his first words."

"What does that make *her*?"

"One hundred and fifty-three years older than you," she said.

"No. No, it's not—It's not right," Thomas said.

"What is 'right'? You need help; someone to show you the future you could have," Cirr said.

"I have no future, it was stolen from me." Thomas pointed at the smouldering pit.

"You're not the first to crawl out of there. You're not the first to have a choice."

"What *choice* do I have? I'd have chosen to stay dead. Find heaven. That was my choice."

"Heaven." Typh snorted.

"You could choose to see this life as a gift, a second chance. Do you have a family, Thomas?"

He didn't answer. He didn't want to tell these people, these Walkin', anything else. Cirr carried on:

"You'll want to see them again, naturally. And you could; the returning soldier falling into the arms of his wife and children. They might even see past the scorched skin and colourless eyes. But you're a changed man. War and death do that."

"So instead I should follow you?" Thomas said.

"We have answers; a way of life for who you are *now*. We can offer you safety. Art, culture, words other than your Good Book."

The life of a damned soul steeped in sin.

"No. There is no way of life. Not as this."

"Think about—"

Thomas turned away. He stumbled from the pit, his legs shaking.

"You're just a child." The voice followed him down the grassy slope. "Black Mountain. When you understand, we're at Black Mountain."

"Thirty-two," Thomas said without looking back. "I was thirty-two years old."

Thomas fled the place of his death.

For three days and three nights he wandered alone. The plains seemed to span the breadth of the world; a rolling prairie, covered by knee-high grass. He explored his new body, but it was empty. He could see skin, burnt and flaked by the pyre, but could not feel anything under it. Pressing where veins used to be, he should have felt his blood beating like a parade drum. Instead, silence. Muscles moved, somehow connected to a greater movement—like his finger bone. But there was no process. He couldn't understand it. He willed his legs to move, so they did, and would continue to do so until he wished otherwise, for ever. There was no growth. There was no weakening. He should be hungry. Thirsty. Tired. He willed himself to feel anything physical, but there was nothing.

With a skin-covered finger he pressed again at his wound. It was a tunnel that ran from his belly, right through his body, and out of his back. The flesh felt like ribbons that fluttered as he probed, his kidney like a mushroom cap—slickly solid.

Pale and dry, the grass crackled underneath his bare feet and around his legs. Half of each foot could feel it; the other halves crushed the blades beneath unfeeling bone. Seeds and stems quickly peppered his worn uniform.

His regiment had skirted the edges of the plains. He'd seen maps that suggested it was a large area. He was alone in a blank landscape. Everywhere he looked more grass carpeted low hills. A map didn't explain that feeling.

Occasionally, he passed a wrinkled tree squatting on the land. Thorny acacias; their only use was shelter. He didn't seem to need it. The sun melted lower towards the horizon each evening, leaving a molten sky. His steady pace matched the retreating light, a continuous cycle of step after step, sunrise after sunset.

As dusk spewed over the plains, the insects started their cho-rus. It was at the edge of his hearing, a bubble of chirps and croaking. After the second night, he forgot the noise was there.

"A way of life for the man you are now. Safety," the Walkin' had said.

"An eternity of sinful existence, a fall into damnation." Pas-tor Gray's words came to him in response. Thomas should be working the fields, helping in the shop, reading stories to his daughter.

As the sun sank on his fourth day, the landscape changed. Gone was the carpet of grass. Gone was the flat horizon. In its stead were the Redlands: stone crags and bluffs; ochre and orange, an earth heavy in clay. The rocks were soft; lots of layers pressed together over uncountable years. Wind and water eroded them, shaping the gullies and cliffs.

Nothing much lived there, save insects, under-mutton and the occasional red-wink. He would be alone with the rocks.

It was a good place to die a second death.

1 : 3

It was getting dark in the shop; Sarah McDermott lit a candle. The flame was warm on her hand. The little light threw shadows down the aisles and against the shelves. As she went, she took stock of what was running low and what wasn't selling this week. The vegetables were a constant surprise. Sometimes carrots would sell as quickly as she put them out. Other weeks they rotted at their tops and their veins turned white and stringy. People were fickle in what they wanted to eat; people were fickle in everything. It made owning a shop interesting.

She listened for sounds of Mary moving upstairs. She couldn't hear anything, but she knew Mary was up there. She just knew. At this time of day, the board-walks would be closing down and Mary liked to watch that from her bed. Sarah liked to watch it too, when she wasn't busy. She flipped the sign to closed and peered out into the street. The thoroughfare was covered in shadow; a moment of dusky darkness before lamps were lit.

The buildings opposite seemed to blur and dance. She rubbed her eyes. It had been a long day. Every day was long. She squinted until the buildings behaved themselves and became clear.

She heard a woman scream. She dropped the candle.

It landed on its side and rolled a little away. Sarah knelt and grabbed it. She quickly blew it out. Men were shouting in the thoroughfare. The flat glow of lamps being lit sparked up and down the board-walks. From where she crouched Sarah could smell dust burnt by the candle. She felt as though she needed to sneeze, but couldn't. Her shoulder was wedged hard against the door. She didn't want to know what was going on. A woman had fallen over, most likely. Or a shaggie had made a bolt for it.

Mary came down the stairs.

"Mum, there's trouble."

Sarah peered back into the shop. She couldn't see her daughter. Of course there was trouble. But it was someone else's. She had enough of her own without rushing into others'. Mary slowly appeared out of the darkness. She looked worried, her little face tight and frowning. It was the look of a concerned adult. And here was Sarah, hunkering down behind a door, trying to make herself as small as possible. As if that would stop anything.

"I'll take a look," Sarah said, forcing herself to stand. "Bolt the door after me, you hear?"

Mary nodded. Sarah passed her the candle—much use it would do.

"Don't come out. No matter what. Not until I know what's going on." There were more shouts. The clap of a rifle rang out, echoing off the shop fronts. Mary jumped. "And stay near the back of the shop."

Sarah hefted the bolt. It seemed heavier than usual. The door had warped this winter and took some opening. The bell tinkled as she yanked the door handle. She stood, her back to the street, and watched as Mary slid the bolt into place. She stared at her daughter's face until Mary disappeared into the shop. "Mum, there's trouble," she had said. This used to be a place without trouble—real trouble. The kind of trouble that takes men away from their families. That makes little girls older before they should be. That makes women stay awake at night until lines appear at their eyes. That was the kind of trouble that was right behind her now and she didn't want to turn around.

Men ran along the board-walk. She felt the wood bend and shudder beneath their heavy boots. There was a crowd growing in the middle of the thoroughfare. There was jostling and pushing and cursing. Other folk watched, like her, from the presumed safety of their doorways. Sarah fought the urge to duck down again. Bullets and guns didn't mind where you were standing.

Someone was in the middle of all those men. Someone was being punched and kicked and pushed.

Sarah looked around in disbelief. Why was no one stopping them? Why wasn't she stopping them? But instead of the crowd getting smaller it got bigger. The air was thick with the sound of deep voices biting off sharp words.

The Pastor came running from the church. His cassock was barely buttoned up. His hair was like a disturbed hive of workers. He held the Good Book in his hand. He reached the crowd and started swinging the book like a club. Heads were clipped and men turned to see the fiery Pastor bearing down on them. They parted under his blows. He was bellowing for calm, which could not be further from his own countenance.

From the centre of the mass of bodies, a man reared up.

"Ma! Pa!" he cried. He looked around frantically—as much as the men holding him would allow. "Ma!"

"Jared," a woman yelled. She was at the edge of the crowd, trying to claw her way in. She was so small and round compared to the bodies blocking her way.

As the mob passed Sarah she got a good look at Jared. The top of his head was blackened and blistered, with no hair at all. The skin was like scorched paper, as if it might flake and turn to ash at any moment. One of his eyes was missing completely. She saw flashes of burnt red clothing, a jacket. An army jacket. This was Jared Peekman. She had said his name so many times in church she had started to doubt he was even real—like most of the names in the Good Book. Jared Peekman had come home. He was a Walkin'.

The Pastor made the sign of the cross.

"Thou art damnèd!" The Pastor's voice carried here, in the street, as well as under the eaves. "Creature of the night."

The mob stopped. The Pastor looked across to the boardwalk. Law-Man Bellis was standing there. His shotgun was slouched in his arms. He had fired earlier, Sarah was sure of it, trying to disperse these angry and frightened people. But what was a gunshot compared to a Walkin'? The Law-Man locked eyes with Pastor Gray. He spat on the ground and turned away.

"He must burn!" the Pastor called, holding aloft the Good Book. The mob bayed for blood. Blood Jared didn't have any more. "We'll save your soul, son of Barkley."

"Ma. Ma, please. Help me," he sobbed. The men, good churchgoing men, dragged him along the thoroughfare. Mrs. Peekman tore at them, at their shirts and their cardigans and their beards. All the while screaming her son's name. Until someone pushed her over. She landed hard on the dirt ground.

"That's not my son," Mr. Peekman shouted from the boardwalks. "That's not my son!" He had to run to keep pace with them now. "My son is dead."

Sarah let them get far enough away before she went to Mrs. Peekman. No one else seemed to care about her. Sarah dropped to her knees and hugged the little woman. Mrs. Peekman fell into her. They cried together. They cried for the men the army took from them. The men they would never get back.

Over Mrs. Peekman's shoulder, Sarah could see men and women bringing wood into the thoroughfare. They would dig a stake into the ground at the far end of town, where there was room enough for everyone. The Pastor would make sure the whole town saw this. The army took men from Barkley. But Barkley's ways were stronger than guns and cannons and uniforms.

They didn't feel so strong to Sarah, with Mrs. Peekman trying to thump her in the chest.

Some of the younger men were mounting up. They were just old enough to be married, a few years younger than Thomas and Jared had been. Bethany Gray, the Pastor's wife, was ordering them about. Their job was to let everyone know—those who lived outside of town. Especially Gravekeeper Courie. There was a way these things should be done. Sarah felt sick. She stopped fighting Mrs. Peekman and took the woman's blows.

Luke Morris was at the Pastor's side. He led the men in clapping and singing. They were going to save a soul today. Hallelujah! He was the Pastor's acolyte. His job had many duties, but at that moment he had to keep the men mindful of the Good Lord. This was not the rule of the mob, but divine justice.

When one song finished he began another. He could barely hear his own voice above the pounding of blood in his ears. He had been an acolyte for almost eight years and he had never had this kind of opportunity to do the Good Lord's work. He spent most of his time lighting candles and sweeping floors. They would save a soul today.

"Hallelujah," Luke cried. Others joined him.

They marched from one end of Main to the other. Luke hadn't had a chance to get a good look at the evil spirit in their midst. He tried to peer through the crowd, but could only see hair and beards and the occasional cheek. It roiled into one mass. Good, honest men were smothering the work of the devil. As it should be. As it should be.

When they reached the end of Main, the Pastor started giving orders. He told a number of men to fetch kindling. Mr. Gregory was given the task of bringing the scented pyre wood from the church. Luke didn't understand; that should have been his job. Eventually, the Pastor turned to him. Despite the Pastor's wild hair and beard, his eyes were calm. He drew Luke aside and whispered into his ear. He had a very important task. Luke could not waver in his faith. Could he do it? Luke nodded. Of course, the Good Lord willed it so. As quickly as his cassock would allow, he ran to the Peekmans' house.

He tried the front door, but it was locked. With righteous fury he pounded on it until the wood itself shook.

"Mara Peekman! Mara, open the door."

He heard the latch slide back. The door opened a crack and a mousy-looking woman looked out: Jared's wife. He burst inside. She fell and landed hard on the floor.

"Where is he?"

"Who?" Mara wailed. She was only a few years older than Luke.

"Your son," he said. He went into the kitchen. He opened drawers until he found a knife. "Your demon son."

"What? What are you doing?" Mara blocked the doorway. He pushed her out of his way. He checked the living room.

"Mum?" The voice was soft but urgent. Luke was at the bottom of the stairs in an instant. At the top was a sandy-haired boy.

"No! Simon, run," Mara screamed. But Simon stood frozen. Luke took each step one at a time. He gazed into the boy's blue eyes. Were there flecks of black there? Signs of a taint? He grabbed the boy's arm. Mara tried to stop him. She was so small. He brushed her aside. He left her in a heap on the floor, weeping.

He took Simon to the church. The boy was used to doing what he was told. And the church was a safe place. A safe place for good men and women. Simon was seven, maybe eight years old.

Luke stopped in front of the altar. There was a large cross with the figure of Jesus Christ. There was great strength and dignity in the son of the Good Lord. His muscles were taut and prominent. His face spoke of all the trials he had endured and how he had come through with his faith intact.

"Say you're sorry, Simon."

"What for?" the boy said.

"For everything that you are."

The boy did so. Luke could feel Simon's thin shoulders shaking in his hands. He took the knife and cut the boy's throat. Luke held him as he died.

Sarah stood with the rest of them. She had made sure Mary was still inside. Other families had brought their children; as though this were another day in church. A sermon with something extra.

Jared's parents were in the crowd, but people kept their distance. Mrs. Peekman was still crying. Mr. Peekman told anyone who would listen that his son was dead, that this Walkin' was someone else.

Jared was tied to the stake. He didn't struggle.

"I shouldn't have come back," he said, looking at his parents. This set his ma crying again and his pa ranting. He didn't even so much as glance their way again. But maybe this was why he came home? So he would be treated in the way that was proper to what he believed. What he was told to believe from the moment he could hear the words.

The Pastor began reading from the Good Book. The crowd was silent. Mrs. Peekman quietened her sobs and sniffs. Her husband drew her close. Sarah hugged herself. Everyone listened to the Pastor. Most people knew the passage; some could even recite it themselves. Nathaniel Courie, the Gravekeeper, surely could. They were the words said when someone in Barkley died. Mr. Peekman denied this was his son, but this Walkin' was being treated as a son of Barkley.

"'. . . Its pyre is fire with much wood; the breath of the Lord, like a stream of brimstone, kindles it. Amen.'"

The crowd said "Amen." So did Jared. Then the fire was lit.

The flames started small. Sarah focused on them. The people around her, the shape of Jared Peekman, the Pastor, they all

blurred at the edges. As the fire grew she could feel its warmth
on her hands and face. She had been cold, without realising it.
The fire felt good. She couldn't help it. The wood creaked and
crackled and Mrs. Peekman started crying again. Jared didn't
look at the flames. He craned his neck skyward, to the stars. He
didn't scream or cry out in pain. Sarah didn't know if Walkin'
could feel the same way a person did. Perhaps that was a small
mercy for Jared.

Then Luke Morris appeared. He was carrying something
wrapped in a white sheet; Sarah couldn't see what. But others
did.

"No," someone called. A ripple went through the crowd—she
could feel as well as see it. People shifted uneasily, many turned
away or looked down.

"That's not right," someone else said.

Luke laid the bundle at the base of the pyre. The flames
quickly took to the sheet. A small face. Sarah couldn't breathe.
The younger adults in the crowd seemed as confused as Sarah.
Why was Simon Peekman dead? The older men and women
shook their heads and muttered.

"What have you done?" Jared shouted. "What have you done?"

"'And all the firstborn in the land shall die, from the firstborn of Pharaoh unto the firstborn of the maidservant; and all
the firstborn of *beasts*,'" the Pastor said for all to hear. "We save
their souls today and rid our town of their tainted blood."

Jared struggled to be free. He cursed and gnashed his teeth
like an animal. Sarah felt her fingernails biting into her palms.
She had to stand very still. If she moved she would hurt someone. Eventually, Jared sagged against the ropes that tied him to
the stake.

"Sorry," Jared said to Simon. Or maybe it was to everyone
there. The Pastor nodded. Nathaniel kept staring at his feet.
Sarah thought of the other men who had left Barkley for the
army, of Thomas.

"That's right. I think at this stage in your training a period of reflection would be most beneficial." The Pastor itched his fiery beard. He never did that in public; Luke considered it an honour he did so in Luke's presence. "A Lent hermitage. Some days in the wilderness. Peace and solitude. Clear mind, body and soul."

"If you think it would aid my journey, Pastor."

"Yes. I almost wish I could join you. Time to think and pray with no distractions." He waved at the door as if to suggest the whole of Barkley. "But, too busy. Always too busy doing the Good Lord's work."

Luke was dismissed. He was to leave immediately, taking only the Good Book, a crucifix and a bag of oats. He picked these up from Mr. and Mrs. Gregory's boarding house. Neither of the elderly couple looked at him as he came in. They were silent for the few minutes he was in the house. They didn't ask him where he was going. Or when he'd be back.

Thomas sat down on a large boulder. Mud criss-crossed his feet like the straps of a sandal. The feet looked almost normal, if a little pale. Squint and they might have passed as human. Would anyone in Barkley squint? The families in the pews? The Pastor as he spoke? His mother, his brothers? His wife?

A black stag-bug emerged from the gap between the rock and the ground. It stopped short of Thomas' foot, its stunted antennae twitching. For a moment the stag-bug stood there and then it scuttled away. Another insect wriggled out from the same gap. It was a flurry of tiny legs with a long scaly body. He recognised it as an ear-y-peg, but it was the biggest one he'd ever seen. The ear-y-peg didn't even stop, but hurtled away from Thomas.

He'd started a migration. Creatures of all shapes imaginable came out from nooks and crannies. Those with wings took to the air, their buzz mixing with the tickle of tiny legs on stone. He watched a colony of crumbers abandon their underground home, washing over the earth like a midnight tide; speckles of white surf dotting the black as larvae were carried out. Thomas

1 : 4

Luke knocked, waited a moment, and then entered the Pastor's house. He was expected. The Pastor had summoned him after Main Street had cleared. The crowd was slow to disperse. Someone had thrown a rock at Luke; thankfully they missed, but he didn't see who it was. He didn't stay long in the street. Could people not see what he had done was for their own good, for the good of the town? He had brought salvation to two undeserving souls. Cleansed them. Allowed them to find eternal joy. He hoped someone would do the same for him—not that it would ever come to that.

The Pastor was sitting by the fire, the Good Book open in his lap. He motioned for Luke to join him. The room was small and sparsely furnished. Luxury went hand in hand with many of the deadly sins.

"You did exactly what was required of you, Luke. Do not let any opinion convince you otherwise."

"Thank you, Pastor."

"What time of year is it?"

"Spring," Luke said. The Pastor narrowed his eyes. "I mean, almost Easter."

had always found crumbers fascinating, with their complex underground towns. Now they fled from him. He was a source of panic.

If the lowest of all the Good Lord's creations scattered at the sight of him, then he was truly a force of evil. A devil. A demon.

Ten paces from where he sat the stony ground fell away to an abyss. Fifty, one hundred, one thousand feet. It didn't matter. He would dive head first. He wouldn't scream. He would wait for the ground to crush his head.

He'd heard that destroying the head was the only way to kill a Walkin'. That and burning them.

It had been a conversation he wasn't meant to hear. A man's conversation; words blown in between smoke on the front porch. Pa, in the rocking chair, a presence beneath a straw hat. Two other men sat on chairs brought from the kitchen. Thomas didn't understand names or places, but he listened well enough in school and church to realise what they were talking about. He was always good at listening.

"Shotgun, straight between the eyes!"

A hand slapped against wood.

He remembered the sound, and the white exploded behind his eyes.

He could see nothing but the red jacket of the man ahead and the canyon walls. But he could hear, he could taste, he could smell; and that all pointed to rifles and dying men. Somewhere ahead were blue uniforms. Same men, different colour. It was funny how right and wrong was watered down into two colours. Was there a time when North and South met and drew straws for them? Or was it pebbles in a bag?

Men parted.

Blue seeped into the cracks.

Thomas fired his rifle. A man fell: dark bushy beard, high cheekbones and brown eyes. Thomas saw the man's skin writhe; purple discoloration swept across his face.

A shot and the red uniform beside Thomas dropped.

A rusty bayonet ran through a haze of gunpowder, before it ran through Thomas McDermott.

There was no pain as his mind came back to the rock and the Redlands. He hadn't moved, but the sun had. It was high in the clear sky, pressing down. Thomas was aware of the heat, but his skin didn't burn. He didn't feel thirsty. He didn't sweat. There was no moisture in him.

When he was a child, the Redlands had been a terrifying landscape of imagination, full of monsters and demons—his childish understanding of hell. He'd bragged that one day he would cross the stony desert, fighting creatures, to rescue a beautiful princess. Mrs. Jackson, the teacher, had scolded him for playing rough as he showed off these adventures. As he got older, he realised the danger of the Redlands was not monsters, but heat and lack of water. He'd never fulfilled his boyhood desire to travel the wastes.

Now they lay in front of him like a smouldering crossroads. A crossroads where the signs pointed "Man," "Walkin'," and "Oblivion." To the west, he would find the Col River and Barkley on its banks. East, the Black Hills and eventually Black Mountain—whatever that place might hold for him. The third option was straight forward, over the edge.

Squawk.

A blightbird landed on the boulder next to him, its head cocked, its big watery eye angled at him. The bird looked healthy, with a full and shiny plumage.

"You're late," Thomas said. Unfurling a wing, the bird groomed its feathers. "Or maybe you're early."

The bird stared at him with a bottomless black eye.

"Rich pickings around here?"

How many carcasses had that eye looked upon? Or, how many living animals had it visited just before they became one more meal?

Countless thousands throughout the ages, the bird seemed to say. Things die, always have and always will. Even you, Walkin'.

Hundreds of years ago there would've been a first meeting of blightbird and Walkin'. The bird might have been feeding on a body and then the body woke up. Maybe the bird had smelt food from the air and flown down to find its meal was still moving. Either way, the world changed in that instant. The following generations of blightbirds must have learnt patience.

Thomas was tired of thinking. Tired of having to rethink every part of what he was. He didn't want to be here. He made his choice.

He stood up.

The bird lifted one claw then the other and turned its head. The other eye was white with blindness. Milky swirls like rainless clouds.

"You've been patient enough," Thomas said.

With every step he took closer to the cliff edge a face from his life appeared. Family, friends, and people he recognised from church and the town. They said nothing, looking at him; some judging, some sad, others hopeful.

Three steps from the edge was Pa, his worn face marked by years in the sun. He stared with tearless eyes. His mouth was set with a too familiar frown. Thomas was grateful for the silence. There would be no kind words.

The blightbird cawed like the tolling of a bell.

Two steps from the edge his wife came to him. He faltered. Such a beautiful face. A nose just slightly too small, red cheeks and a narrow mouth. Her long hair. On their wedding night he'd pulled loose the braids before they shared a bed. His finger tips could still feel the strands set free from their tight weaving. But those fingers were changed, burnt.

The blightbird cawed again. It wasn't an eager sound, but confident.

One step from the edge was his daughter. Thomas fell to his knees. Her hazel eyes. She would be older now, her face different. Would he recognise his own daughter? He felt the chill of shame. He had abandoned her. She might need him, despite his skeletal hands and charred skin.

"I'm here, Dad."

1 : 5

No farmers or craftsmen came to the shop to sell goods on a Monday, so Mary had nothing to put away. The minutes dragged by as she wandered past shelves full of potatoes; carrots; wool; dye; knives—kitchen and hunting; plates; honey; bread; shoes, sandals and socks; mallets; pegs; needles and thread; candles; matches; pipes and pipe grass; riding tack; bird fat; and sharpening stones. It was like a grown-up version of the far corner of the playing patch. But instead of sugary sweets and pennies the adults swapped vegetables and fat coins.

Turning a corner, she caught her doll on the edge of a shelf. She watched as its head rolled across the dusty wooden floor; the sack weave was coming loose everywhere. She'd forgotten the doll was in her hand. Picking up the head, her fingers found the thread that ran the length of the doll. A quick knot and the head was back on.

The doll was a gift from her father. Mary called it Stripe, after the pet stripe-dog he'd had at her age. She was getting too old for dolls, but she wasn't allowed a stripe-dog and sometimes she felt lonely. The other girls teased her for playing with "dollies,"

so in school she kept it hidden at the bottom of her bag. They
didn't understand. Every now and again she would reach into
the bag and touch Stripe's rough skin.

It was getting late and her mother would soon send her
upstairs. Mary would hear the muffled sounds of Sarah closing
the shop as she closed her eyes.

"Still playin' with dolls, eh?" Mr. Adams said, rubbing at his
nose. Mary hadn't noticed him standing there. He looked thin
and hungry.

"Pardon?" she said. She'd been thinking about sneaking out
tonight. She'd go to the river again, as long as the moon was out.

"I said, playin' with dollies are ya?"

"No, Mr. Adams. I don't play with dolls." She glanced up at
his black teeth and bald head. When she was little she thought
Mr. Adams told a lot of lies: lies made your teeth and hair fall
out, so her mother said. Now, she knew that happened to all old
men. She stared at the nearest shelf.

"That so?" Mr. Adams said, leaning forward and snatching
Stripe. "Easy now, Mary, just wantin' a look at 'im."

Stripe seemed to wriggle in Mr. Adams' dirty fingers. They held
the doll tight, like a blightbird's claw. Mary could feel the heavy,
smelly breath pouring over Stripe as if it were her own skin.

"Yessir, he's taken a tumblin' all right. Would give 'im a new
eye if I were you, girlie, yes I would. People might think he was
lookin' nasty like." He sniffed. "Might get into trouble." He
broke into a wheezing laugh.

"Bed time, Mary; come leave Mr. Adams alone," her mother
called from behind the counter.

"'Tis no bother, Sarah, just seeing ole Stripe was a' right,"
Mr. Adams said, stiffly straightening his legs. He gave back the
doll.

The ugly man started talking about the army; Sarah was nodding along. She gave Mary a wink and cut across him to say: "Off
now, up to bed, Mary."

"Rules is rules, eh, kiddo?" Mr. Adams said.

* * *

Mary climbed the wooden stairs to her room. She shut the door behind her, careful of the rusty hinges. She had wanted the day to be over quickly.

Her room was simple. In the corner there was a wash basin and shard of broken mirror. Against the wall was a rail where she hung her plain black dresses and white aprons. A little wooden bed was next to the window.

She jumped onto her bed and looked out. The sky was a punctured blanket, little pinpricks of Pastor Gray's heaven peeking through. She saw Uncle Peter driving his wagon back from working the fields over at Caleb's farm. He raised his hat to Mr. and Mrs. North; they nodded back, and carried on down the board-walk. Barber Barringsley stood at the door of his shop, smoking a pipe. She waved to him, but he didn't see. He tapped out his pipe and went back inside. He drew the curtains across the big window.

The street became quiet. No wagons rolled past. The shops were closed. With a sigh, Mary lay down. She pushed at the back of Stripe, feeling for the hard roll of paper hidden there. It was a note from her father and a small picture of him.

"Keep it a secret," he'd told her. "You know the rules." By the teachings of Barkley she shouldn't have anything on paper, other than the Good Book. Her memories of her father were allowed, but not this token to remember him by. For that, she would risk a few strokes of the cane.

The window was open; it was a warm night. The breeze stirred just enough to move the hot air around the small room. There was little need for the rough cotton sheet, but it was odd being in bed without it. She heard footsteps on the stairs and closed her eyes, if only to pretend.

Sarah opened the door and tiptoed into the room. She wondered if she should close the window, but the night was so hot and stuffy. There was a time she'd wished Mary could grow up somewhere else, on a farm. They could tend the woollies together and never have to talk to foul-smelling men. Thomas always wanted his own farm; said it was in his family's blood. Judging by how awkward he had been behind the counter, Sarah didn't deny it.

The man in uniform had come to the shop. She'd understood the moment she saw him. He put the letter on the counter, tipped his hat, and left without a word. She'd managed to stay on her feet and half-read the lines through the tears: Thomas McDermott . . . dead . . . battle. She'd thought, stupidly, how strange it was to read a letter in Barkley—that she was breaking the rules.

Thomas used to read the Good Book to Mary at bed time, bringing the words to life. He found the heart and soul of each verse; found the story and the humanity in the teachings. The Pastor made the Good Book burn with conviction; Thomas made it sing.

She forced thoughts of her husband from her mind, refusing to be sucked down into a grief she had no idea how to climb out of. There was Mary and she was enough. Thomas was gone and as dead as if he were buried up at Courie's. But, when Mary was asleep and so calm and safe, she couldn't help thinking of him.

Sarah had to swallow hard and take deep breaths. Breathing was easy to forget and sometimes she would wake her daughter with a fit of coughing. She sat down by the wardrobe, knees tucked beneath her chin. The master bed was too big, too lonely. Here, by her Mary, it was right to sleep.

Her mother was asleep by the bed as usual. Mary put on her dress. She reached around and did up as many buttons as she could. The top two were still undone, but she didn't mind. She carefully stepped into her shoes. Sneaking out would be so much easier if her mother slept in the big bedroom. It would just be better if her father were here—then Sarah could sleep in a bed and Mary wouldn't have to keep looking for him. Everyone would be happy again.

Easing the window open, she slipped out onto the awning that covered the board-walk. She had to be quiet and not wake Mr. and Mrs. Gregory next door. She tiptoed to the edge and peered down. The wooden lattice had holes big enough for her hands and feet. She could climb, like any of the children in Barkley. Sometimes she didn't want to, that was all, whatever Michael Farly said. She tightened her grip on Stripe and then jumped down into the street.

The wind had picked up. It blew the sand across the streets of Barkley, wearing away at its buildings and people. It got inside Mary's rolled-down socks, scratching her ankles.

Shadows loomed in every alley. The familiar was dark.

Mary wasn't afraid. She felt pulled towards the river. On the grassy banks, she had played games with her father and listened to him read. Now, her mother never wanted to go. Whenever the river was mentioned her smile would become a flat line and her voice would grow short and hard. That's where Mary decided to search for her father.

The ground was uneven beneath his knees. Thomas dropped his hands from his face and opened his eyes. One footstep away the earth opened up. He had no idea how far he would have fallen, how many feet the canyon stretched down. Rocky outcrops on the canyon walls reminded him of the pyre pit. The fall could have lasted an eternity. It would have been a fitting punishment. Though was the path he'd chosen any different? It too would last for all time.

More questions bubbled into his mind: would there ever be a punishment? Was there anyone, the Good Lord or otherwise, to judge him and mete it out? Had he done anything wrong? He'd wanted an end to these questions, an end to the uncertainty. To spill them out onto the orange soil at the bottom of the canyon.

Mary had stopped him. No matter what he had become, he was still a father.

He yelled. An expulsion of sound and doubt that echoed beyond the canyon. He got up. This was his test, his forty days and forty nights in the desert squashed into a single moment. The devil had tempted him, offered the false way with its twisted promises.

He turned his back on the abyss. The blightbird still stood on the stone, hopping from one foot to the other. The unflinching gaze of its black eye sized him up. Flicking its head, the white eye bid him farewell as the bird took to the air.

The choice was east or west: Barkley or Black Mountain. The living or the Walkin'. He checked the sun as he picked his way across the rugged Redlands. He was heading north. The choice was east or west.

The living or the Walkin'.

He wandered on. Each footfall pounded with the arguments for and against. A family, but as a Walkin'? Others who were Walkin', but strangers?

The sun began to set. The Redlands paled away into a grey landscape. Thomas had been watching his feet, their simple one-after-the-other movement. Now, he noticed the buildings.

It was a town or maybe a village, a mile in the distance. Dusky silhouettes dotting the low hills. No light came from them.

Thomas followed an old road. He stepped between patches of flat, black rock. Grass and weeds sprouted between each piece. The more isolated parts of Pierre County still had neglected tracks like these, but everywhere else they'd been cleared long ago, people finding other uses for the stone.

The sun was leaving trails of purple in its wake. Then it was gone.

He was standing at the beginning of what he guessed was the main street. The broken road ran straight along it and out through the other side of the town. The air was still, but every so often a creak broke the silence. He saw a sign clinging to a post by one hinge.

It said: "Miracle." He gave a dry chuckle.

Leaning into a hole where a ground-floor window would've been, he looked around an empty room. The stone underneath his fingers was loose. It became dust in his hands. There were many tiny holes and gaps, like the burrows of woodworm. He had never heard of a stoneworm. Going further down the street, he saw all the houses were made of the same material.

The extent to which they'd suffered at time's hand varied, but none was untouched. A few were blackened. Others were little more than foundations, spaces that once meant something to someone.

There was a larger ruined building, too big to be just a house. It dwarfed the church or Elder Richards's office in Barkley. A thousand people could fit in something that size. Stone steps led up to a massive entrance. It must have been a grand sight in its time. Curiosity tugged at him.

He peered in through the gloom. Rubble covered the floor. The ceiling had collapsed, scattering across an entrance hall. Thomas went carefully, trying not to disturb anything.

Another opening stood gaping on the other side of the room. As his eyes adjusted to the darkness, he stared into a vast chamber. There was line after line of cotton-covered seats, most broken. It was staggering. How could enough people be in one place to require such a room? The rows reminded him of church, which was the only explanation he could think of. Folk must have come here to worship the Good Lord, or perhaps the heathen gods of their time. The thought made him shudder. What evil acts could've been performed to such an audience?

He heard something move behind him.

Caw-aw, the blightbird called. It stood on the rubble, performing the same dance of one foot raised after the other.

He hurried past the bird and out of the building. It was good to be outside again. He wanted to be away from this corpse of a town. It was a husk. Once it had been home to many people. Had it abandoned them, or had they forsaken it?

He heard the blightbird cry behind him. At the end of the street, he could see the open horizon of the Redlands. Never had such an endless nothing been so welcome a sight. Maybe there was a worse fate than living for ever: being trapped, or left to rust and ruin like Miracle.

"Hold right there," a gruff voice called. It came from every direction, echoing around the thoroughfare.

Thomas tried to find the source.

"I said don't move." The heavy clank of a rifle's action—a sound Thomas knew all too well.

1 : 6

He stood still and raised his hands.

"You stole that uniform?"

"Why would anyone steal a uniform?" Thomas said. Turning slowly he saw a man with greasy black hair leaning over a rubble wall, rifle aimed. "Most try and get rid of it, like you." He risked a guess, seeing the man wore a threadbare and stained vest—the kind soldiers wore underneath their jackets.

The man spat out of the side of his mouth.

"Just my luck; found by a bag o' bones. I ain't goin'; I'll shoot you dead before I go back."

"I'm not here to take you back. I'm like you," Thomas said.

"That so?" The rifle didn't move.

"The army and me, we left each other behind." Thomas was enjoying talking to someone again.

"Army doesn't leave nobody behind."

"Does when you're dead." He waited for the shot, waited for the lead ball to fly cleanly through his head. He waited for an end at the hands of someone else.

"True enough. Don't think that means I won't shoot you." The man had a week's worth of stubble on his chin.

"So, what now?"

"I should chase you outta town, that's what. Pissin' Walkin', always showing up where you're not wanted," the man said.

Thomas had nothing to say to that. He'd been a Walkin' for a matter of days and before then he'd never met one.

"Your kind don't feel the cold, but I got a fire going," the man said eventually, lowering the rifle.

"I've always liked watching a flame," Thomas said, wandering over to the ruined house. A waist-high wall was all that remained of the front. He followed the man through crumbling corridors to the back. He saw the glow of fire seeping out of a room. Inside, the man had gathered a stool, a flimsy bed frame and a colourful patch blanket.

"Name's Karl. Karl Williams." Karl leant the rifle in a corner and put out his hand.

"Thomas McDermott." They shook.

"Done a real number on you, eh?" Karl said, nodding at the bare bones and burnt skin on Thomas's hand.

"Not enough."

Karl sat down on the stool in front of the fire. The orange light eased his tired-looking features and Thomas saw a man four or five years younger than himself. Karl's face was long and drawn, his cheeks pocked and his eyes bloodshot. He probably hadn't slept in the weeks he'd been running. Thomas sat on the stone floor.

"So, what regiment?" Karl said, poking the fire with a stick.

"Second Pierre."

"Pierre? Real country boy, then. At least you ended up on your own back porch."

"You're a long way from home?" Thomas said.

"Could say that; I could see the sea from my kitchen window. You got a family?"

"Used to." It was like being back in camp: two men talking around a fire about home and life before.

"They dead too?"

"No. But I can't see them like this." He raised his bony hand to the light. "I'm dead to them."

"Aye, back home they don't make Walkin' too welcome," Karl said. "They're around, mind. In the streets, some even workin' in fields and markets. Funny, my ma will buy leather from a Walkin', but not meat." He put more wood—a broken piece of ceiling beam—on the fire. As it caught, black smoke rose into the air. "There's rules for Walkin' in Bar County: can't buy a house; not allowed out after dark alone; 'ave to make themselves known to the authorities on arrival; that kind of thing."

"I don't expect much of a welcome anywhere. Though, you didn't chase me off. A lot of men in the Protectorate would have shot me on sight."

"You live in the south, you join the Protectorate. Besides, nine days in this rocky armpit and I haven't met a soul. Man needs some company every now and again; keeps him sane. I've been talking to a lot of rocks."

"Me too," Thomas said. "Do you have a wife? Any children?"

"Two boys. They'll run me into an early grave—excuse my meanin'—if the army doesn't."

Karl busied himself with the fire. Thomas stared at the yellow tongues licking over wood and ash.

"So, what's it like to die?" Karl said.

"I don't remember. All this feels strange, parts of me bone, parts of me skin. The wind blows and half of me feels it."

"There's Walkin' in my family, my grandpappy says. He's lookin' forward to it, crazy ass. Says it's the best mistake people ever made, all those years ago. We tried to cure one problem and created another instead; he used to get a real kick out of that. He thinks he'll get busy with all the things he never found time for. What are you gonna do with the years?"

"I wish I knew. What does anyone do with forever?"

"Get bored, if you ask me."

"Have you ever heard of Black Mountain?" Thomas said.

"Can't say I have."

"Might be the only place for someone like me. Lots of Walkin'; someone told me it's safe there."

"You tried killing yourself?" Karl said in an off-hand way, as if suggesting a solution to damp in a hay loft or a toothache.

"Yes. Couldn't, my daughter . . ."

"Want me to do it?" The question was offered as a favour, one soldier to another.

He felt like a little boy again; not thinking, just doing. He didn't know why he was here or why he was a Walkin'. He had decided not to jump over the cliff edge. Was it the right choice? He had stayed for Mary, but maybe he would do more harm than good. He would have to face a future where all he loved had died long ago.

"I'm not ready yet."

All the teachings of J. S. Barkley were about preventing a man becoming a Walkin'. There was no guidance if his teachings failed.

"What about you? What are you going to do now?"

Karl shifted on the stool. "I'll stop here for a while, there's plenty of huntin': under-mutton and red-winks. I'll keep my distance from the fellas in uniforms. Then, somehow make my way home."

A young man, his life ahead of him; he had a plan. He had a home to struggle back to. Thomas envied Karl Williams, the greasy-haired deserter.

Stepping quietly, Thomas left the room. The fire had gone out soon after Karl had gone to sleep. Thomas had watched the embers for a while, thinking empty thoughts of never growing old, never having more children, and getting bored. As the first rays of dawn gradually lifted the darkness, he'd decided to go. Goodbyes would have been awkward.

On the edge of the town called "Miracle," Thomas turned his back on the rising sun and headed for Barkley.

1 : 7

Sarah was cold, despite falling asleep in her clothes again. Rubbing her arms she stood up. She glanced at the mirror. When had she become so old? She pulled at her hair. It used to be golden, but now she had to add honey to get any kind of colour. Her eyes were paler. Her skin drawn.

Mary's bed was empty. Sarah looked out of the open window. The sun was still rising; she hadn't slept too long. Perhaps Mary had woken early and was already downstairs.

"Mary?"

She went onto the landing. The master bedroom door was open.

"Mary?" she called, leaning in. But she knew no one was there. The air was still and stale. The bed tightly made.

Downstairs, the shop was quiet. Dust hung in front of the windows. Sarah held her breath, trying to hear the scratches and taps and thuds that might be her daughter.

"Mary?" she called again.

She went back up the stairs, taking two at a time. Her skirt caught under her foot and she fell with a cry. The cold wood cut her forehead; time slowed, a drop of blood stretched down like candle wax.

"Mum?"

Sarah froze. She couldn't take her eyes off the blood on the floor; didn't want to look up just in case she'd imagined the little voice.

"Mum? You've got blood on you."

A hand brushed Sarah's cheek. The fingers were delicate. She pulled her daughter tightly against her, tears falling onto Mary's hair. Sarah wiped her face and gave a laugh of relief.

"Where have you been?"

"I'm here, Mum."

"I was looking for you; where have you been?"

"Nowhere, I was right here," Mary said.

"But I . . ."

"I'm hungry, Mum."

In the kitchen, Sarah opened the curtains. Mary pulled out a stool and sat at the table. She sat Stripe on the table top.

"We have some under-mutton stew and some bread. How does that sound?" Her knees were shaking, so she leant back against a dresser. Mary nodded.

The heavy smell of meat and broth filled the room.

"Mum, where did Dad find Stripe?"

Mary had asked this question so many times.

"Well, when you were little, your dad was in the Midcountry with the army. They were marching up and down the land. One day, he and some friends were gathering firewood to keep all the men warm, when they found a woman—"

"The lady in the forest," Mary added.

"That's right. Some men from the North were trying to hurt her. Your dad stopped the men and made sure they would never come back to bother her again. She thanked him and saw he had a daughter, because she had special sight that could see into the hearts of people. And there you were, right in your dad's heart."

"Me?"

"You. What he had done was dangerous, and all he cared about was coming home to you. So the lady gave your dad a doll. A present for you." Sarah stirred the pot. Her face still stung, but the bleeding had stopped. She hoped it wouldn't bruise.

She took a wooden bowl from the cupboard and poured in the stew. Then she cut two slices of bread and gave them to Mary. Sarah didn't feel hungry.

Mary took to the food as if she hadn't eaten in a week. Between mouthfuls she said:

"She was a Walkin," wasn't she?'

This question was new. Usually the story ended with the giving of the doll. Sarah sat down at the table.

"Why do you say that?"

"Because you said she had magical sight. I wonder if I'll become magical, when I die."

"Mary, you mustn't say things like that."

"Why not?"

It was a juggling act; some answers would only breed more questions. But Sarah didn't want to lie.

"Well, it's like the Pastor said in church. Remember?"

Mary shook her head.

"He said the Walkin' don't go to heaven like good people. And that's very sad."

"Is Dad in heaven?"

It was like being run down by a herd of charging shaggies.

"Yes, I think he is." She tried to hide her doubts. The army didn't follow the strict rituals of Barkley. No one, anywhere in the civilised world, wanted folk to become Walkin'. But Thomas was lost in battle. Would the army have taken proper care of his body? There were situations nobody could control; she'd run her mind ragged with all the possibilities.

People thought she wouldn't hear, thought she had no idea, but she knew folk had been whispering; especially since Jared. Their gossip didn't matter; Thomas had told her already.

* * *

They were sitting on the river bank, the evening breeze rippling across the water. Thomas had been quiet all day. Summer was almost gone and he would start helping with the harvest soon, which meant less time together. He would be bone-weary each night. She didn't want the sun to set, the season to change. She felt her stomach beneath her linen dress. Was it bigger?

Thomas's hand touched hers.

"Our son," he said, smiling.

"Our daughter," she teased.

He snatched a kiss. He hadn't shaved in the months since they were married. His chin tickled. Lying back on the woollen blanket, Sarah stared up at the sky and watched the sun paint the clouds.

He cleared his throat.

"I want to be a father."

She couldn't see his face.

"You haven't got much choice," she said.

"No, I know. It's just . . . I'm not sure I should be."

She sat up, putting her arm around him.

"You will be a great father."

He was quiet for a while.

"When I was young," he said eventually, "I woke up one night from a bad dream. I could hear Ma and Pa talking outside. He sounded angry, nothing strange about that, but I was curious. I peeked out behind the curtain. A dead face looked up at me. It was so sad. Now I'm older, I know why. At the time I screamed. I was terrified because I recognised the face: it was my aunt."

"Your aunt?"

"I would have told you before, but I thought you'd leave me. It was selfish."

"What are you saying?"

"You have to understand," he said. His eyes were wet. "It could be in me. I could become one of them."

Her heart was pumping so fast the whole world seemed to jump. She took her arm away.

"How could you?" she said. Her voice was cold.

"It doesn't change who I am, doesn't change how I feel."

"It changes who you *will* be!"

"Sarah—"

"How could you? You didn't tell me? And now we have a child." Her voice grew louder with each word.

"I'm sorry—"

"Damned blood! My baby, my child?" She was shouting.

"Do you still love me?"

"Of course I still love you," she screamed.

"It will be all right," he said.

"Why didn't you say something? What will we do?"

"Put me on a pyre. No one needs to know."

"And the baby?"

"Don't," he said.

"When it dies?"

"Don't."

"When it *dies*?" she shouted.

"Then our grandchildren will burn him. Or her."

She let herself fall into him, feeling the beat of his heart.

"Ashes, or I never see you again. You stay dead to us."

Not a day ended without her wishing away those words. If she could only unstitch them from the past. So many actions were forgotten, but words like that stained for ever. Thomas. Her husband. She would give anything to see him, just once. His arms shutting out the rest of the world. Walkin' or no, she still loved him.

"Right," Sarah said, shaking away her memories. "We'd best get you ready for school."

Mary finished her breakfast. She'd wiped the bowl clean. Sarah followed her upstairs, noticing her neck and arms were covered in dust.

"Mary, why are you so dirty?"

"I don't know." Mary stopped, one foot on the next step.

Sarah shooed her daughter up the stairs, wielding motherly sounds like a broom, brushing her daughter into the bedroom. Mary's fingers fiddled the buttons of her nightie undone. She knelt down in the corner and began to wash her face. Sarah stared at yesterday's dress, now a wrinkled heap on the floor. Grubby yellow streaks flashed against the black.

"Mum? My hair?"

Sarah moved away from the discarded clothes and picked up Mary's brush. Kneeling on the floor behind her daughter, she unpicked the two long braids. Little clouds of dust puffed into the air as each strand came loose. Sarah noticed the brown water in the wash bowl. She looked hard at Mary's face in the mirror.

"What *have* you been doing?"

"Nothing."

Sarah's head felt as muddied as the bowl. The whole morning had been strange; the usual routine of waking up, eating, and washing had changed. Even Mary's hair was different, older, as Sarah ran the brush through it. For a moment they looked at each other in the mirror. A woman stared back at Sarah, until Mary looked away.

"Did you sleep all right?" Sarah said.

Mary shrugged.

Sarah rebraided Mary's hair, the two large weaves branding her young, unmarried. Still a child in the eyes of Barkley. But not in her mother's. This morning they seemed out of place.

"Hurry with your dress, or we'll be late," Sarah said, standing up.

Main Street was stirring into life as Sarah and Mary headed along the board-walk. The shops on each side opening up. Barber Barringlsey was in front of his, putting to good use his brittle twig broom. The Smithy was clearing his yard, his apprentice sulkily shovelling the leavings of the last shaggie. Windows were wiped. Signs polished.

Barkley in the morning; there was such a sense of purpose to everyone and everything. The air was fresh and new. The sunlight was a ready yellow, not a tired and spent orange. There was hope in the morning.

Turning off Main into an alley, she heard the shrill voices of children echoing against the wooden houses. The school came into view as they rounded a corner. It was a simple building: a single floor—much like the church—with Barkley's whitewashed wooden walls.

She missed the houses she'd grown up around, all different colours; some made of stone, some of wood. The city was much more interesting to walk through. So many sights and places she'd taken for granted as a girl—fountains, statues, grand houses with gates, wide streets lined by trees, shops three storeys tall, and pubs. They didn't seem real any more, as if she'd spent her childhood daydreaming. At one time she would have instinctively crossed the street to avoid a group of drunken men. Now, she could barely remember what a drunk looked like.

The only feature that set the school apart was the playing patch—a little square of fenced-off ground where children ran and tumbled and played. It was as though, rather than keeping the children safe, the white fence protected Barkley from their untempered imagination.

Opening the school gate, Sarah ushered her daughter in. She watched Mary walk slowly across the playing patch—like Moses and the Red Sea, Mary parted the waves of youngsters. Behind her, the rushing water of "catch-my-neighbour" and "stuck-in-the-sand" closed in. Sarah turned to go.

"Mrs. Gray." Lois Wellins pulled at the teacher's hand, staring up with her big, expectant green eyes. Loud sniffs punctuated each word: "Matthew just bit me."

Sarah stood by the gate.

"Matthew Smith!" Bethany called.

The playing patch stopped.

One boy was slow to notice and bumped into another. Sniggers rippled out amongst the motionless pupils.

"I didn't do it," a boy said.

"Didn't do what?" Bethany moved further into the patch.

"Bite her."

"Who said anything about biting?"

"I—Well, I didn't do it."

Bethany snatched the boy's ear and made him stand beside her. Matthew would probably end the morning with bruised knuckles.

Sarah went home, following the sandy roads that cut between the houses. Shapes seemed to be drawn into their surface by the breeze, only to be wiped away again.

1 : 8

It was early morning when Nathaniel Courie walked the dirt track to the graveyard where he worked. He heard a noise in one of the bramble hedges and stopped for a moment. Tiny creatures moved about their business between the branches and thorns. Insects appealed to him; they knew what had to be done and did it.

Tails, a black mouser, stepped out of the hedge. He was a bruiser with a neck as thick as his shoulders, which gave him a hunched swagger. His fur was wiry, like an old broom. Tails was the other Gravekeeper and did the job well. Nathaniel called him "Tails" because that was only thing left of the mouser's work.

"Mornin', Tails. Sleep well?" Nathaniel said.

The mouser purred, rubbing its head against his leg.

"Me neither."

Nathaniel would likely be alone at the graveyard today, as he was most days, with the exception of Tails. He had nearly stayed in bed.

Barkley's cemetery was a respectful distance outside the town, on the low-lying hills just before the Redlands. It was large—too large for a town like Barkley. He stopped at the entrance, underneath the stone archway, and pinched his arm. He did so every day, looking on at the headstones.

Willows ran along the four wide walls of the graveyard. Nathaniel had planted many of these trees as a youngster. They had seen generations pass through the arch and into the ground.

"Willows break a harsh wind," his father once said. "But their real value is they never stop mourning. Folk appreciate that."

He started towards the east wall, where Tails sat peering out of the cemetery.

"Found one that bites back, Tails?"

Miaow.

"Well, what is it then?" Nathaniel said, leaning against the wall. Stones littered the ground on the other side, as if a giant paw had swiped at the wall. "What's happened here?" Tails leant further, sniffing. The mouser hissed and bolted. "Easy now, Tails. What's got into you?" But the mouser was gone, lost amongst the graves. "Well," he said to himself, "the rounds first, then I suppose we'll go about fixing this mess."

Blood pounded in his face and ears. He'd been leant over too long, taken too long to decide. Each rock had to be picked up, handled for weight and shape, and remembered in relation to all the others. The wall had to fit together piece by piece, otherwise it would fall.

The morning was lost in that pile of stones and now the afternoon was wearing thin. Weak sunlight played across the graves, brushing the ochre soil.

"Blood and bones," he muttered. "If I can't even right a drystone any more, I'm no use to nobody."

Straightening, he heard the steady thud of hooves. A cart was coming down the path, churning up dust. It was still too far away to make out the driver, but he knew who it was. Caleb Williams drove the only grey shaggie in Barkley: a heavy-set animal with the patience of a saint. Couldn't mistake the pair and no other shaggie made that kind of sound. It approached like a storm.

Stepping away from the wall, the Gravekeeper surveyed his "workshop." Weeds were creeping up by the Farlys. That was tomorrow morning accounted for. The willows in the south end would need tending again; the lower branches were beginning to cover some of the headstones. And there was the wall. Simple work. He should have been a gardener.

"Nathaniel, you work-shy old digger," Caleb Williams called from the seat of his cart. Crates of vegetables jostled and bumped on the wagon's bed as it slowed.

"Sat down again, Caleb, I see. Letting this poor animal drag you around."

"Sampson doesn't mind, do you, boy? He likes a good challenge."

Nathaniel stroked the shaggie's nose. "Where you headed?" he said.

"Town. Dropping off these." Caleb took off his straw hat and motioned to the back of the wagon. He'd been a solid man, squarely built, a man of the mountains, as he used to say. Seasons had passed, muscle had turned to fat, and he'd lost his hair. However, he'd kept his sense of humour.

Nathaniel hefted a leek and looked up at his friend.

"Well, these are barely worth taking to town. I'll save you the trouble." He took a potato. "And the embarrassment."

"Now listen to me—"

"And don't you cause that girl any trouble. Lord knows she's having a hard time."

"Sarah? Wouldn't dream of it." Caleb glanced at the cemetery and flicked the reins. Sampson stood there for a moment and then clearly decided it was time to leave.

The house was set back from the track, in a hollow. Compared to the exposed graveyard his home felt like a burrow: warm and secure. He had dug out and levelled the ground, many years ago. Lydia, his first wife, had brought him fresh juice during the hot days.

Dry-stone walls and willow trees lined the path to the house. They never stopped mourning.

The porch steps creaked. All across the front of the house the white paint was beginning to flake. He marked off another day to paint it. How many days did he have left? He took off his boots. Red mud coated the leather and he leant over the porch fence to scrape it off.

Lydia's hand, warm and delicate like the departing light, would rub his lower back. She knew he'd be tense, a day's work bunched there, alongside all the tears and grief that he brought home. Laying her head on his shoulder, they would just stand together.

"There's tea in the pot, when you come in."

He turned to see Rachel holding the door, smiling. He was remembering Lydia and it was obvious that Rachel knew. She had known from the very beginning and loved him for it.

"I'll share you, if that's the only way I can have you," she'd said. He couldn't let go of Lydia; she was still in this world and that was his fault. Whether or not she enjoyed the Walk, whether she was happy, whether she hated or loved him, he could never know. As a Gravekeeper, he had deliberately failed to do his job for her. He hid her body in the shed, wrapped in sheets and surrounded by rose-scented logs. He knew how quickly a body should rot; he knew what she'd become. By morning she was gone.

"I'll be right there."

Rachel looked down. Her sandals would need mending soon. He would do that for her; she wouldn't even have to ask.

The smell of freshly ground chamomile leaves, their time in the sun split and crushed and dried, drifted out onto the porch.

"How was your day?" Rachel said.

"Not good."

Nathaniel walked into the kitchen and took a seat. He looked at his wife. Her hair was tied back today, stopping in a short, blonde ponytail. She looked younger. Loose strands played across her face as she busied herself at the cooking pot.

"Something took a chunk out of one of the walls. It'll take a while to right; no idea what knocked it about." He idly spun a potato on the table top. The oak table had been a gift from her father. Nathaniel had made the rest of the kitchen: the chopping tops; the cupboards; and the chairs. "Caleb gave us these vegetables. He asked after you."

"No he didn't," Rachel said, placing a log on the embers.

"I haven't forgotten my promise. Have you?"

"Of course not."

"Good. We'll go to the hives after we eat, then. That's if you still want to?" he said.

Rachel left the fire and stood behind him, putting her arms around his shoulders.

"I can't wait." She kissed his neck. She smelt happy. "I've put some under-mutton in the stew."

"Need anything done?" he said.

"We need more firewood."

Nathaniel kissed her arm. It tasted earthy. He could see the dust of Barkley, marking her as a woman of the town just as much as the dress and apron. He stood and stretched. His arms and legs ached.

The firewood was behind the house, beneath a lean-to. Nathaniel stooped to check the three logs he'd placed outside the shelter. They were as wet as he could hope for. Picking up a few from the dry pile, he went back to the kitchen, where the smell of the stew had chased away the chamomile leaves. He could chart the progress of the sun through the scents in his kitchen: burning embers at dawn; herbs in the morning; tea in the afternoon; stew in the evening.

The meal cleared the day's dust and dirt from Nathaniel's mouth. It wasn't until he ate something that he realised how much sand he had unwittingly chewed. He savoured every bite: the rosemary dancing on the meat, the stew hot but not scalding. They finished and he cleared the plates.

"Does your veil fit now?" he said, leaning against a cupboard.

"Yes, I just took out a few stitches. The gloves are a little tight, but I haven't found the time."

"You can use mine."

"Won't you need them?" she said.

"No, not with the smoke. They get in the way. If you pick up the veils and my gloves, I'll get the smoker ready."

The smoker was a metal tube he'd found when he was clearing stones in the graveyard. The Smithy had fixed a small set of bellows to it. Nathaniel split one of the wet logs and put half in, alongside a bit of kindling taken from the cooking fire. A careful press of the bellows and the log caught. He split the other logs and stuffed the pieces into a bag.

The hives were a short walk from the house. They were once in the back garden, but Lydia had hated them. Lying in bed, they had argued through many nights over his workers. She had shouted and screamed, balling her fists until they were white. The buzzing; the fear of being stung; how he never took her feelings seriously; all were stabbed at him with venom.

"I could have married the Elder's son, don't forget," she'd spat. He could still feel the passion of her words. His hands shook.

"Ready?" Rachel said.

He blinked.

"Aye, smoking nicely."

She took his arm and they walked out past the herb patch and the weeping willows and onto the hills that embraced Barkley. As they walked, Rachel spoke of all the chores and touches of her day. How she'd washed the bed linen, though it hadn't quite come clean on one corner; and when she'd swept the kitchen a big huntsman had scuttled away, nearly frightening her to death. Nathaniel could tell she was excited. He knew his wife desperately wanted to share his love for the workers; she'd said that anything important to him was important to her. But he wondered how much of Lydia's hatred for the workers was on Rachel's mind.

"Best put the veils on," he said, pumping the bellows. A lattice of white cotton covered the landscape, as if he were half asleep. The hives slipped into view. At first glance they resembled stripped tree trunks, cut and laid on their side, ready to be hauled away. He squeezed her hand. "Don't be afraid, the smoke will make them sleepy."

He unclipped the lid of the first hive and blew more smoke into the air. Rachel peered over his shoulder. The hive boiled, like the under-mutton stew; shapes floating into sight and then drifting back into the roiling mass. He glanced at his wife.

"Now," he said softly, "I know you want to, but don't touch anything yet." Her breath flew past him, dancing on his veil. "It's too early for honey, we're just checking on the lady of the house."

The queen was on the central frame. She was longer than the others and had no stripes. But it was the blue dot of paint with which he'd crowned her that gave her away.

"Well, that's a shame," he said.

"What's a shame?"

Nathaniel pointed to an area of the comb that wasn't yellow like the rest, but a milky white.

"That's the succession. She's been with me for a good many years now."

"What will happen to her?" Rachel sounded genuinely concerned; she had such a love for all living things. He knew she hadn't killed that huntsman.

"Either they will let her die naturally, or smother her."

"That's terrible."

"I'm not sure which would be the greater mercy. If it were me, I'd rather not see my replacement."

He returned the frame and checked the hive wasn't damaged in any way. With winter slowly taking its leave there was little to do except make sure the workers were alive and safe. Over the next few weeks, as spring took hold, there would be an explosion of breeding and gathering and a new queen to dot. It was a good time for Rachel to see the colonies, while they were small and quiet.

"How about the others?" she said.

"Let's take a look. Those queens are younger, so should be all right."

The other two inhabited hives were fine, healthy-looking colonies. The final hive was empty.

"I may move a colony there this spring, haven't decided yet."

"They feel so different from one another, like different people. It's odd."

He turned to her. In the smoke, amongst the workers, and behind the veil, her hair looked darker. He had to blink away the image of Lydia, standing there, smiling at him. Breathing suddenly felt painful.

"We—We should be heading back."

She took his arm.

"I know this wasn't easy, because of her. Thank you."

Nodding, he led them back to the house.

The bed sheets were cold against his back. He wriggled, enjoying the feel of clean cotton. The candle had burnt itself out. Moonlight sketched the room in chalk on a black canvas of bed, floor and bodies. A window was open; he could see his breath as he sighed. Rachel was still awake. He felt her breathing through the grass mattress, but not slow and deep.

When they got back he'd washed his hands in a bucket outside, pressing a day's worth of dirt from the wrinkles. He'd looked at himself then, in the muddy water that blurred his face. The water had been warmed by the fire, by her.

He shifted onto his side. Her back was bare and silver-streaked; it rose to his hand and Nathaniel winced. Soft. How could he deserve that kind of soft? There was nothing he did, in any part of his day, which could justify his touch on her back. But he ran his hand down from her shoulder. She'd said, their first time together, that he could play with her back all night.

Rachel turned her head and he kissed her. Her hair tickled his dry tongue. She pressed, kisses snatched and pushed. He tried to match them, but kissed her neck instead. She murmured.

She would want to face him now. Let him take control as she lay back and watched the whole act play out. A cuddle. A kiss. And goodnight. Strip the food, cook, and eat. She would do it all thinking of him.

He wouldn't be thinking of her.

Wood smoke wrenched at his nose. He wanted to see Lydia's hair spilling down onto the sheets in black ringlets. He wanted something to change. She started to twist, but he dropped his hand between her thighs. Her breathing became heavy.

He imagined Lydia's face on the pillow. Her body felt wrong.

He pulled at her and closed his eyes.

He grabbed her thigh, her stomach, her breast. She slapped against him. She was bigger, fatter, a different woman. She moved, and he followed.

The calm of the past five years shattered to the pounding of blood in his ears.

For once he was eager. Her sweat stung his tongue. That was how she tasted.

They tensed and Nathaniel fell on her back; ragged breaths against her skin.

He could feel Rachel's surprise. His hands shook as he pushed himself out of the bed. The moon glared large in the window and he had to cover his eyes.

"Why didn't you burn her?" Her voice was quiet and even.

Cotton lined his mouth.

"Because I love her."

"Would you burn me?"

"No."

1 : 9

Luke Morris wasn't in church. This weighed heavily on him for a number of reasons. Foremost, he was the Pastor's acolyte. As such, there were duties he usually performed on the Sabbath. He lit candles. Greeted the men and women and their families and closed the doors after them. Handed out prayer books. But without Luke the Pastor would have to do these menial jobs. Or worse, his wife.

This was the first Sabbath service Luke had missed in all his years. Even when he had itching-fever as a child he insisted he attend. He had slowly worn his mother down until she had no choice. He sat at the back with two pews between him and anyone else. It was one of the best services he could remember.

Now, instead of sitting on a pew, he was hunkered down on hard rock. He hugged his knees under his chin. To lean against something, to sprawl like an ignorant farmer, would be an unacceptable luxury. The black wool of his cassock scratched his chin. He hadn't shaved for some days. A beard wasn't appropriate for a single man, but he was sprouting bristles harsh enough to brush a floor.

He worked some saliva back into his mouth. It was a clear spring morning, not hot but dry. The Col River was fifty or so paces in front of him. It looked silky today, barely making a sound as it flowed by. He could feel the water in the air. It stroked his cheek and pressed on his forehead like a soothing cloth. When he breathed through his nose he could taste the cool water. But he didn't open his mouth. He'd taken a handful of water at dawn and sucked it down greedily. That greed, that base desire, earned him a thirsty day.

Luke was in exile for Lent. He had wandered out of Barkley with no direction. There was no destination. He left town for wilderness, buildings for bluffs, and sin for purity.

Would the Good Lord be upset with him for missing the service? He was holding a service of his own, in a way. His self-denial was an act of prayer. He didn't have a roof over him, or pews, or a congregation. But wasn't this spot, a shady bend in the Col River, just as good a place to worship as the church in Barkley? The Good Lord was everywhere. It made sense for His flock to be everywhere too. He imagined giving a sermon to the river, gesturing to the bluff behind him, to the little holes that riddled the rocky face. Casting his gaze wide over a congregation that covered the Redlands and stretched all the way to the horizon.

He shook away the fantasy. He took the Good Book from his pocket, determined to focus his mind on something holy. He read until his tongue felt like a leather belt and his ankles ached. Then he read some more.

The next day Luke woke to the sound of angels. Their trumpets were high-pitched and glorious. Their radiance warmed his face. He opened his eyes. His face was pressed against the rock. Fine gritty sand grated his skin. It wore away these rocks and it would do the same to him. There were no angels.

Luke sat up. There was a man on the bluff. He was fat, but somehow managed to move nimbly from ledge to ledge. He was whistling. Luke would need a suitable penance for his foolish and probably blasphemous half-dream. He looked around for his glasses. Before sleeping, he put them a few paces away so he wouldn't roll on them. They were scratched and old—old long before his mother insisted he needed glasses. He put them on and the fat man suddenly had edges. Almost at the top now, the man visited each of the little holes he could get to. He would need wings to reach the rest. Then he climbed back down, all the while whistling. Luke recognised it as a hymn. Probably the hymn the congregation sang yesterday. He wished he had been there. He envied this fat man. That was a deadly sin. But it wasn't Luke's fault. He was supposed to be alone in the wilderness. Not visited by whistling ignorants with no understanding of holy matters. Luke winced when the man came towards him. It was Caleb Williams.

"I'm sorry, acolyte. Didn't mean to wake you," Caleb said. The man seemed to wriggle in his fat folds. "I just like to whistle when I'm checking the traps. Otherwise I have to listen to 'em whimper." He held up his hand. A brace of under-mutton hung limply from their ears. Luke's stomach growled. Was this farmer trying to tempt him? The devil chose a strange garb, but then Lucifer was guile incarnate. He would not appear to Luke in his hornèd finery, stepping brimstone and spouting evil. Caleb was sweating.

Luke tried to clear his throat. "I should have been awake at dawn," he said, eventually.

"You look like you needed the rest. In a bed."

"The Pastor knows why I am here."

"I'm sure he does. Can I offer you meat?" Caleb held up the under-mutton again. Luke gave a dry retch, his hand to his mouth just in case. He shook his head. Caleb paled, but said nothing as he headed off towards town. His cart must have been near by. Luke couldn't imagine the man walking far.

Glancing at the sky, Luke noticed it was almost midday. His slovenliness was added to the tally. He went to the river to get away from the smell of dead under-mutton as much as for some water. He allowed himself half a handful.

* * *

Luke spent the afternoon wandering along the river bank. He took off his sandals. The damp mud cooled the bottoms of his feet. After a while he looked back and saw his footprints. They made him smile; they were his journey. Not just away from the bluffs where Caleb Williams checked his traps, but from his role as an acolyte. Soon he would be a Pastor in his own right.

He needed to find another suitable spot to continue his period of Lent. Shelter was important. He would risk sun-madness without the shade and too much wind distracted him from his reading. Sprinkling some oats into his hand, he chewed a pinch-full at a time. His stomach tightened around the flakes of food. The persistent ache of hunger was becoming less and less important to him. This week of fasting was perhaps the most exciting time in his life. Maybe even more exciting than the day he became an acolyte, or when they burnt Jared Peekman. He was growing, spiritually. He could feel it. He smiled as he chewed his oats.

But he had to be careful of self-worth. Pride. He put his sandals back on. The blisters on his feet were worthy of this moment. His body wanted to go barefoot. His soul demanded sandals.

He eventually found another set of small bluffs. This time both sides of the wide river had rocky formations the height of Main Street. He would miss the view from his old spot, but for tonight it would suffice. He sat down and watched his shadow lengthen.

1 : 10

If the offering is a burnt offering from the flock,
from either the sheep or the goats,
he is to offer a male without defect.

Leviticus

BOOK 2

2 : 1

Someone just pushed Lois Wellins. Mary had wanted to do that before—Lois was an annoying little brat. She would cry to get attention and then blame you for it. She'd attached herself to Eunice recently, like a bloodsucker. A big, green-eyed bloodsucker.

She heard Mrs. Gray yell something and all the children stood still. She felt inside her bag, rubbing her thumb along Stripe's sack-weave. Michael was being told off. He probably didn't do it.

The other boys and girls gradually started moving again; chase and the silly games they played. Noise bubbled louder and louder, like a cooking pot. Mary went to a corner, where it was quiet.

She knelt down, her back to the patch. There were no houses around the school. She looked out onto an open area, trying to find something to draw. There was the grass, a couple of rocky bits, and a thin tree. It wasn't much of a choice. With her finger, she started at the bottom of the trunk. She made it tall and mighty. Straight up into a big cloud of leaves. Next, she imagined a red-wink underneath. It was difficult to draw something small in the sand with her finger, so the red-wink was the size of the tree. She giggled. The red-wink could trample the tree. It would eat everyone.

"Mary McDermott!"

Mary looked round; Mrs. Gray was blocking out the sun.

"You scrub that out this instant," Mrs. Gray hissed. So far none of the other children had noticed what Mary was doing. She stood up and kicked at the sand.

"You'll stand by me, right here, until we go inside."

Without a word, she did as she was told.

The schoolroom smelt like old skin. It was the smell of many fidgeting hours, over many fidgeting generations. The taste of a child's desire to be outside.

Mary stood at the front of the class. The other children, all in their seats, looked at her with wide eyes.

"Mary has done something very naughty. Later, we will talk about why it was naughty," Mrs. Gray said. She was holding the switch. Mary held out her hands, knuckles facing up.

The air whistled and her hand stung. She winced. It didn't hurt that much, but doing nothing was a bad idea—Mrs. Gray took that as a challenge. Another thwack. Her fingers caught fire; red knuckles. That one did hurt. Mrs. Gray had hit the same spot twice. The last one luckily missed the marks, but the tips of her fingers now throbbed.

Mary went back to her seat. She sat in the fourth row of chairs and on the left-hand side. Everyone was ordered by their age: youngest at the front, eldest at the back. Girls on the left, boys on the right. Like the pews in church, the chairs were hard wood with straight backs. There was no comfortable way to sit on them. Mary was tired and it was difficult to sit up straight.

That morning she had woken up with stones jabbing in her back. Beside her, the Col River lapped at its bank like a wrinkled blanket. The sun had been rising but wasn't full enough to chase away the shivers. Picking up Stripe she returned to her home, to her mother.

She hadn't found her father.

Now, she watched the dark crowns of the children in the rows in front. There was little else to look at. Blank walls in a blank room full of blank faces. The ceiling was low; she had spent many mornings staring at the flowing wood grain.

These days, Mary was one of the lucky ones: she sat by a window. Wagons passed, but each one was the same as the last. The men driving wore the same black trousers and white shirts. With the playing patch between Mary and the road, she couldn't see their faces.

Mrs. Gray's voice droned on at the front of the class. Was everyone else listening? Or were they falling asleep too? The teacher was reading from the Good Book. The only book. Those same pages flooded Barkley; a copy in every house and in every hand. All other writing was forbidden. In school, they were taught how to read from that one book and nothing else. Mary wanted more; she had a thirst as deep as a well.

The two older girls in the school had once told her that far away, where non-Leyists lived, words were written on people. They'd whispered, in the corner of the playing patch. Mary had pretended to be impressed, but knew they were lying. She didn't think Eunice and Siaha knew anything of the world outside Barkley. They only cared about losing their braids.

"'—yoked together with unbelievers—'"

The words came lifelessly from the page, out of Mrs. Gray, and into the musty air of the room. She was reading it all wrong.

"'—what communion hath light with—'"

Mary didn't listen. She didn't have to. If pushed, and it would take some pushing, she could recite almost all of Corinthians. Her father used to give the epistle power and understanding. Without him, it shrivelled and died. Weak like that, she found holes and questions. Not answers.

She'd brought the questions to Mrs. Gray. Cupping them in her hands, like precious water, only to have the teacher spill them onto the sand. Mrs. Gray answered Mary with the verses she already knew. In the following weeks she had got as far as the steps below the Pastor's door, before his fiery head passed a window and she ran.

Mrs. Gray closed the Good Book. It never closed quietly; as if it was angry.

"And now, children, we turn to the spoken teachings of J. S. Barkley, founder and father," Mrs. Gray said. Spoken, not written.

"Amen," the children said. Three repetitions, followed by Mrs. Gray's own lesson for the morning, and the day would be half over. It was only Tuesday.

"'Live a plain life: family, worship, and the soil—repentance for our ancestors.'"

The children echoed the teaching. Their piping voices sounded foolish to Mary, they twisted and broke the words.

"'The Second Fall was born of the written word. Only the Good Book is to be written and read.'"

The children echoed the teaching. All, except Mary.

"'Jesus Christ rose from the dead. He was the Good Lord's first example, and we follow it by burning the body.'"

The children echoed the teaching.

One of the small boys in the front row raised his hand.

"Mrs. Gray, did Jesus' mummy burn his body?" James Turner said, whistling over his "s" sounds. James' brother, Paul, had recently died of a fever. Mrs. Gray moved out from behind the table and crouched down in front of the boy.

"No, James, she did not; and that's why Jesus came back to life. The Good Book says the last thing the resurrected Jesus did was to light a fire for his friends. Then, as his spirit returned to heaven, tongues of fire came to rest on each of those friends. Our Barkley realised the Lord's message: through fire our spirit will not stay in this world, but journey to paradise. So you see, your mummy used fire to set Paul's spirit free. All right?"

James nodded and waved up at the ceiling to his brother. It could've been funny, but no one laughed.

Mrs. Gray straightened and smoothed her dress. Mary knew what every girl in the classroom was thinking, because she was thinking it too. "Will my hair be that pretty when I'm married?" She looked from the teacher to her own braids. Did Mrs. Gray like wearing those dresses? Was Mary alone in hating clothes that made everyone the same? She couldn't be. They itched like damnation.

"Today, I will talk about another part of John Sebastian Barkley's teachings. Sometimes, as James just saw, our Barkley's words can be confusing. What he means, what he wants us to think and do, is not always clear."

Mary stared out of the window. Much of Barkley's rules were obvious, common ideas that made sense: don't hurt people; help those in need; burn bodies when people die. It made the rest of the rules seem strange. Strange and frustrating. Why no books? No drawings, no tales, no nothing other than the Good Book. Reading, but no writing? She thought the Good Book was important and wonderful. But wouldn't other stories be good to read as well? Her father had told her of heroes and quests and princesses; hushed words when her mother was still closing the shop. He'd have the Good Book open and ready in case Sarah came in.

"In the first teaching, we speak the words 'repentance for our ancestors.'" Mrs. Gray was going slowly for the younger children. Mary sighed as loudly as she dared. "To repent is to say we are sorry for what we have done. But Barkley tells us to repent for something our *ancestors* have done. Why would he say that?"

The children were silent. Then, a small hand jerked upwards. "Yes, Lois?"

"Because our ansisters were naughty."

"That's right, they were. And we say sorry for all the naughty things our ancestors did by doing what?"

"Living a plain life. *Family*, *worship* and the *soil*," Mary said, exaggerating each word. It was a game she played with Mrs. Gray: give the right answer but in a challenging tone. The teacher would be caught like a fish on the river bank. As the seconds raced past, the only thing she could say was, "That's right," and move on before the other children noticed.

The corners of Mrs. Gray's eyes and mouth tightened.

"You see, many years ago, before the Second Fall, man lived without family, without worship and without any care for the soil. It was not how the Good Lord wanted us to live. Our ancestors were *lazy*, so He took away the mechaniks, took away their dark and evil magic."

"Took away the books and the drawing and the music," Mary said. Her mouth fell open. She'd only meant to think that.

"Actually, Mary, He did not," Mrs. Gray snapped. "J. S. Barkley did. Our Barkley saw the Good Lord's disapproval and showed us the right way to live. He gave us a town in which to live this way. He saved our souls. Tomorrow, I will tell you exactly *what* he saved our souls from."

Another old lesson Mary could ignore.

The children filed out of the schoolroom, clunking down each step. They formed a single line, Mrs. Gray leading the smallest at the front—James. Eunice was the last one out. It was her job to close the door and the gate as they went out onto the street. Men riding shaggies wandered down Farborough, the thud of hooves like a drum for the children's march home. It was important to be quiet around shaggies. They were unpredictable and could kick a man if scared. As one plodded past their line, Mary's whole body tingled with the desire to jump out and scream. But she didn't.

Mary stood in front of the shop. An afternoon with her mother lay behind the door: learning how to keep a floor tidy; when shelves needed filling with food or clothing; how to make small words with dull people. These lessons were better than the ones in school.

In the late afternoon, before supper and bed time, she was allowed to run and play and see the other children. Instead of playing, she decided she would go to the river and draw in the wet mud. She would draw people and birds and anything at all, and watch the water wash them away.

"Are you going in or not?" Mrs. Gray said. Mary looked up at her aunt. It was easy to forget she was part of the family. She was married and had a different surname, but that wasn't why. Mrs. Gray was the teacher; that's who she was. Did she ever stop and just be a normal grown-up? She was coming into the shop as the teacher.

Mary opened the door and Mrs. Gray followed her in. The line waited outside, Eunice now in charge.

"Hello, Sarah. I wondered if I could have a brief word." Mrs. Gray stood at the counter. She was shorter than Sarah by almost a foot, but the teacher had a way of looking down at someone.

Mrs. Gray was actually very pretty, with long eyelashes and curly hair. But there was an edge to her. Maybe it was because she spent all day telling children off, or because she was married to the Pastor. She had fierce eyes.

"I caught Mary drawing in the sand again," Mrs. Gray said.

"Again? But I told her last time." Her mother's cheeks turned red. "Mary, upstairs, now."

She went to the stairs and clomped away on the third one. Then she sat down.

"What was she drawing?" That was her mother.

"Does it matter?" Mrs. Gray said.

"No. It won't happen again, I promise. It's been difficult; she misses Thomas."

No one said anything for a while.

"Well, it's forbidden. She knows that."

The bell of the shop door chimed.

"How could you be so silly?" her mother said.

2 : 2

An appreciation of distance is always framed by an understanding of time. To a human child, tomorrow could seem a hundred miles away. A twenty-minute walk, from one side of a town to the other, is a vast and tiring expedition. But as they grow, the world around them shrinks. Over the years they shift their expectations of time, of what could and should be achieved in a single day. They begin to think of the future and the past. They lose a minute-by-minute existence, an immediacy of needs and wants. This is the transition from child to adult.

And then, everything is reversed. The world shrinks again. It takes twice as long to walk anywhere; confined in their homes, only the most essential journeys seem worth the effort. Thoughts turn to making the most of their time. The past holds too many memories; the future, only an end. This is the transition from adult to elder.

An example: a boy dreams of the Redlands. They are an expanse of adventure and possibility. As he grows into a man he discovers that the map of Pierre County disagrees—the Redlands are a set of lines the size of a thumb. His adult eyes realise the relative scale: big, but a space that has its limits. Then the man becomes elderly. He looks on the same map again and marvels at the sheer size of that rocky wasteland.

There is only one disruption to this cycle. For some it is final, for others only moments. To those lucky enough to be born again, time becomes infinite and distance is reduced to nothing.

This is the transition from human to Walkin'.

—transcribed from *Transitions*, a lecture in the
Black Mountain Common Consensus of Winters 2919—Councilman Cirr speaking

Thomas travelled all day and all night. He spent the time remembering, not just the big things but every small detail he could of Barkley. His family. His friends. The way Main felt on a busy day. The lamps being lit at dusk; their soft light getting stronger as the night became darker. But most of all, he thought about the day he became a soldier.

Thomas had joined the line of men outside the church. He recognised most of them. Some were barely older than boys, others married men with families. Paul Richards was in front of him.

"What's this about, Paul?" Thomas said.

The Elder's son couldn't stand still and kept putting his hands in his pockets and taking them out again.

"I overheard . . ." Paul glanced about to make sure no one else was listening. "I overheard it's a draft."

"What's that?"

"I don't know."

Thomas scratched his beard. It always itched. A beard was the tradition for married men in Barkley. It was a way of keeping things in perspective—not even a wife was as annoying as an itchy beard.

Thomas tried to ask more questions, but Paul wasn't interested. He just shrugged and kept his head down. The line shuffled forwards. Thomas stepped into the church. The pews were empty. It was cold without all the people. And so quiet. At the front the men were lining up. The Pastor, Gravekeeper Courie,

Law-Man Bellis and a bunch of strangers stood a little way off, talking. Elder Richards was directing everyone where to stand. It came to Thomas's turn and the Elder took him by the elbow.

"Right up front, Mr. McDermott."

The Elder had never called him "Mr. McDermott" before. Thirty men all told, in three lines. Some of the younger men looked restless, like Paul. The older hands seemed bored. Thomas was at the end of the front row. He looked along it. He knew all the men by name and family. They were all farm boys. Paul was standing in the back row.

With a bang of his stick, the Elder called for quiet—though the men weren't making a sound. The Pastor, the Law-Man and the strangers came to stand alongside the Elder.

"First, thank you for coming down so quickly," Richards said. "This man here is Lieutenant Morgan from the Southern Protectorate Army. He has a few things he wants to say to you boys, so listen carefully."

Morgan was wearing a heavy-looking red jacket. Its buttons were so shiny they caught the dying sunlight. His trousers were matching red, though the knees were scuffed. He wore calf-high boots in polished black. Somehow the dust and dirt of Barkley hadn't stuck to the boots the way it stuck to everything else. But most of the men were staring at Morgan's moustache. It was bushy and greying and sat on his lip like a fat mouser. His chin was clean-shaven. Thomas knew what the other men were thinking, and he was thinking it too: was Lieutenant Morgan married?

"Gentlemen," Morgan said, clearing his throat with a loud humpf. "I come here today to offer you a great opportunity. History is being made, right here in our blessed country. You too can be a part of something glorious."

Someone in the lines sneezed.

"There is a menace wandering the streets of our nation. The Walkin'." Morgan made to spit at the word, and then remembered where he was. One of the boys couldn't help but snigger when Morgan swallowed. "The Walkin." An evil the likes this land has never seen before. I don't have to tell you men. Your Pastor has explained your feelings on the matter. So I will just say this: join the Southern Protectorate and keep your families safe from this scourge for ever.' Lieutenant Morgan stepped back, his boots slapping the wooden floor.

The Pastor came forward and led them all in a prayer. Thomas bowed his head like the rest of them, but couldn't help glancing at the men next to him. They looked as confused and afraid as he felt. Walkin' in the streets? That didn't happen in Barkley. And didn't a man best protect his family from his own home? Thomas had heard rumours of armies and wars. It was the reason you couldn't get bananas in the shop these past years. *Amen.*

"Thank you, Pastor," Richards said. "And thank you, Lieutenant Morgan. Now, boys, now is your chance to volunteer for this magnificent cause. Just step up here and do the right thing for your town and your country."

No one moved. 'Keeper Courie started coughing. Thomas was fairly sure Nathaniel was really laughing and trying to hide it. The Elder glared at everyone and no one in particular. He waited. Thomas, like many others, shifted his weight from foot to foot. Hands were run through hair. Noses pinched or blown. But not one of them budged an inch.

"I didn't want to do it this way," Richards said. "Ten men will join the Southern army today. Either by volunteering or by draw." He let the men consider that for a while. Still no volunteers. From the altar the Elder picked up a leather bag. He shook it. "There's white pebbles and red pebbles in here. Draw a red pebble and you're part of Barkley's representation to the Southern Army."

The Elder went to the first man in the front row. Jared Peekman. Jared looked at the Pastor, who nodded to the boy. The pebble came out red. Jared had a wife and son. They were moving out of his pa's place that summer. Jared held the pebble in his hand, staring in disbelief. He didn't know what it meant, not really, and neither did Thomas. War took bananas out of shops, not men out of their homes. Not Barkley men.

The next pebble was red. And the next. When it came to Thomas's turn, the Elder couldn't look him in the eye.

The shop bell chimed and Sarah saw Rachel Courie come in. The plump woman hesitated as the door closed behind her and then busied herself amongst the vegetables. She usually came in on a Wednesday afternoon to fill the Courie larder.

Mary was still putting out the stock Caleb Williams had brought in that morning. Sarah heard her daughter greet Mrs. Courie, before her attention was drawn back to the counter and the woman standing in front of it.

"You'll give me three silver for each of the wax, and two for the tallow?" Mrs. North said.

"I'm afraid so."

Mrs. North looked hard at the candles laid out on the polished wooden counter. Her eyes narrowed. She gave a sharp nod.

"Thirty-three silver then."

"I make it thirty-five," Sarah said.

The chandler gave a rare smile.

"Thank you."

Dropping the silver into her purse, Mrs. North paused. Her apron was covered in grease marks; she'd come straight from her work. She blushed and quietly said "Good day." The bell chimed again as Mrs. North left.

Mary appeared from the end of a row. Dust and dirt marked her face, which was set in a dangerously neutral expression. Sarah knew that face well. Mary had been kept indoors these last few days.

"So," Sarah said brightly, "I thought we could have a picnic today, after we shut the shop. Go up to the hills and see the whole town."

"I'll put those candles away next." Her daughter was trying not to smile.

"Is there anything special you want to eat?"

"Not really," Mary said.

Sarah moved the candles to one side, keeping the wax and tallow separate. The Pastor would want the wax candles for the church. She hoped he didn't want them all. Three silver each would be a generous addition to her regular donations. At times it was a struggle to keep track of everything that came in and out of the shop—especially to the church. But over the years, she'd developed an excellent memory. All the prices and all the levels of stock were ordered neatly in her head.

"Good afternoon," Rachel Courie said, her arms full of food. "Five potatoes, three onions, two courgettes and some beans."

Sarah counted up the price, named it, and helped Rachel put the vegetables into her basket.

"How is Nathaniel?"

"He's well, thank you for asking. That business with Jared Peekman was difficult for him."

"It was for all of us," Sarah said.

Rachel smiled weakly. "It's silly, but he feels somehow responsible. Like he could have been there for Jared and . . ." Rachel adjusted her dress. The wool was tight around her waist. "He says there will be plenty of wax this year."

"I hope so. The winter would be torture without candles," Sarah said.

"We rarely use ours. Nathaniel is always so tired when he comes home."

"It must be very hard, being the 'Keeper."

"He gets lonely, I think. The graveyard is so far from town, and folk that visit want to be alone."

There was a moment of uncomfortable silence. Sarah had visited the graveyard two days ago. Alone.

"Well," Rachel said, "these vegetables won't stew themselves."

Sarah shut the shop door and locked it. She looked out onto the street, seeing Rachel struggling with her full basket; Caleb's cart still hitched in the street; and many other familiar folk walking along the board-walks. There were children playing on the edge of the thoroughfare. They laughed and ran and shouted.

She flipped the wooden sign on the door to "closed" and went back to the stillness of the empty shop.

"I think I'll put some oranges in the picnic, how does that sound?"

"All right, Mum."

Sarah laid out the patchwork quilt on the brittle yellow grass. On these hills it was knee-length and stiff, prickly hairs standing on guard if you rubbed it the wrong way. Mary sat down and started pulling apart pieces that stood at the edge of the blanket. People called it bone-grass.

When Sarah had first come to Barkley, children used to bury each other under handfuls of the stuff. After a while, the girl or boy underneath would jump up and pretend to be a Walkin'. The hairy bone-grass would stick in their woollen cardigan or skirt. A little imagination and these were exposed bones and rotten flesh. The resulting games of chase had a fear only children could enjoy.

It was a bright, cloudless evening, though a chill ran with the breeze. Sarah could see the whole town from here: the jumbled rows of wooden houses; the two main streets with their board-walks; the church; her shop; and Elder Richards's office. It was all smaller than it felt.

She knew almost everyone. She'd assumed it was because she ran the shop, but really, there weren't many people to know. They would come in and chat briefly whilst buying or selling goods. But they didn't stay long. The men seemed nervous, the women sharp. Since Thomas had gone, no one had stopped for a drink or dinner. She used to like entertaining, though Thomas didn't. He would sit through it for her. He was always charming.

Rebekah's monument stood on the far side of town, a tower of rusting bars that criss-crossed like the weave of a basket. It was fragile and very old. Once it was tall enough to touch the clouds, so the stories went. There had been more on these hills, in a line that went all the way to Pine Ridge, but most had crumbled and fallen away over the years. The Pastor said they were a work of our ancestors; it was important to remember their mistakes.

Childless couples still came from all over the county to try their luck in the shadow of Rebekah. Folk said it was a good shape.

Sarah hadn't visited the relic with Thomas, hadn't needed the monument's help to get pregnant. In fact, the place they had gone flowed across the land, wide and shallow. The Col River: the source of water and life in Barkley. She was drawn to it, to the memories of time spent on its banks with Thomas. She had to shut them out or she would lose herself there.

The picnic basket was full: cured meat, Indi figs, cheese, and two oranges. Mary's face brightened when she saw the sweet fruit.

"For later," Sarah said. She felt a moment of pride when Mary accepted this and cut off a piece of cheese.

"What happened in the street the other night?" Mary said.

"What night?"

Mary finished chewing. "The trouble. You were gone a long time. I saw a fire at the end of Main."

"Oh, that," Sarah said, taking a long drink. "One of the farmers wanted to burn some wood they didn't need. But it was too close to someone's home."

"People sounded angry."

Sarah shrugged. "It was silly. But people get angry for all sorts of reasons."

"Whose house was it?" Mary said.

"Um, the Peekmans," I think.'

"Jared Peekman?"

Sarah started to pack away the plates. "I think I see someone at those worker hives." She pointed to a nearby hill.

"They're 'Keeper Courie's."

"Want to say hello?"

Sarah checked the sun as Mary peeled an orange. She packed away the rest of the picnic.

The man was covered by a veil, but Sarah could tell it was 'Keeper Courie from the way he walked. It was a confident but modest way of moving, born of the respect of others combined with a sense of duty. Sarah liked him.

"Hello, 'Keeper. I hope we're not disturbing you?" Sarah said.

"Not at all, Mistress McDermott. If Mary here wants to see the hives, I'll show her, with your permission."

It was strange seeing only half the man's face; as if he were at the edge of her vision, out of focus. His nose and brows rose out of a darkness created by the veil, the shadows shifting as he spoke. But his voice was calm. A deep and soothing sound, as if he didn't just say the words, but hummed them to a tune of his own.

"If it's no bother?" Sarah said.

"No. No bother."

Courie took off his veil. He looked worn, like a rock-face that stood in defiance of the wind. His eyes were startlingly blue, yet the colour had a tint of something else. Sarah realised she knew that tint; it was in the mirror every morning. He put the veil on Mary; it was far too big, so he told her to hold on tight to stop it slipping.

"Should be a good year for honey, if this weather keeps," he said to Sarah.

"What's that?" Mary pointed to something in Courie's hand.

To answer, he lifted the item and pressed lightly on a set of small bellows. Smoke wafted into the air.

"Makes the workers sleepy. Otherwise they might not be happy to see us."

The two of them walked towards the hives; Mary's questions like flashes of lightning, followed by the rumble of Courie's answers. Sarah sat down and watched. She fiddled nervously with the grass. She was sure nothing bad would happen, but couldn't help feeling uneasy. Thomas used to scold her, saying she was Harrying the girl. She hated that old story: of Harry Herris who caught a bright-lie made of gold and in trying to keep it safe killed it. "It's just a rope-swing, stop worrying," Thomas had said. What if she fell off and broke her neck? "What if the sky fell tomorrow?" It was an annoying response, and she had said so.

The hives came to life.

It was sudden and she could feel it, like the wind changing direction. All the hives were emptying; plumes of workers rose from each. Their buzzing seemed to surround the hills in an instant. Courie stopped and put his hand on Mary's shoulder. They were still some way from the hives.

"'Keeper?" Sarah tried to call over the noise. Her voice shook.

He looked around, confused. His mouth was moving, but she could hear nothing but the beating of a hundred thousand wings. Her daughter was only twenty paces away, but she could barely see Mary. A curtain had been pulled down between them.

2 : 3

Courie took Mary's hand and turned his back to the hives. Sarah saw the doll, Stripe, fall slowly from her daughter's grasp like a leaf in the autumn.

The air emptied.

"Stripe," Mary screamed. Courie kept hold of her as she wriggled to reach her doll.

A cone of workers rose from the ground, like a tiny hurricane. At the base of this swirling mass, lying in the bone-grass, was Stripe. He was covered from head to toe in workers. Only his green button eyes were uncovered. The buzzing calmed to a deep hum. It sounded like a mouser purring.

"What are they doing?" Mary fought to be free as Courie carried her over to Sarah.

"Easy, Mary. They won't do the doll harm. Maybe they're just curious," he said, but he didn't sound convinced.

"What now?" Sarah said.

"I don't know. I doubt we could make the workers leave him. But they won't leave the hives either." Courie paused, his hand scratching his beard. "Wait here."

He took the veil from Mary and pressed on the bellows. He approached the winged hurricane. More smoke muddied the air. He bent down and with an outstretched hand picked up a leg of the doll. Workers oozed onto his white glove. Courie moved away from the hives. The further he went, the more workers lifted off from the doll.

"Next time, we'll leave Stripe at home, eh?" he said, handing the doll to Mary. She stared at it.

"I'm so sorry, 'Keeper," Sarah said.

"No harm done. Only seen them like that once before, back when they were my pa's. He'd bought some leather shoes from a river trader. Workers changed, like today. He couldn't figure if they were angry or curious. He wasn't stung."

"What did he do?"

"He walked away, then went back to the river trader and raised all kinds of hell. Eventually, just to be rid of Pa, the man admitted he'd bought the shoes from a Walkin." Pa came home and buried the shoes far from the house. Said they were tainted.'

Mary and Courie were looking at her. Thank you, Thomas, she thought. Thank you for this mess.

"Well, that *is* a strange story," she said. "I can assure you, 'Keeper, it won't happen again."

With Courie and his hives fading behind them, Mary said: "'Cursed be he that smiteth his neighbour secretly.'"

Sarah didn't reply as they trudged through the bone-grass.

Thank you, Thomas.

The sun was still full, but its edge breathed down onto the horizon. It would be dark by the time they were home.

As the sun set, Luke Morris shivered. He hadn't moved from this spot for two days now. He counted sunsets and lost track of hours. The bag of oats was half empty. He ate like a bird, picking crumbs out of his own hand in jerky, nervous movements. His arms looked delicate and he could feel his ribs through his cassock. But he wasn't hungry. His vigil for the Good Lord sustained him. He wasn't hungry. He was lonely.

Earlier, he had noticed a line of crumbers marching along the hot rock. They moved in single file. Luke wondered if the front crumber was important, older, or just knew these parts better than the others. They all seemed content to follow. He started talking to them. Asking where they were going, where they had been, and what they looked forward to. They kept marching. He was overcome with the urge to crush them beneath his sandal for ignoring him. It was a hateful thought. He stood up slowly. His joints creaked like a barn door. He looked for a switch or stick with which to cleanse himself, but there were no bushes in sight. Instead, he picked up a sharp-edged stone from the side of the Col River. He clenched it in his hand. He squeezed until his knuckles turned white and blood lined his fingers. Drops of red touched the blue water, expanded, and then disappeared. He put the stone in his pocket and waited for the bleeding to stop. It didn't take long.

He now hefted the stone in his other hand. It was stained a reddy-brown. Sinful thoughts could be atoned for. The Good Lord was forgiving. And Luke was lonely.

The moon was heavy in the clear sky. It would be a cold night. As he walked, he rubbed his arms to keep warm. Barkley wasn't far away. He wasn't returning from exile. He was reminding himself of what he left behind. Or couldn't.

Main Street was asleep. It wasn't late, but too late for a stroll along the board-walks. Luke ducked into a back alley. He passed locked doors and small, fenced-off patches of ground. One or two were looked after, growing shrubs that smelt bitter. He didn't want to be seen. The Pastor would find out. In this town nothing stayed a secret and Luke couldn't face the Pastor's disappointment. Twice in the alley Luke almost turned back. He was indulging himself, and at a time when self-denial was the Good Lord's will. Going without food or water was easy. Denying himself the sight of her wasn't.

Behind her house he found a barrel to perch on. The alley was dark, but candlelight spilt out of the top windows. He was desperate to see her. Just a glimpse of her face. He willed her to walk past once and he would be sated. His exile could run indefinitely. He peered upwards, cursing his weak eyes. A window was fogging up, or had blindness finally come to him? He wiped his glasses and strained to see.

There. The soft curve of a shoulder. Bare. Hair spilling onto her back. He took out his crucifix and began to rub it between his thumb and forefinger. His hand stung from the cuts but he embraced the pain. She went out of sight. Luke almost fell off the barrel. He prayed she would return. He was answered—her back turned, she stepped into a bath. Then she was gone. In his other hand, Luke grasped the sharp stone.

He waited, but didn't see her again. The candles went out. He stayed for as long as he could. Dawn was coming. He left the alley, running his bloodied hand along the wooden wall. Touching it wasn't like touching her, but he would remember how it felt nonetheless.

2 : 4

Mary sat watching the huntsman's web in front of her. It stretched across the back of the tired-looking pew. The fat shoulders of the Levin family rolled over the top edge. There were large cracks up and down the pew, probably because the Levins were so big. It certainly creaked a lot. The cuts in the wood had been there so long they were smooth. She liked to run a finger down them, but this Sabbath a web was in the way. The threads clung to the pew as if by magic. But she knew it wasn't the kind of magic that was bad, the kind that Pastor Gray preached against, the kind of their ancestors. This was a natural magic from the Good Lord. Delicate and complicated.

She hadn't spotted the huntsman yet. Some cracks were quite deep and there was a little hole in the corner. The hole was her guess: more private. Huntsmen liked doing things on their own.

From the front of the church she could hear Mrs. Gray listing the week's announcements. Everyone—including lots of adults—fidgeted on the hard seats; their bony bottoms trying to find a comfortable way to sit. It was just like school. But Mary was sitting very still. She wanted the huntsman to come out. Mrs. Gray finished, the Pastor came to the front, and Mary's patience was rewarded: the huntsman's long legs trickled out of the hole, like a leak in a bucket. Its body was small and black.

"When we doubt the word of the Good Lord, we *disgrace* ourselves," the Pastor said, beginning the sermon. Mary could see his red hair and dark cassock at the edge of her vision. He was getting closer. "And when we doubt the word of *our* fathers, we disgrace ourselves."

Despite its legs, the huntsman seemed tiny on the web. A smudge on a blank page.

"The Good Book tells of two such doubters, who shamed the names of Aaron and Miriam." The Pastor moved further down the aisle, into the centre of the congregation. The huntsman stopped on its spiralling home. "They challenged the beloved Moses, chosen of the Good Lord. Doubters. Fools, amen."

"Amen," came the echo. Mary breathed the word heavily and the web shook. The huntsman stood its ground, swaying.

"They questioned his visions, questioned the very gift of the Lord. Fools, amen—"

"Amen."

"—to question the gift, which was His word." The Pastor stood for a moment; his voice was steady and unusually quiet. Mary wanted to watch the animal, but she couldn't ignore the Pastor.

"So, the Lord appeared to Moses, Aaron and Miriam; because that is the nature of the doubting mind. Weak, it desires proof when it needs faith. And He said:

"'Listen,'" the Pastor roared. Mary and her mother jumped, and others did too. The word was so complete it filled the church. It was too big a word for their little town: it was the word of the Good Lord.

"'When a prophet of the Lord is among you, I reveal myself to him in *visions*, and I speak to him in *dreams*.'"

Pastor Gray's voice dropped again, back to his own.

"For seven days Miriam was exiled. Cast out. The fitting punishment for going against the will of her father."

"You must *never* go against the word of our Father. Nor the word of your own."

Never. It was a long time, and when Mary met her father in heaven, never would still be happening. People were always saying "never" and "for ever," but they rarely meant it. People other than the Pastor.

"For that is the road of damnation and exile."

The Pastor went to the front of the church and her attention turned back to the huntsman. It casually slid across its web. Something was caught, struggling to be free. Mrs. Freeman, who lived on Main in a big old house, leant in to whisper:

"Looks like he's done for." She nodded at the web.

Whatever the buzzing creature was, the huntsman was now eating it. Or so Mary thought. Nothing was really happening. The huntsman could've been kissing it. Finally, in the silence that followed the end of the sermon, the black smudge went back to its hole. Left behind was the insect, but she could almost see through it, as if it was empty.

"Didn't want that bit," Mrs. Freeman said.

"I wonder how long the shell will last," Mary said.

"Won't last for ever." Mrs. Freeman and her mother stood up, but Mary stayed looking at the web. The two women left her there as the congregation gradually filtered out of the church. The shell of the insect still hung on the sticky threads. Perhaps, like her mother washing the dishes, the huntsman would clean up later.

Was the web its only home? She thought about how big the huntsman was and then how big its web was. It would be like living in your bedroom. But, the huntsman could move its home. She couldn't. It was a gift the Good Lord gave His huntsmen, but not her. She was more like the insect: stuck and wriggling to be free. Free from what, the insect didn't know; not until it was too late. She was caught in something, something she didn't understand but could feel all around her. Sticky threads of people and words. And she didn't know where her huntsman was.

She wanted to destroy the web, but didn't. Instead, she carefully plucked the insect shell off. Opening the pocket of her dress, she dropped it inside. The huntsman started to come out, but must have thought better of it.

The sound of people talking outside was strange to hear in the empty church. Their mumble echoed faintly. The pews and altar were peaceful, as if they were resting after the service. Mary did the same each Sabbath, lying on her bed. She would close her eyes and imagine she was somewhere else—a place without flaking walls and rough sheets. There would be mountains, great peaks that challenged the sky. And trees, so green they were almost painful to see. And streams, with water clear enough to drink and warm enough to swim in. Her father would catch fish, her mother prepare the picnic. They'd talk and play games she was too old for, but she wouldn't care. Maybe the pews dreamed too.

Mary got up and turned to go. There was another person still in the church, sitting near the back, and he was looking at her.

"Hello, Mary," he said.

Luke Morris stared at her. He had small dark eyes behind his glasses. He'd always made her feel self-conscious, but there was something else now. Mary's cardigan buttons were undone.

He stepped in beside her as she walked out of the church. Outside, they stood on the porch as the rest of the congregation milled about and gossiped. She blinked away the glare of the mid-morning sun. It was a cold clear day, still as the grave. That's what all the buildings looked like in the weak spring light: big gravestones.

"How are you? How is your mother?" Luke said.

"Very well, thank you." Mary searched for Sarah. Her mother would talk to Luke instead. The crowd all looked the same: the women in black dresses and blonde ponytails. They blurred together, one stream of drab colours and forced smiles. Mary's eyes hurt to look at them. Her head felt heavy, her knees weak.

She'd gotten up too quickly. Taking a deep breath, she tried to listen to the acolyte.

"—don't you think? Mary?" He said her name in a strange way, like it was covered in honey. "Don't you think the Lord *does* show Himself in dreams and visions? To normal people?"

"Maybe, Mr. Morris. But you probably have to be special, not normal."

"Special. Yes," he said softly. He was looking out at the crowd.

"But," Mary said, "to the Good Lord everyone's special, so . . ."

He smiled at her.

"I think everyone's special too. I've been away from the town, but I had to come back for the sermon. For the people."

The acolyte drifted off into the crowd. After a few more deep breaths her head cleared. Watching people was always interesting, especially when they didn't know you were there. These minutes after church were the real reason everyone came. They all acted like good Leyists—some even meant it—but organising trades and gatherings, work and play, that was the value of the Sabbath. No one worked today, of course, but it was the seed of the week ahead.

Still shading her eyes, Mary saw Mrs. Gray stop and speak to people, no doubt parents asking about their children. Her mother would likely do the same; to check Mary hadn't been drawing again. She had, she just hadn't been caught. Drawing in the playing patch was silly, she knew that, but she'd been bored and angry. With what she couldn't remember. It was rarely one thing that got you angry.

Elder Richards was hunched over, talking with a little knot of men. The Law-Man was one of them. He was shaking his head and leaning back. No secret those two didn't like each other. Adults were a lot like children sometimes. Her uncles, Aunt Hannah, and her grandparents started off towards the cart-hitch. Finally, Mary spotted her mother. Sarah had also noticed the rest of the family. Her face was set in flat lines, tense.

"Luke Morris says hello," Mary said when she reached her mother.

"Let's go home. Are you hungry?"

"Like a huntsman without a web."

"Pardon?" Sarah said.

"Never mind. It was something Dad used to say." It wasn't, but Mary didn't wait for a reply. She wanted to get home to the quiet of her room and leave this dusty town behind. She could dream herself away and when she woke up, there was always the river.

Two days without water. Two scarred hands and two aching feet. It was worth it. Whenever Luke thought of her bare shoulder, he forced himself to swallow. Each time was like eating dust. He thought about her often. There was nothing base or tawdry about her taking a bath. He hadn't been aroused at the sight—not physically—and he wasn't when he recalled the moment over and over. The shoulder was like the unfurling of an angelic wing. It was a symbol of purity.

He had found some more shade at a different part of the river. Here, the water raged. The surface was a jagged mess of white peaks like a scrunched-up tissue. But somehow it still looked soft to the touch, airy. The river narrowed between two outcrops of solid stone, forcing more and more water through the gap. It would never burst these walls, but it would wear away at them—one fleck of dust at a time. In the distance, Luke could see the placid and wide stretches that were the normal way of the Col River. He could go there with little trouble. But he was enjoying the deafening roar of something alive, as it bounced between the rocky walls. The sound washed away everything—his hunger, his thirst, his questions, the Good Book. Almost everything. It couldn't force her shoulder from his mind.

The bag of oats was open next to him. He had tried eating at roughly midday. He couldn't manage it. Looking at the dry whiteness—so different from the river—he doubted he would ever eat again. He was sweating in his cassock. This long into his exile he ignored his own smell. It was a dank sweetness he simply lived with. He could bathe in the river. But he was unworthy of bathing. He was no angel.

He was looking once more at his inedible oats when he saw it. The river was coming alive. It spat a ball of white foam onto the bank, not twenty paces from where he was sitting. Luke carefully took off his glasses, rubbed his eyes, and looked again. The ball of white was still there. He tried to stand. His knees were sharp with pain and he sat back, tears coming to his eyes. He let them flow without crying. With his hands, he eased himself up. He took each step like an old woman—one foot forward, the other scraping the dust to meet it. His hips locked. He rubbed at them, willing blood into his legs.

It seemed to take the entire afternoon to cross the gulf of twenty paces. As he drew closer, he saw the ball of white was actually a baby woollie. Luke looked around for more of them, a mother perhaps, but found nothing. The little thing was alone. He was close enough to touch the woollie. It didn't run from him. Instead, it seemed to be pawing at the dirt as if it was looking for something. Luke put his hand out to touch the soft creature. It turned and ran ten or so paces and resumed its pawing. Bending down, Luke tried to find whatever the animal was looking for—something to eat most likely. He brushed away at the dirt, all the while the river shouting at the side of his head, but couldn't uncover whatever the woollie was looking for. Standing, he almost fell. He put out his arms to steady himself. He felt dizzy, the ground tilting wildly beneath him, the small woollie like a fulcrum for the world. He vomited a mix of dust and stale air. The woollie seemed only interested in its new patch of dirt. Luke stumbled forward. He sank to his knees and again the woollie skipped back. There was a divot where the woollie had been. He squinted. He called to the animal. He dug frantically at the spot, grabbing handfuls of sand and dust until he reached the moist earth beneath. He kept going. More and more earth; he piled it next to him. He hit stones and his nails bled. There was nothing there. He started to laugh. He laughed until he started to cough. The woollie carried on paw-ing at the ground.

Luke tried to reach the woollie. But as he came closer it skipped off. It never raised its head from its search, somehow knowing when Luke was near. He couldn't see the animal's eyes or any part of its face. He squinted, trying to find a feature to focus on, but his gaze seemed to slide away. Eventually, the bluffs tapered down to the river bank. The water was calmer here. The woollie didn't make a sound when it scratched in the dirt or when it performed its backwards shuffle. Luke had to concentrate to stay on his feet. He no longer tried to catch the woollie. He decided to follow it. Luke wasn't surprised when it turned away from the river and started backing towards Bark-ley. At any moment he expected to see a wayward flock of wool-lies or a frantic-looking shepherd. But there was only a blanket of empty and rolling earth, dry and cracked, broken by the occa-sional stubborn bush.

It was dark. Luke couldn't recall the sun setting; the sky turn-ing from blue to orange to black. He blinked, his eyes gritty and tired and begging for water, and it was night. The going was slow. It would take him days to reach the town, if that was in fact where he was being led. The woollie seemed to possess infinite patience. It dug its little holes until he caught up then started over in another spot. It never looked up. Not once.

Through the haze of hunger and thirst and dust, Luke came to realise this was no ordinary woollie. This animal was look-ing for something, something spiritual. It had taken itself away from the flock and headed into the wilderness. The two of them, pilgrims, had found each other. They would help one another in their search. He knew this, as he ignored the ache in his knees and the shooting pains that struck like lightning in his feet. His stomach was nothing more than a knot in a piece of string. The woollie kept moving and so would he.

Luke woke to find himself still walking. He had been drifting in and out of sleep for some time. He couldn't remember the last time he had slept or what it was like to lay his head down and accept the darkness.

There were lights ahead. He had to shield his eyes from their brightness. As the lights grew closer they bathed the woollie in dirty orange. This angered Luke, but all he could do was keep walking and try to stay awake. He knew this place, those lights. It was very familiar but he couldn't summon the memories. They skipped from his grasp, like his fluffy guide. He glanced back and saw a trail of holes stretching into the night. He stumbled and almost fell. But the Good Lord watched over him; wanted him to find the truth in this place, in the dirt, in his soul. *Hallelujah.*

The woollie led him into a labyrinth. Away from the lights. Wooden walls surrounded him. The smell of shaggies was strong in the air. He fumbled towards the smell—it was warm and wet and he was tired. But the woollie kept on and the shaggies grew fainter and then were gone.

They turned a corner and Luke knocked into something heavy. He hit the ground hard; his arm caught under his weight. The breath was chased out of him creating a puff of dust. He couldn't move. His legs were someone else's. He was watching another body. It was a barrel that had tripped him. A barrel full of lust and envy and all kinds of sin. Heavy enough to knock any man down.

Inches from his head, the woollie pawed at the ground. He still couldn't see the animal's face. Its digging grew frantic, nuzzling one moment and scraping the next. It bleated. The sound trumpeted through Luke like a blast from heaven. His ears were close to bursting. The woollie raised its head from the ground in what looked like triumph—an offering. In its mouth was a piece of bone-grass.

Then it was gone. Luke passed out.

Luke dreamed. Then he woke. Then he dreamed. In some dreams he knew where he was. In others he was lost.

He was lying in the dirt. His head rested awkwardly against the rough wooden slats of the barrel. He didn't have the energy to move it. He blinked and blinked; his eyes felt like a gravel path. He recognised the back of the house. This was *her* house. He had been here before. Many times. He glanced at the sky but couldn't see the moon. It must have been behind him. The alley was painted in a pure white; one even coat applied by an almighty brush. The windows gleamed, but this was not from inside. She was sleeping. Her daughter was sleeping. He closed his eyes.

2 : 5

Thomas stood on the bank of the Col River. He had done so many times before, but this time was different. He couldn't feel the water as it rumbled past him. Couldn't feel its pounding matched in his veins or in his chest or in his head. The river was loud but it sounded empty. Rocks and rapids cut the surface to white shreds of foam that shone in the moonlight. He could go farther and find a quiet place to cross, but he was tired of not being home. Karl Williams could see the sea from his kitchen window. Thomas couldn't remember what was outside his. It was at the back of the house, but every time he tried to picture it he couldn't.

He plunged one foot into the river. The water wrenched at his leg, but he held firm. He was ready for the water to be cold. It probably was. He had no awareness of the water itself. He didn't seem to be getting wet. There was just the pull, just the force of it. He planted his other foot in the silty riverbed. He kept his feet wide apart and knees bent, trying to make a solid structure out of himself, out of bones and muscles and quiet organs.

Every step took a long time. If anyone was watching, it would look funny: this man swinging his legs high out of the water then bracing against the pull. This Walkin'. He looked around for the blightbird that had been following him, that seemed to appear at his weakest moments, but the sky was empty.

The water streamed through his right leg. He had lost a lot of skin beneath the knee. His calf was being pulled away from the bone, like when he used to ease meat off a well-roasted joint. He needed to make it to the other side before the Col River claimed one or two joints for its own.

He quickened his strides. There was no strain. The work was not difficult or tiring, like a day in the fields. He felt the same as when he started. It would not be long now. He would be home. What was he going to do when he got there? He couldn't walk down Main calling Sarah's name. He would start a panic. Some people would not be happy to see him. Elder Richards. The Pastor. His Pa.

He slipped.

His leg, the one that was coming apart, suddenly went from under him. He dropped into the river. The water poured into him. It rushed through his arms and legs, down his throat, behind his eyes. It filled his stomach, his lungs. He struggled in panic, flailing to find the surface or the bottom or anything other than water. But he didn't choke or drown. He snatched at a rock, getting enough purchase to grab hold with both hands. The river roared at his face. He forced his feet down. He was three, maybe four steps from the bank. He concentrated everything he had on those steps.

He stumbled onto the sand and curled into a wet and shivering ball. He wasn't cold, but his body shook. He opened his mouth and water drained out. Struggling onto his back, he gazed up at the night sky while he waited for the shaking to stop. The moon was behind a bank of clouds.

Those fleeting moments, when he had been under the water, he did not panic because he might die again. It was the thought of being so close to Sarah and Mary and not to see them one last time.

Barkley appeared on the horizon in an orange glow, like the first rays of dawn. Thomas moved faster. The water had almost entirely left his body; seeping out of the cracks and gaps that fire and a bayonet had made. His legs worked fine, though he was aware of the space between his calf muscle and the bone. Air whistled where the water had been. It wasn't with every stride, but often enough. Another thing to get used to.

He stood at the edge of town. Main street was well lit, even at this hour of the night. Lamps, some oil but most of them candles, chased away the shadows. There would be no place to hide on Main. He skirted the side of the first building—Mrs. Freeman's house if he remembered correctly. Behind Main was entirely covered in darkness. His eyes adjusted instantly. The windows were all empty, but he ducked anyway. He waited and listened. The shop was right at the centre of Main. He counted off the buildings as he passed: Mrs. Freeman's, the tanner, Elder Richards' office. The houses had small back doors, with little patches of ground fenced off for gardens of sorts. Mrs. Freeman somehow managed to keep shrubs and herbs alive in hers. He could smell their sharp flavour. Having to skulk like this, keeping low in the back alleys, didn't sit right. But it was the only way.

Ahead was a faint glow. Thomas stopped. It could only be one small candle. It came from the back of a bigger place, that sprawled out into the alley. He crept closer. The musky stink of shaggies assaulted him. He had grown up with that smell. It had floated through his house and through his hours of work. And he had forgotten it. Now, seemingly in revenge, the heavy air of manure and fur and trampled straw covered him. He came closer to the candlelight.

There was a piercing whinnying. It came from one shaggie, and then another, and another. They were screaming. Loud thuds accompanied the high-pitched whines. Thomas stayed very still. Anything could have spooked the shaggies—everybody knew some shaggies were skittish and nervous. Anything, but it was most likely him.

A bang shook the stable wall next to him. And again. A board cracked. A shaggie was lashing out.

He had to go quickly, before they tore down the Smithy's stable. He ran past the entrance, through the candlelight.

"Hey! Who's there?"

Thomas dove into the shadows and kept running. The shaggies were still whinnying and stomping and that stable boy would have his hands full for hours. Thomas looked back to see him peering out of the stable entrance, but Thomas was too far away now. The boy went back in to calm the shaggies.

Thomas counted the back doors he had run past. It wasn't far now. There was a gap between the buildings. He could see Main and its flooding of light. He pressed himself against the alley wall. He stopped at what he guessed was the right place. The garden was bare of any life. Sarah couldn't grow a thing. There was no farming in her blood. Empty crates were stacked neatly up against the fencing. Crates that would have held food and tools and all kinds of goods. And would again.

He opened the gate latch as carefully as he could. He stared up at the windows, imagining his daughter and wife. Their looks of horror. A creature of the night stealing into their home. He shook away their scared faces. The back door was locked. He tried it again, hoping it might just be stuck. It didn't budge. The door had hazy glass panes. He could see through to the kitchen; the table where he had eaten meals with his family. He looked around for a rock or piece of metal to break the glass, but found nothing.

He flexed his hand into a fist. What little skin he had left became taut and strained. People wrapped their hands before breaking glass—Peter had done that when they were kids, breaking into Caleb Williams' shed. Thomas peeled off a patch of his uniform. It didn't come easily. It was burnt onto his skin. It didn't hurt, but he wanted to keep as much of himself whole as possible. Eventually, he had enough to wrap his hand.

The first blow didn't break the glass. Back along the alley the shaggies were calming down. He tried again. This time the glass cracked. Once more and a large chunk of the pane fell to the ground. It narrowly missed his foot. Reaching in, he unlocked the door. It swung inwards. He stepped into his house.

When Luke next woke, his crucifix was in his hand. He gripped it. Some of his scabs and cuts opened and blood begrudgingly slicked the wooden cross. He wept from the dream he'd been having. It was lost to him now, but he remembered the happiness. It was something he had touched. Held in his arms. A very real happiness and he silently cried to have left it.

His vision was blurred when the man appeared. Luke wiped his eyes, smearing blood across his cheeks. But this was not a man. The figure was garbed in a fiery red. Great black wings furled and unfurled from its shoulders. Where it trod the ground erupted in geysers of molten rock. Unbound sin emanated from it, buffeting Luke like a gale. Luke retched painfully. The knot of his stomach managed to creep tighter. He held up his crucifix, blood dripping down his wrist. The devil stood watching her house. It searched for a sign of life, a sign of the purity that Luke himself had glimpsed. Luke tried to call out. To stop the creature of the night. All he managed was a pathetic rasping sound. It was enough to get the devil's attention. It turned.

Thomas. The creature had the face of Thomas McDermott; the lost farmer, the lost soldier, the lost soul.

The devil-Thomas willed the house's back door open. Its wings dipped to enter. Luke hurled his crucifix, but it skidded uselessly across the ground. He prayed for strength. He forced himself upright. In no state to face Lucifer's minion, Luke stumbled towards the church. The Pastor would help. Help save Sarah McDermott.

* * *

The kitchen was silent. There was a faint smell of woollie; he spotted the bone still on the sideboard. It had been expertly stripped of its meat. A lucky pet would get the bone tomorrow. Thomas ran his hand along the table. His knuckles tapped and scraped over the even surface. He touched one of the stools, hoping it might still be warm, hoping he might be able to feel it if it was. But he couldn't. He glanced out the window: an alley wall and the roof of another house. If he saw Karl again, he would tell him.

On the stairs he tried to make as little noise as possible. He took each step slowly, deliberately, focusing on his feet, not daring to look up in case someone was there. Halfway up he stopped. He turned. This was a bad idea. What could he possibly have thought would happen? That Sarah would cry tears of joy and open her arms to him? That she would be blind to the gaping, dried wounds? That her fingers would lie to her as they touched his face? If she was still sleeping he would not wake her. He would hammer the image of her face into his memory and hope that would last for ever. The door to their bedroom was slightly ajar. He summoned the strength to push it open.

The bed was empty.

He almost collapsed with relief. The worry of what his wife would say was momentarily gone, cheated. He began shivering—as he had at the river—and closed the door. He sat down on the corner of the bed and touched the starched sheets; again wondering if they felt warm to a normal hand. He looked around the room. It was just as he'd left it. His two spare sets of boots were lined up against one wall. They were dusty.

Where was she?

That she could have remarried had not crossed his mind. How long had he been gone? He didn't even know. The time he was in the army, alive. The time in the pit; the fire still burning. The journey here. It would be long enough. Things like that could strike like lightning—he knew *that*. Sarah was most likely in another man's bed. He gripped the sheets. He could have come here and found them together.

The bedroom door opened.

He looked up to a crack of gunfire and a cloud of smoke.

2 : 6

The ball hit him in the ribs; one buckled under the blow.

"Sarah," he said.

She dropped the gun. He stood up. Slowly, he walked to her. She stepped backwards, her hands clasped over her mouth, until she hit the wall.

"Sarah, it's me. Thomas."

She shook her head, over and over.

"I'm sorry," he said. She burst into tears. He tried to hug her, but she pushed him away.

"No," she said, her voice thick. "You can't be here!" And then she came to him. She hugged him fiercely, ignoring the bones and dead skin. "Where have you been?"

He hugged her back for as long as he could. He made sure his fingers did not touch her skin. He couldn't bear for her to feel him like this, on her body. She kept on crying, hot and wet against his chest.

"I didn't know if I should come back," he said. "I needed to see you."

"Mum?" Mary came out of her bedroom. She was rubbing the sleep from her eyes. Thomas turned away from his daughter. He didn't want to frighten her. Sarah took Mary by the hand. "Who is that?" Mary said.

"Just an old friend."

Thomas stayed silent. An old friend. If he was in any doubt a Walkin' could be hurt, it was gone. Sarah came back and they went into her bedroom. She looked into his face for the first time. Her hand traced the charred skin.

"I had my suspicions. I didn't want it to be true." She touched his cheekbone and shuddered. "I've regretted it every day."

"Regretted what?" he said.

"When I told you ashes or never again. I've missed you."

"I haven't thought of anything else. I had to see you both."

"It will be better if she sees you in the morning," Sarah said. The morning. He had not thought that far ahead. She must have seen it on his face, somehow. "You are staying?"

"I don't—"

Someone banged the shop door, hard.

"Mistress McDermott? It's the Law-Man. We heard a gunshot?"

"They'll go away," she whispered, gripping the front of his uniform.

"No, they won't," Thomas said.

"It's in there! The demon. I saw it myself. Spawn of Satan!" More banging.

"They will break it down," he said.

"Sarah!" called the Law-Man.

"You can't," she said. "They burnt Jared already. And his son." She ran to the doorway. "Mary," she hissed.

"I'm sorry. I had to see you again. It was selfish."

Sarah went into Mary's room.

A bang shook the front of the house. The door wouldn't hold long. He went to a wardrobe. He took out a shirt and trousers. He quickly put them on. They were so loose on him, he felt like a child in an adult's clothing.

"You have to take her with you," Sarah said. "They'll kill her."

"What? Why would they do that?"

"I told you: they killed Simon Peekman because Jared came back."

"I didn't know. I—"

"Mum? What's going on?" Mary was still half asleep, but she was fully dressed.

"I know one place that might be safe," he said.

"They'll follow you—the Law-Man, the Pastor. Why did you come back?"

He hugged Sarah. "I love you."

"Mary, you have to go with this man. He will take care of you."

"But, Mum—"

"Just do as I say," Sarah shouted. Mary was confused, but her mother's tone was clear enough. Thomas took his daughter by the hand and ran down the stairs. He reached the bottom just as they broke through the door.

"There!" someone yelled. Thomas went as quickly as he could through the kitchen. Mary was awake enough to be frightened now and ran with him.

The door frame exploded next to Thomas. They were out in the alley.

"He's out back," the same voice called. Thomas heard the gun cock again. He kept low. More wood behind him splintered under the weight of lead shot.

They reached the stable and an idea hit him. He ran right in. The shaggies went berserk. They threw their heads up, pulling desperately against their ropes. Some pawed the ground with their front hooves; others slammed the walls with their back set. Mary stood looking from one animal to the next. He opened the first stall. The shaggie backed away from him, as far as it could go, right into the corner, which suited Thomas. He undid the knot and circled the stall. The shaggie kept one quivering eye on him. Then it saw freedom and bolted.

"What the—?" the stable boy burst into view.

Thomas ran at him, knocking him down. "Sorry, son," he said. He released as many shaggies as he dared. He chased them into the alley, dragging Mary as close alongside them as he could, careful of their thrashing, metal-clad feet. The shaggies poured through the gaps to Main. From the angry cries of men, they were causing enough problems. One shaggie was caught between Thomas and the alley wall. The poor beast ran as quickly as its hairy legs could take it, always watching Thomas. He kept pace. The edge of town was in sight.

A man stepped into the end of the alley. Thomas couldn't see his face. He fired. The shaggie seemed to lose its footing and went down. It happened slowly. Somehow the movement appeared graceful, deliberate. The sound was awful; the shaggie shrieked, then gurgled, then rolled like thunder.

Thomas was on the man. He was old, his beard gone to white. Thomas wrenched the rifle from the man's shaking hands and yanked the butt upwards into his chin. The man dropped with a lot less noise than the shaggie. Thomas left him his gun.

Running, Thomas didn't look back. The shouts of men grew softer as he went. It was a shame about the stable boy. A shame about the shaggie and the old man. But he kept the sight of Sarah in his mind; her touch on his cheek, the way she had hugged him. And now he had a purpose. His daughter was with him. He had to keep her safe. He kept them moving until Mary fell down, exhausted.

Mary woke with the sun in her eyes. She closed them. Her body was sore. Her face, arms and legs stung. She wasn't in her bed. She had slept on the ground and her back ached.

She groaned and sat up. Wiping one hand on her dress, she rubbed at her face with the other. What had she done last night? She couldn't remember much. She didn't remember sneaking out, but how else did she get here? She pressed her fingers against her eyes. She'd had a dream about someone in their house. Someone her mother knew.

"Hello, Mary."

The voice came from a man sitting near her. He was in a loose shirt and trousers. Underneath the thin white cotton of his shirt she could see a shabby-looking army jacket, the same colour as the army men that had come to Barkley. His uniform looked burnt: great holes with singed edges. It wasn't just his clothes that were burnt. His skin had burns all along it too.

She gasped, covering her mouth with her hand. She looked away, trying not to be rude and stare. He looked horrible.

"I'm not the prettiest picture, I know," he said.

She glanced over at him and away again.

"How—how do you know my name?"

"Times I wondered if I'd recognise you. But I did, first moment."

She couldn't see or hear the Col River. Couldn't hear any birds either. The ground was a dirty yellow. Had it really happened? Did this man take her from her home?

"I should be, should be getting home." She tried to stand up, but her legs wobbled and she dropped back down.

"You can't, Mary. They'll hurt you if you go back."

"My mother; she'll be worried." Mary got to her knees gradually, careful not to look at the stranger.

"Your ma, yes she will. She probably won't open the shop today," he said.

At this, she looked right at him. Really looked at him. Her mouth fell open. If she weren't so fuzzy, she would have screamed. Part of her knew she should scream. Most of the man's face was missing. His whole left cheek was gone—she could see his teeth, all mucky and brown. His left eye seemed to hang in plain air, above scorched bone. Bits of his forehead were blackened, and there were singed rings with bone beneath.

Bile rose in her throat.

"It's that bad, is it?" he said.

There was a Walkin' sitting opposite her. Within spitting distance was someone who had died and come back to life. It looked like somebody even tried to burn him. She began to shake all over.

"I—I—Home."

"I can't take you home, Mary. And it's my fault." He looked away. His normal-looking cheek was facing her. She sat staring at him.

If she could move, she could run; but would she be fast enough? Even if she was, which direction would she go? Did Walkin' get tired? Would he keep chasing her?

"How—how do you know my name? How do you know my mother?" she said slowly.

"I didn't expect you to recognise me; been gone a while. Drop you in an Easter parade and I'd still pick you out from two streets over." He wasn't looking at her. "Isn't a complicated way to say it: it's me, Mary. Your dad."

Silence yawned between them. She gazed at the black marks on the back of his neck. Suddenly they grew, blotting out the world. She took a shuddering breath, but it was too late. She was falling down into the shadow.

2 : 7

Thomas had thought she might be scared or revolted, maybe run away from him. He had no plan for fainting.

He hesitated. She was still breathing. He knew he should go to her, but what if she woke up? What if she saw him, a fleshless beast, towering over her? Things had gone well to begin with; as well as could be expected. That was until Mary actually realised what he was; *who* he was tipped her over the edge.

He was being stupid. He went over to her. When he had left, her hair had been almost white. Now it was much darker. She was still in braids, as she should be. But she was growing up fast and he'd missed a lot of it. He knelt beside her. She had fallen onto her back. Her calm little face looked up. The sun was getting higher. The morning chill was fading; it would be a hot day. Not a problem for him, but he needed to get Mary into some shade. She would need water. And food.

Food. He hadn't thought about food for weeks. It was strange; he had forgotten something he'd taken for granted his whole life. The river was close by. He still had his leather flint kit in the pocket of his uniform. If they could catch something, they could cook it. As gently as he could he picked Mary up; one arm under her knees, one under her shoulders. She was as light as summer rain.

Mary didn't stir as he carried her across the rough, rocky plateau. They weren't in the Redlands proper; the river was less than a mile away. Scrubby bushes and bent trees were still dotted here and there. He covered ground quickly; the river was getting fatter on the horizon. There was a set of small bluffs to the south as the river wound its way round a corner and carved its path through the rock. It would be as good a place as any to find shade. As a child he had rarely ventured that far, but when working for Caleb he'd trapped for under-mutton there. He hoped the farmer wasn't checking his traps this morning.

The water was quiet, drifting calmly along. Luckily, their side was in the shade. He eased Mary down on a dry bit of bank and stopped to look at her. He had watched her sleep for the few hours before dawn, just enjoying being close to his daughter again. He would watch again now, but she needed something to eat.

Caleb had traps all over these bluffs and had checked them every day when Thomas worked for him. Or his help did. The first dozen Thomas checked were empty; limp pieces of wire in front of cup-sized holes. He didn't wander too far, in case Mary came to.

The next one wasn't empty. It was a small under-mutton, not much more than a baby. Its head was through the trap, but the wire had cut down into its neck. Thomas could see the red raw skin; it had struggled, which caused the wire to tighten. The animal's eyes were wide open, but covered in a film of dust and dirt. Its mouth the same.

As Thomas came closer it sprang into life. Whimpering, it wriggled frantically.

"Easy now," he whispered. "Won't be long." He reached down, taking the under-mutton firmly. The neck snapped like a shaft of bone-grass. Pushing at the side wires, he took the animal out of the trap.

He went back to Mary. The whole thing left him feeling out of place. He had been a human, a creature at the top of the heap. He'd killed other animals to live. Then he died; the natural way of things. But now, he was back and killing again. Not for his own sake, but still. He'd come back into the bigger chain of life and death—and he didn't know if he belonged there.

He looked at the lifeless body of the under-mutton. He didn't care to think about it much. What he did care about was unconscious by the river. She had shifted away from the rock, cuddling her knees close. He gathered some dry wood. There was no shortage—most of the brush here was slowly dying. He set a fire against the cliff, same as he'd done a thousand times in the army. Someone might see the smoke, but there was no helping that. She needed to eat before they went any further. The wood was dry at least.

As he put the flint to work, he glanced over at Mary. Camp talk had been about wives and children more often than not. Old and young men would share stories about their families. Now he could share a story or two with his daughter, if she'd care to hear it. A strange, forgotten feeling came over him. He was looking forward to her waking up.

Mary could smell something like burnt skin. Was it the Walkin'? She hadn't noticed a smell before, or maybe she couldn't remember. She kept her eyes half closed. He was sitting a little way from her; the thing that claimed to be her father. Every so often he poked the fire. The smell was coming from something on the end of a stick, propped over the flames.

Her stomach rumbled.

"I didn't know how to wake you," he said.

She sat up. To her relief she saw the river. She could make her way home from here. Maybe.

"Have a drink. This is almost ready." He gestured towards the stick. The fire made spitting noises.

She thought about saying no, about standing up and walking away. But she *was* thirsty. And hungry.

The water stung her skin as she washed her face. It was almost too cold to drink. She cupped her hands and slurped. She hadn't realised how dry her throat was. The scratches on her forehead and cheeks burnt a little. She dried her face with a clean-ish bit of her dress.

"I'm glad you kept the doll."

She turned back and saw Stripe sitting in the shade. She had been carrying him in her dream.

"You're not my dad."

"'I will love you always. I will come back to you,'" he said.

They were the words written on the note she kept in Stripe. No one knew about the note. No one, except her and the man who put it there. Her father. She had found him. But it wasn't him.

"You're . . . you're supposed to be in heaven," she said quietly.

"That's what I thought."

"Your brothers and sisters, what're their names?"

"Peter the eldest, then Bethany, Hannah and finally Samuel," he said.

"When did you meet my mother?"

"The day her family came to Barkley. I can remember Ma was none too happy. Never was." He poked the fire, which was going out. "I helped them unload their cart. I was taking down some bags when the prettiest little thing popped her head round. Told me to 'be careful with her cases' before gliding off. Peter didn't stop gawping. She was a beauty."

Mary's chest grew tighter the more he said. Her mother said they first met at church, but her father always insisted it was her first day in town. There was no doubting it. Her father had come back, but as a Walkin'—an abomination, an evil spirit.

Every lesson, every sermon she'd sat through, all said this creature was an agent of the devil.

But that agent was her father.

She felt dizzy. She tried to keep breathing, to not black out again.

He got up and came over to her.

"I know it's hard to understand."

She stared at the broken skin and exposed bone. Her father was there, beneath it all.

"This wasn't supposed to happen," he said. "They were supposed to do the right thing. But they didn't. I just wanted to say goodbye, that's all."

She snapped to.

"What?" she said.

"I came back to say goodbye."

"No. No, you said you would come back to me."

"But, Mary, I'm ... this," he said, spreading his arms. "I ruined everything. But I promised I would keep you safe."

Her eyes and nose were streaming. She coughed and spluttered.

He hugged her, but she fought. There was a workers' nest swarming inside her. But one worker buzzed louder than all others: want.

She wanted her father.

2 : 8

Sarah prepared some breakfast. She fried eggs over the fire, cut and buttered four slices of bread, and put out two plates. She got as far as putting out the cutlery before she stopped. She stared at Mary's plate. At the empty stool.

The back door was open and swung on its hinges in the breeze. She hugged herself. She had tried to close it, but the frame was a mess. The shop door was flat on the floor. The wind ran right through the building, like her daughter used to after school. She ate an egg without tasting it.

"Sarah?"

Law-Man Bellis knocked and came into the kitchen. He seemed taller today. And younger. His skin still had the ghost of wrinkles, but it had colour. It was whole. She wanted to touch his face; to chase away her finger's memory of Thomas's paper-skin. He sat down opposite her.

"How are you?" he said.

"Have some breakfast, Bellis. I made too much."

He looked at the extra plate.

"I've got some boys working on the shop door. They're good boys; they'll do it right."

"You didn't need to do that," she said. But if he hadn't, how would she have put the door back? She didn't have any tools. Then she remembered the shelves of hammers, nails, and more things she barely knew the name of. Selling something was different from being able to use it. Bellis had tools. They were strapped around his waist in a thick leather belt. He probably bought them here.

"I'll get to work on that," he said, motioning to the back door. "But first, why don't you tell me what happened."

On her plate, half an egg oozed its yellow insides. It spread at the pace of seasons, slowly engulfing crumbs. She watched it as she spoke.

"A man broke into my house last night."

"Did you recognise him?"

"It was so dark."

"Sarah, was it Thomas?" he said.

She had to lie. Since Thomas took Mary down the stairs and out of the house, Sarah had been preparing for this moment. She imagined it would be difficult; she had to be convincing for Mary's sake. The voice shouting "spawn of Satan" haunted her. Someone knew. It was her word against theirs.

But it was easy. She wasn't lying; she told the truth. "I don't know who it was."

"Did he hurt you?"

She shook her head. "He took Mary. He took my daughter."

"We heard a gunshot."

"I missed," she said. "He pushed me to the floor. He grabbed Mary. I couldn't stop him." She started to cry. The tears weren't fake; Mary was gone. She might not see her again.

"Was this upstairs?"

She nodded. "My bedroom."

"Can I take a look? Maybe I can fix the damage." Bellis got up. He was heavy on the stairs. She followed the sound of him on the floorboards. He took a few steps and then stopped for a while. He did this many times. When he came back, Sarah's egg yolk had grown a skin.

"Can't see where the shot went," he said.

"I don't remember."

"That's okay. At least there's no mess. Not like what I did here." He went over to the back door. She watched him work. She had nothing else to do. No one would come to the shop today. News of last night would spread like a sickness—sour faces and shaking heads and more than enough tutting. One or two people might be concerned for her. They would wait a respectful time before popping in. Those who did would be interrogated for more details. How was she doing? Was her hair a mess? Had she washed the dishes? Did she cry?

Bellis cleared away the splintered wood. He was smoothing a kink in the door frame. She didn't know why, but she liked the look of it; the curving break in the straight line.

"I'm sorry," Bellis said. "I'm sorry I missed him."

Mary's face was buried in his chest. His shirt scratched against her skin. It was nice, as though she was scrubbing off her doubts and worries. Mary could smell burnt wool but nothing else. She'd thought Walkin' would smell terrible. She had found a dead red-wink once; guessed someone shot it. The smell was rancid and she gagged. But her father had no scent, like he wasn't really there.

He was stroking her hair. Her mother only ever brushed it; but before bed time he would stroke her hair and she would fall asleep.

His hand felt uneven. Hair caught in it, like knots in a comb. She ignored the pain.

"You eat your fill. Then we have to get moving," he said.

She drew away. She forced herself to look at his face. All of it. She would have to accept that was how her father looked now. Patches of normal, patches of dead. He wasn't all that frightening, now she knew what to expect.

He turned his head. From this side it was as if nothing had happened. He was a little pale, as if he'd been bedridden from one church service to the next. It was the same flat nose. The same wide chin. He still had the scar near his ear. She didn't know how he got it and he'd probably not tell her, even now.

The fire had almost gone out when they sat down. Her father prodded the embers and handed her the makeshift spit. He had skinned a young under-mutton, gutted it, and taken off the head and paws. She didn't want to know how.

"Our Father, who art in—" Mary glanced at her father. She always prayed before eating, but she felt silly, as if she'd just said the wrong thing in front of her parents' dinner guests.

He shrugged. She skipped the prayer. The meat was stringy and tough, but she tore into it nonetheless. Her stomach continued to rumble. Juices ran down her chin and she wiped them off with the back of her hand. Manners didn't seem to matter either. He was watching her eat. With a mouth half full, she said:

"Want some?"

"No, darlin." I don't eat.'

"You don't eat? What, nothing?"

"Nothing," he said.

She took another bite and chewed.

"That's sad," she said eventually.

"You know, it probably is. That smells pretty good."

She carried on eating, though he wasn't watching now. The breeze picked up, sending smoke right at her. She coughed and moved to the other side of the fire. The wind changed and the smoke followed her.

"Blood and bones!"

She winced, expecting to be told off.

Instead, her father laughed. It was a dry sound—like the shuffling of hay stalks.

"I haven't heard that one in a long while. Don't worry, I won't tell your mother."

She smiled.

Sitting in the shade, the muddy sand cool through her dress, she finished the meat. Bits were still between the bones, but she didn't like getting her face right in there. It was silly, she'd eaten the animal anyway, but that's how it was. There were things you didn't do. And that was your choice.

"Done?" Thomas said, holding out his hand. She gave the spit to him. Standing up, he walked to the river's edge and tossed the remains into the water. The carcass bobbed down-stream a little, and then disappeared.

He sat beside her. The fire had gone out and no longer smoked.

"Does it hurt, your face?" she said.

"No. Nothing does."

"Can I?"

He nodded.

She stood in front of him. Slowly she ghosted her fingers along his cheekbone. It was like stone. She touched the dark red area below, a little curtain of meat. It was hard, not like the under-mutton. Lines ran down it and she thought of the bark of a tree. His skin was like paper, the edges almost sharp.

His teeth were black with soot. He gave her a nip, making her jump.

She giggled and touched her own cheek. It felt nothing like his. Everything was softer, wetter. Even his teeth were dried out.

"What was it like, dying?" she said quietly.

He looked away. She was beginning to think he hadn't heard her, when he said:

"There was a lot of pain, but not for long. The man who got me did the job right; made a mess of me. Then, nothing. I can't remember anything that happened after."

"And what about . . . when you . . ."

Again he took his time before answering.

"It was like waking up from a nap in the afternoon. When you're not sure where you are, what part of the day it is, even who you are. But worse."

"Can I see where he got you?"

"Don't tell your mother," he said. He lifted the bottom of his shirt.

The hole was small, a black circle that went deep. She could see through it. The skin around it was puffy, an angry red. He was right; inside was a mess. Colours all mixed together: purples, reds, yellows, greens and whites. It was like a field full of different flowers.

"The man had a knife strapped onto his gun. They call it a bayonet. He put it in and twisted it right round."

"Who was he?" she said.

"I don't know, darlin.' Just another soldier on the other side." He pulled down his shirt.

The morning was everything he had come back for. He couldn't stop looking at her, watching her every move. He wanted to memorise it all: how she tossed her hair from her face; how her brow wrinkled when she concentrated; and her smile. He had been forced to leave a girl; he'd come back to a young woman.

He could not believe how smart she was. He grinned like a fool with pride. She talked about school, working in the shop, the people she saw and spoke to. She had a good eye for detail and a way of understanding folk. He could see Sarah's hand in that. Mary certainly didn't get it from a country boy like him.

"Have you met people like you?"

"Yes, I've met other Walkin." Not many.'

"Really?" She was excited by the idea. He could see why—it was Barkley's fault. The Walkin' had been called evil, the devil's minions. To a child they seemed exciting and mysterious. As a boy he had felt it too. The truth, or his take on it, wasn't so interesting.

"The two I met seemed normal enough. They talked about the place they live. There's lots of people like me. They have the space to do whatever they want."

"Do they draw?"

"I think so."

"And they're allowed to draw? Do they write words too?"

"I don't know if anyone tells them not to; it's not like Barkley. As I understand it, they have a lot of time to fill," he said.

"I want to see them."

He tried to explain that really he knew nothing about Black Mountain. It might be dull for a child. There might not be any food there. He assumed that she'd be the only living person, but he didn't know for certain. He didn't even know if she'd be allowed to go inside—if there was an inside. He said it might take a week or a month or a year to get there, over desert and mountains. There would be long climbs; sheer drops; paths so thin a billy-beard would wince; and no water for miles around. The more he talked, the worse it sounded to him. What was he doing?

"I don't care," she said. "I ran away each night to find you."

She was right. And he did owe her. He owed her something he had plenty of: time. She wasn't the only one who deserved this time together.

Mary was about to say something, but was stopped by the sound of whistling. They both heard it. The hymn of St. Anne. Someone was checking the traps and that someone was whistling.

"Caleb Williams," Mary said.

"We need to hide."

"Why? Caleb's a nice man."

"Your ma said they would follow us. They want to hurt you because of what I am. What you might become. That's what they did to Jared and Simon Peekman." He grabbed her arm and pulled her away from the water.

"Caleb won't burn me," she said, but she let him drag her off the bank and into some scrub.

"Yes, he would."

Caleb would think he was doing the right thing. Saving the girl's soul. Caleb was out here looking for Mary. Maybe the whole town was. Already they were hiding as if hunted.

2 : 9

Nathaniel was the last to arrive at Elder Richards' office. He hitched Buster and went quickly into the building. Veronica Klimp was sitting at her desk. When he entered, she looked up from her copy of the Good Book. She looked tired. No doubt the Elder had woken her late last night and kept her working through the day. If he was awake, so was she. He took off his hat and smiled what he hoped was a sympathetic smile.

"The Elder says you're late."

"Not everyone lives on Main," Nathaniel said.

"They're in his chambers."

"Don't get up," he said. "I know the way."

He hurried along the corridor. He was tracking mud onto the Elder's carpets. Served Richards right for making him rush into town. But as he stood in front of the chamber door, he realised it was Veronica who would have to clean up his mess. He knocked and went in.

". . . and it was no ordinary man! It was Satan's spawn."

"Yes, Luke," the Elder said. He was sitting behind his large, dark wood desk. In front of him were the Pastor and Luke

Morris. Law-Man Bellis stood a little way off, leaning against the wall. He clearly wasn't happy despite appearing at ease; he was whittling away at his fingernails with a six-inch blade. The chamber was warm—a brazier holding coals sat in the corner. More carpet filled the sizeable room. Chairs were arranged in front of the desk. A basin and a standing mirror were the only furniture to suggest this was a private room. It wasn't private today. The two holy men turned when Nathaniel came in.

"What's going on?" Nathaniel said.

Luke launched into his story. The young man looked awful. His cheeks were hollow. The hands he gestured with were almost skeletal. The gist of it was someone had taken Mary McDermott in the night. Nathaniel sat down heavily in one of the Elder's big leather chairs. Luke was making some pretty extravagant claims about who that "someone" was.

". . . and the evil that rolled off this creature—"

"Thank you, Luke," the Elder said. "Now, if you would leave us?"

Luke looked to the Pastor who nodded just a fraction. Richards didn't like that, but managed to sit on his anger. The young acolyte left the room muttering.

"I say again, what's going on?"

The Pastor turned to Nathaniel. "My acolyte has been in self-imposed exile, a pious enterprise to cleanse the soul. He has fasted. He hasn't slept. But someone *did* take Mary McDermott from her home last night. There was a gunshot. This we know as fact."

"But no demon took her," Bellis said. "I saw him."

"Luke isn't lying. He saw the events as a holy man might."

"A demon with the face of Thomas McDermott?"

"I think it's fairly clear that Thomas returned to Barkley in the same manner as Jared Peekman. As a Walkin'," the Pastor said.

The men grew quiet. Nathaniel remembered that day clearly: the pyre, Jared, and his son. He was sure the rest of them were remembering too.

"Just what are you suggesting?" he said.

"We send a party to find them. We have a duty to their eternal souls." The Pastor looked at every one of them in turn. "If Thomas did indeed take Mary, and he is indeed a Walkin," then both *have* to burn on a pyre.'

"I don't kill children," Bellis growled.

"Wait, wait here a moment. What happened to Sarah?"

"She's fine," Richards said. "Upset and shaken, but fine. But she says it wasn't Thomas."

"Is she sure?"

"Either way. We must get back the girl," the Pastor said. "If her father is a creature of Satan, then our course is clear."

"It isn't so clear to me," Bellis said.

The Pastor rushed over to him. "Is your faith so lacking? Do you doubt the Lord? Our founder and saviour, J. S. Barkley? Where, Bellis? Tell me where does your heresy lie?"

Bellis didn't flinch under the gaze of the Pastor. He pointedly put away his knife. Nathaniel could not have been so calm were it him.

"I don't—"

"You won't have to," the Pastor snapped. "Luke will. You will need him to perform the rites. And you, Gravekeeper, will be needed too."

Nathaniel floundered. What did this have to do with him? He tended gravestones. The Elder came to his rescue before he managed a word. "Now see here, Pastor, none of this is decided."

"This is a matter for the church. Two souls are at risk. We need to act quickly. Bellis, Luke and Nathaniel must ride out at once. Every hour Mary and Thomas are farther away."

"If it is Thomas," the Elder reminded them.

"Why do I need to go?" Nathaniel said.

"On this, I agree with the Pastor," Richards said. "Jared Peekman was the first Walkin' we've ever dealt with; until now our ways have always stopped that from happening. Jared was . . .

difficult. People are asking questions. We can't have it happen again, not in the town."

"Bring them home to bury," the Pastor said.

"For Christ's sake!" Bellis said, slapping the wall.

"Yes, Bellis. For the sake of Christ, He who taught us the way."

The Law-Man stormed out of the room. Richards let the dust settle.

"He will do it. He might not like it, but there's one thing Bellis will always do: uphold the law."

"I will need a day. To get the urns ready," Nathaniel said, not quite believing what he was agreeing to.

The Pastor nodded. Then he too left the chamber, gliding triumphantly out the door. This was a significant moment for the red-haired preacher. The Elder squirmed in his seat.

"What are we going to do, John?" Since they were adults, Nathaniel had called his friend by his first name only twice—on his wedding days.

"Hope Sarah is right."

2 : 10

*At this, she bowed down with her face to the ground.
She exclaimed, "Why have I found such favour in your eyes
that you notice me—a foreigner?"*

Ruth

BOOK 3

3 : 1

Our lack of dreams is a difficult and contentious subject.

Ancient thinkers attributed a great deal of importance to these vivid but often forgotten images. They suggested that dreams were the work of a deeper subconscious. As such, they are the playground of the repressed. Anger, hatred, love, lust, envy—the true emotional content that humanity hides not only from each other, but from themselves. Powerful feelings require a powerful outlet.

Dreams can prove so potent as to cross the boundary between waking and sleep. They can influence the actions of an individual the following day—inspiring fear, malaise, or a sense of well-being. Many old religions utilised the dream world as a conduit between deity and worshipper. There are accounts of walking-dreams: men and women and even children acting physically whilst deep in slumber.

But, brothers and sisters, do we not feel anger? Do we not feel love? Do we not envy the work of others? Every time I'm foolish enough to pick up a brush, I know I do.

Where is our outlet?

I submit to the forum: Memories.

We have a previous lifetime—be it eight or eighty years—full of vividly remembered moments. Those same emotions that escape the net of human sensibilities within dreams can be found in our memories.

There we find solace and experience. That is our outlet.

—transcribed from *The Human Condition*, an open forum in the Black Mountain Common Consensus of Winters 2920—Councilman Cirr speaking in response to Chairman Immu's remarks on humanity's need for sleep

The sound of whistling faded as Thomas took Mary away from the river. They were as quiet as grain-thieves when they left the bush. Whoever was checking the traps was down on the bank.

They passed the rest of the afternoon trudging along. He asked her about school and the other children. She said she had so many friends it was hard to keep up. She talked about the town gossip, about the Easter parade and the dance after. He asked about boys and she said they smelt funny. Mary didn't complain once. The land changed colour slightly. There were fewer scrubs and trees. They'd come to the Redlands proper.

This could be the most stupid thing he had ever done, in a long line of stupid things. Why break with the habit of two lifetimes? He'd been told he was a fool for marrying Sarah; the upstart girl who hadn't been in Barkley more than three years. He felt a fool for waiting that long.

The wisdom of that particular choice was walking next to him. Her brow was knitted. Perhaps she was also wondering if she'd made a mistake. She would have plenty of time to think about it in the days or weeks to Black Mountain.

Thomas tried to keep the going easy, avoiding the bluffs and gorges that veined the Redlands. Once or twice that afternoon they had to back-track after coming to a cliff edge. Mary still didn't complain.

The sun was large in the sky ahead of them. The clouds, like fluffy fat grubs, were stained yellow.

"Dad. You're not wearing any shoes."

He glanced down. "You're right, darlin.'"

"Don't your feet hurt?"

"No. I can feel the rocks, but they don't hurt," he said.

"I'm thirsty, Dad."

"I know you are. Just a little further and we'll get you something to drink. And eat."

He hoped he remembered the way to Miracle—the ruined town where he'd met the deserter Karl Williams. Karl would share his supplies; maybe even give them some extra to go on with.

Thinking of Karl brought back memories from his time in the army. It felt a long time ago. So many nights sleeping under canvas, talking by a fire, going hungry—they all melted into one. He had only been in a real battle three times. Survived two of them. There were plenty of skirmishes. Red coats sneaking around in the night. Muzzle flashes like falling stars.

There was a howl in the distance. It rang across the plain.

"Was that a red-wink, Dad?"

"I'd say so."

"It sounded bigger. Are were-winks real?"

"No. They're not."

It was early for a red-wink; they usually only called at night. Unless it was a warning. Could the animal sense Thomas from this far away? Or was there something else out there to be worried about?

They pressed on, but it was a losing battle—the sun was falling. What would he give to Mary? What could he possibly catch with his bare hands? It wasn't his scent, but somehow even the lowliest critter knew he was there. He'd have to try. And hope for rain.

"Dad, what's this?" She bent down. In her hand was a lump of black rock.

"It's good news. We follow it."

"But where did it come from?"

He'd forgotten how tiring a line of questions could be. He hoped she had grown out of the "why" stage—he remembered that from before he left. He remembered falling straight to sleep each night.

"It's called blacktop. In the old world people drove carts on it. It was all over the place; couldn't walk a mile without stumbling on some."

"What happened to it?" she said, looking closer at the lump. Parts of it caught the last rays of the sun.

"Like the good Pastor says." He put on his best Pastor Gray voice: "*The past was no match for the Good Lord.*"

"Dad!"

He laughed. "But he's right. See all that grey scrub? Not exactly fields of the stuff, but it's enough. Breaks through the blacktop like pie crust."

"Can I keep this?"

"If you want to carry it," he said.

She put it in her pocket.

They followed the blacktop towards what remained of the sun. The shadowy boxes of Miracle stood framed by the molten disk. How the town had stayed standing this long, he didn't know—wasn't much sense in it. What did Automated Man want with this place? What drew them to live here in such numbers? Most of the old world cities and towns had been ransacked, so his fellow soldiers had said. People took everything useful and left the rest. Miracle clearly wasn't useful.

"Dad, isn't that a . . ."

He followed her pointing finger. She'd seen it before him, so there was no use denying it.

"I think you should stay here," he said.

"No, I won't."

"Mary."

"You're going to stand there, half a cheek missing, and tell me I can't see *that*?" she said.

"You've spent too long with your mother. And your grandmother."

But she was right. What was a man hanged by his neck in comparison to him?

Thomas gazed around the surrounding hills. You could hide a whole battalion in the crumbling walls of Miracle, if you had a mind to. But he couldn't see anything and it wasn't the kind of place worth staying at.

He knew it was Karl before he got there. The tree was huge and old, with thick low branches, from which the body dangled. He expected Mary to be shocked or frightened. She only looked intrigued.

The army had left the man to die in his undergarments. That, and the churned ground speckled by hoofprints, told the story. A deserter the army caught up with. Thomas walked around the trunk of the tree. They hadn't even stopped long enough to carve his crimes. Or, they had some sense and not the heart to call it that. Every one of the soldiers who hanged Karl understood. They would have felt the same urge—home, family, anything but war.

Mary reached up and touched Karl's foot.

"Cold." She circled the body. "What did he do, Dad?"

"He got caught."

She didn't ask what for. She was either too clever or too sensitive.

"What are we going to do?"

"Cut him down, I guess," he said.

Karl's neck was raw. The rope was stained with dried blood. His tongue lolled in his mouth, fat and purple. His white eyes bulged like boiled eggs.

"Shouldn't a dead man smell? Shouldn't there be birds and specks picking at him?"

He stared at his daughter, amazed. He really knew nothing about this little woman.

"I suppose so. But maybe not; if he's going to be a Walkin' maybe things leave him alone. Either way, we should cut him down."

"If he's going to be a Walkin' what's he waiting for?" she said.

"I don't know, maybe a miracle?" Thomas laughed at his own joke. But it was a hollow sound and Mary didn't join him.

Night was coming on quick. Thomas stood at the bottom of the tree. He held the little skinning knife between his teeth. The climb was easy enough thanks to the wide gaps in the bark and the branches. He shimmied along the branch holding Karl.

"Stand back a little, Mary."

He took to the rope. He might as well have used his nails—the knife was small and not very sharp. He hacked and sawed. Eventually he loosened enough threads and the knot started to slip.

"Look out."

It went. Karl hit the ground with a loud thump. Thomas started back down. A blightbird landed on the branch. Thomas almost lost his grip.

"Blood and ashes!"

The blightbird cawed. Flapping its wings loudly, it settled on the tree.

"Don't let it get Karl," Mary called up.

He grinned. "Don't worry. It ain't that kind of bird." He climbed out of the tree. He checked Mary was all right and then went to look at the body. Loosening the knot, he slipped the noose over Karl's head. He thought about throwing it away, but Karl might want it—a kind of explanation.

"We can't leave him here," Mary said.

The blightbird cawed. It jerked its head from side to side.

"No, we'll move him. That one," he gestured to the branch. "One Eye Blind I call him. Rascal lives on annoying the likes of me."

"Dad. It's rude to call people names."

Another caw. One Eye Blind hopped from one claw to the other.

"People, darlin'." He picked Karl up under the arms. "Vermin is different."

Caw.

"Noisy vermin at that. We'll put Karl in the first house. We'll need a fire tonight—so we'll borrow his."

As they went, Mary gathered kindling and as much dead wood as she could carry. The body wasn't heavy, just awkward. Halfway to the town, Thomas dragged Karl up over his shoulder. The blightbird didn't follow them, but its calls did—soft shrieks from the tree.

Thomas approached the buildings cautiously. As far as he could tell, nothing had changed on the main street. He couldn't see any tracks in the ground either side of the road. Could be the army didn't come into the town; caught Karl on the outskirts, hunting or fetching water maybe.

Mary's eyes were plates. She scampered from one house to the next. She leant in over the empty windows. Peered in through the open doorways.

"These houses aren't made of wood. Is this stone?" she said.

"I think so."

"Not like any stone I know."

"That would make two of us," he said.

He dropped Karl on the floor of the first house they came to that had a roof. He put the noose down in Karl's lap.

It was a bright night, with a big moon.

"Some of these are huge," she called, her voice echoing amongst the ruins.

"Try this one."

He took her to the cavernous building he'd stumbled into the first time. As they walked up the stone steps Mary said:

"Like church."

"That's the right of it."

Inside, they both stood awestruck by the size of the main chamber. It had lost none of its effect. Large sections of the ceiling had collapsed, but the impression of the room was still there. All those rows of broken seats.

Outside, Mary shook her head, but didn't say anything. Thomas led her to the house Karl had lived in. He heard the scuttle of longtails as they came to the back room. He soon saw what they were after.

Strips of meat hung over an unset fire pit. Large, from what animal he couldn't say, but definitely not under-mutton. They were well smoked. He tried to find Karl's gun, but there was only a half-empty box of shells on an upturned crate. Mary was still standing in the corridor.

"What? He's not going to need the food," he said.

"But . . ."

"Here." He picked up the large water-skin hanging over Karl's old bed. She took it and drank. "Whatever happens, he won't need that. Or these," he said, cutting down the meat. Using Karl's blanket, he wrapped up the strips. If there had been any other food the longtails had got to it.

He took the water-skin and handed her the meat.

"Thank you, Karl," Mary said to the room.

He set and lit a fire. Mary sat eating on the bed.

"What if he wakes up?" she said between mouthfuls.

"I'll be here. We'll have a good ole chat."

"What if he doesn't?"

Thomas had no answer for that one.

3 : 2

Nathaniel pulled the bed-covers up to his nose. Rachel had drawn back the curtains. He looked out onto a cold morning; the sun was hiding behind a bank of dull clouds. Today he wouldn't go to the graveyard. He wouldn't be going there for some days. How long, he had no idea. But today he had to make the urns.

"Are you getting up?" Rachel said. She sounded annoyed.

"I was trying to avoid it."

"Nathaniel Courie. You can't hide in bed, not at your age. You should know better."

"Yes, I probably should." He moved so he was on Rachel's side of the bed. There, the blanket smelt like roses. It was still warm.

"There's bread and cheese in the pantry. I'm going into town. You'll need more food when you go."

"You could find me a bag of those rusty-almonds," he said.

"Oh, could I?" She leant down to kiss him. Her hair tickled his ear. "Don't go."

"I have to. If it was my choice . . ."

She nodded. She kissed him again, harder.

The sounds of Rachel moving about the house drifted away, until he could only hear his breath as it hit the blanket. He got up. He passed the dresser where Rachel kept her washing soaps and scents. Over the years she had changed the way the house smelt. She'd changed the way it looked, too. That dresser used to be next to the window.

Some mornings the view from the bedroom would stop him in his tracks. The light made the bone-grass into a lake; the still impression of endless swaying. He pulled himself away.

He could smell the damp, fresh morning as he went into the garden. The water bucket was full, but Rachel hadn't warmed it. A cold wash was the best way to wake up. It would sting and seem like torture, but feel righteous afterwards like all things good for you. His hair stood on end and his skin turned red as he ran the cloth along his body.

He watched the little movements in the garden—the leaves, the petals, the grass.

He scratched his chin. He went to the pantry. Pulling the curtain aside, he winced. Two onions, some bread, a small lump of cheese and an apple. He was glad winter was over. He took the bread and cheese, and sat down at the table.

The shed door creaked, another little job that would have to wait until he returned. Something niggled at him; a job he'd forgotten. The front wall? The windows? Something needed doing, but that was no surprise—finishing one job created two others.

His shed at home was a bigger version of the one at the graveyard. Most of the tools were the same. There were some extras for the vegetable patch—stakes, a hoe, tools for digging small holes. But the main difference was the clay wheel. The dust made him cough. He checked over everything, looking to see if any water had found its way in. The roof seemed sound. Everything was dry.

He pulled the wheel out onto the grass. The wooden legs scraped along the floor. He took it a little way from the shed, almost to the middle of the garden. He didn't like having his back to either the house or the garden gate. He went out the back gate to the kiln. It was a few paces from the hedge, nestled in a dip in the hills. As tall as his shoulder, it was small and had only one shelf. Firing urns was all it ever did. Rounded at the top, the sides uneven, it reminded him of a wild worker hive turned on its head.

Opening the waist-high door, he was relieved to find he'd cleaned the fire pit after last time. His father drilled that into him—"Don't put off a job, boy, it'll only be waiting for you." He reached in and lifted out the sag-box. Flecks of hardened clay and dust rained out. He banked up the fire and took his flint set from his pocket. It took him three tries before a spark caught. He waited until the flames took hold, the bark breathing orange and red, then added another log and closed the door.

At the gate he stopped and watched the activity on his lawn. Insects zipped silently from one side to the other, a foot or so from the ground. He followed each until he lost sight of it and another came along. Bigger creatures buzzed from hedge to lawn to vegetable patch. Bright-lies bounced around Rachel's flowers. He brought it to a brief halt, stomping across the grass to the shed. He might have scared a few things, but they'd move on and forget him. It all kept going, regardless of his worries.

He picked up the sack of yellow clay. Breaking off two handfuls he began wedging it on the worktop. Deep thuds echoed in the shed, like the parade drum on Main. He broke the lump in two, squeezing it back together in his hands. Keep it moving. Thumping the worktop.

At the wheel, he put his foot on the pedal and began an easy rhythm. The bat picked up speed, levelling off in a steady spin. He pulled his wash bucket closer and dipped his hands. He sprinkled drops on the bat, the water spreading with the motion, changing the wood's colour from a dusty cream to a wet brown.

A red chalk dot marked the centre of the bat. He eased the clay lump as close to that mark as he could. The clay took, turning, and he held it there.

He hunched, bent over the wheel. His back didn't ache, but it would that night. Especially without a bed to sleep in.

Up and down on the pedal, nice and easy.

The wet clay slid under his cupped hands. He raised his fingers, a slight pulling movement. The lump followed, becoming taller and thinner. The clay appeared to stay still whilst the bat ran, but his eyes lied. His hands knew the truth. He pressed gradually inwards with his thumb. The ball yawned open. He steadied it there. Taking his hand from inside, he dunked it into the water bucket. With two fingers he inched the hole wider, pulling them back towards his body. He kept it spinning.

Carefully, he squeezed. The urn grew; pulsing upwards.

Clay water stained his forearm. The lip was up to his elbow. Feeling his way, he pushed gently at the point three quarters up the urn's height. There it became fat; the curve of a mother's hips. The tips of his fingers pinched the top. Closer and closer he brought his hands together, until the hole was only a few inches wide. A final touch, he pulled the lip flat, like a bud unfurling. He slowed his foot a little at a time, until it stopped. He took the wire that hung from the wheel and slid it under the base. His hands and arms were covered in dried clay. His foot throbbed, ghosting the motion of the pedal.

It was all soothing. A thought hadn't troubled him the whole time.

And now he hated himself for doing it. No matter how smooth, no matter how he shaped and moulded, the urn was still supposed to hold the ashes of a little girl or a man. Or a Walkin'. One person lost to another. A simple clay urn. Black powder and memories would fill it. A symbol to remember—like the headstones, like the graveyard. Folk went there to remind themselves of relatives they'd lost; they left remembering the family they still had.

A simple shape. He'd made an urn for Lydia, but he'd been guilty of leaving out more than just ashes. He'd forgotten what he had. Rachel was a part of this urn; everyone left in Barkley was. Each urn was a little different. He was well practised by now, but they were never exactly the same. This one was narrower than usual, but still only a foot and a half tall. And he had another to make today.

He went to the kiln. He felt the heat as a slight change in the air. He opened the door and eased the paddle in.

Back in the garden he did it all again. It was midday by the time he finished. The second urn thrown, he sat at the wheel. His hands were a chalky grey. He dusted them off. With a nail, he idly peeled dried clay off his arms.

"Nathaniel?"

He jumped; he hadn't heard Rachel come back. She stood behind him, resting her hands on his shoulders.

"Sorry, I was years away," he said.

Her hands tightened ever so slightly. Such a simple movement, but it was everything: all the times he thought of the past; the slips when he confused the two of them; simple words that could hurt; but most of all, her patience and love. It cut, and drew apart the curtains he had held tightly closed. Men— Nathaniel had no illusions as to how women worked—could be so blind.

He took her hand, it was cold but soft. So soft. He cupped it between his own. He would keep her there from now on, surrounded by his attention. It was no less than she deserved.

"When I come home it will be different. I promise."

She squeezed his hand. "It's all right."

"I promise."

Luke knelt before the altar. He held his arms in a cradle; as he had done for Simon Peekman. Beside him, the wooden floor still bore the stain of Simon's blood. Mrs. Gray had scrubbed as hard as she could, but it wasn't enough. It was a mark that had to remain, under the eyes of the Good Lord. Luke carried it with him, also. Not in shame, but in pride. He had done the Good Lord's work here that day and he continued to do it.

He stared at the crucified figure of Christ. It was carved in a light wood. Christ's head was angled to one side, his gaze averted from his followers. Luke had tried every spot he could but, no matter where he sat, Christ would not look him in the eye. But they shared so much.

Luke's hands were covered in scars. He picked at one on each hand, right in the middle, until it bled. He heard the church door open and close. A single set of footsteps echoed along the aisle. He didn't turn to look who it was. He didn't need to.

"Hello, Luke."

"Pastor."

"I'm sorry I have to interrupt your meditations," the Pastor said. He was standing a few paces behind Luke.

"No need. I find myself often deep in thought, these days." He looked again at the stain on the floor.

"As is right. If only more men spent time in contemplation; their paths would be clear."

"My path is not so clear to me, Pastor."

"Let me help." The Pastor began to pace. "You have shown great fortitude. The Good Lord sees everything. Your service has been noticed."

"Has it?" he said, failing once more to meet Christ's gaze.

"Of course. So much so, that the Good Lord has provided you with another opportunity to serve." The Pastor paused.

"The McDermotts," Luke said, the name filling the empty air between him and the eaves.

"Yes." The Pastor placed a hand on Luke's shoulder. "It will be your great trial, acolyte. There will be many obstacles—both of Satan and of man."

"The Good Lord grant me strength," Luke said.

The Pastor gripped his shoulder. There was pain. There was burning. But Luke did not buckle; he kept his back straight. "*He* wills it," the Pastor whispered in his ear. The man's beard tick-led Luke's neck. "You are an instrument of the Good Lord. Never forget that. The men who travel with you are not so strong. Their faith is flimsy. Barkley *needs* you, Luke."

"Then let me go alone. Unburdened by unbelievers."

"If it were my decision. Sadly, even men of Barkley interfere with holy matters. But you do go alone. Only you can rid us of these two devil-spawn. You will not fail me."

Luke's entire upper body started to throb.

"I will do what has to be done."

"Amen." The Pastor released his grip and patted Luke's shoulder.

It didn't take Nathaniel long to pack the rest of his things. A change of clothes, a raincoat, his rifle, sleeping blankets, and food. They wouldn't be gone long. He said as much to Rachel as she helped him. He said it many times, mostly for his own benefit.

Rachel cooked lunch as they waited for the urns.

"Last hot meal for a while," she said. She was smiling, but it was strained. "You will be careful?"

"Of course."

"What would I do if . . . ?"

"Don't worry yourself. We're just going to find whoever took Mary," he said.

"No you're not." She looked at the empty space where his rifle had hung.

They ate the meal in silence, Rachel sniffing every so often.

Nathaniel packed his gear onto Buster. The shaggie took the load in his usual stoic way. He put the clothes and supplies in well-worn saddlebags. He strapped the urns to the top of the bags, one on each side. He checked three times they were tied down tight. Rachel stood on the porch, watching. He went over and drew her into a hug. For a moment she resisted, and then she went limp in his arms. She shook as she cried. He told her it would be okay.

"Everything will be better when I come home," he said. "I keep my promises." She looked up at him. He kissed her forehead. "I have to go."

He mounted. Rachel passed him his rifle. Her hands were shaking.

"It will only be a couple of days," he said.

"I love you."

On the track he looked back twice, but he didn't wave.

As usual, Nathaniel was the last to arrive. Bellis, Luke Morris and a few others stood outside Elder Richards' office. The acolyte was already in the saddle, looking eager to go. He tutted as Nathaniel eased Buster alongside the other shaggies.

"Morning, Elder, Veronica," Nathaniel said, tipping his hat.

The Elder turned. He had been speaking to a small knot of people—most of whom were from the McDermott family.

"Good, you're here." The Elder took Nathaniel by the arm and led him a little way off. "Four of you going—yourself, Bellis, Luke, and Samuel McDermott."

"A McDermott boy? Is that a good idea, considering?"

"Ma McDermott insists the family is represented." Richards glanced sidelong at the McDermotts. "I'm sorry, but I couldn't have her bothering me every day until you're back. She's a . . . persistent woman."

He knew Samuel to look at and by reputation as a steady worker. But what kind of temperament did the boy have? Was he the Pastor's man, ready to light a match under everyone? And it might be his brother out there. Nathaniel could only imagine how that would play on a man's mind—he himself was an only child.

"How well does he know the Good Book?" Nathaniel said.

Richards leant closer. "I would think he's too busy in the fields to read much. But he's young."

Nathaniel nodded. "I'll keep an eye on him."

"You might not be able to spare it."

Luke Morris was making a fuss. "Your gossip is an agent of the devil. It costs us time."

"We'll catch up to them," Bellis said in his even manner.

"The Good Lord doesn't reward idle words."

The Good Lord also had infinite patience; a shame his most devout followers rarely shared the virtue. They mounted and rode out of the town with no fanfare. No one waved them good-bye or wished them well. The Elder, Veronica and the McDermotts watched them go in silence. They received similar stony stares from folk on the board-walks. When they passed the shop, Nathaniel made himself look at the front. He was relieved that Sarah wasn't there.

3 : 3

Mary stretched and rubbed her eyes.

"Morning," Thomas said.

"Did Karl come?"

"No."

"Can we see him before we go?" she said.

"All right, if we're quick. I'll put the fire out, you gather your things."

They left Karl's room tidy. Mary looked uncomfortable taking the food, but Thomas insisted. Better guilty than hungry.

Karl hadn't moved. His jaw was slack, hanging down on his chest. He still didn't smell—it was just a matter of time before he woke up. Karl had mentioned Walkin' blood in his family; that his grandpa said as much. Thomas was no expert, these things could take years for all he knew, but it would happen.

"Good luck, Karl," he said.

It had rained during the night. Clouds covered the sky; one colour in every direction. He hoped it would stay dry, for Mary's sake. The wet stone buildings had an odd smell. A musty damp, but with a bite.

They left Miracle. A blightbird circled overhead. One friend was still around. Thomas had never seen the Redlands after rain. The whole land seemed to be busy making use of the water.

"Did you sleep, Dad?"

"No. Another thing I don't do."

"But how do you dream?" she said.

He almost stumbled. Dreams. He'd forgotten about them. Mary was looking at him, her little face frowning.

"It's all right. I have memories of you to keep me going," he said.

It was true; he had spent those first nights awake but dreaming of his family and home.

"We'll make new ones then. New dreams for you." Mary smiled, but she looked tired. He had no idea how long it would take to get to Black Mountain. It could be many, many nights of sleeping on rough ground.

This was the farthest into the Redlands Nathaniel had ever been. They had been riding for two days now. At first, the going was difficult. They left the track that led out of Barkley and headed into the scrub. The ground was uneven beneath Buster's hooves. It rolled and jutted like the surface of the Col River and was just as unpredictable. The earth itself was not far from the colour of his clay. It was cracked and dry and it was only spring. Looking at it robbed his mouth of saliva and made his throat itch. Buster carefully picked his way between the thorny bushes. The four of them zigzagged across the land. It was not the quickest way to travel. The sky had a few wisps of cloud but was otherwise clear. From the saddle, he could see for miles in every direction. The vastness of it made him shiver, despite the warm morning sun. This over-fired clay ground stretched on for ever. In such a place, they should be able to see their quarry. Two tiny dots. Two crumbers in the palm of the Redlands. But Nathaniel saw nothing but bushes and cracked earth and empty sky.

It was past midday when Bellis got off his shaggie. The rest of them stopped, spread out as they were, and waited. This wasn't the first time the Law-Man had dismounted. Luke leant towards Bellis, straining to see what was happening. Samuel looked bored. He stroked the tuft of hair between his shaggie's ears. Bellis knelt by a thorn bush.

"Anything?" Nathaniel said.

"Is it them?" Luke said.

Bellis shrugged and got back on his shaggie.

According to Bellis they were going in the right direction. He didn't tell the rest of them how he knew that, just that he *did* know. Luke muttered. But Bellis was the only one of them who could track more than their own breath in a cold morning. Samuel had found missing woollies before, but that wasn't the same.

They resumed their slow meandering across the Redlands. That night, they made camp in a hollow. There was no wind, but the feeling of shelter was a comfort after the days of open ground. Samuel stayed with the shaggies as the rest of them liberated firewood from scrawny bushes. When they returned, they compared thorn wounds. Luke's hands looked the worst, covered in scars and holes and wet with blood. He insisted that had little to do with thorns. Bellis shook his head at the acolyte but said nothing.

Samuel was the best at starting a fire. He handled flint like Nathaniel handled a shovel or Luke the Good Book.

"I've spent nights watching the woollies," Samuel said when asked about this proficiency. The McDermott boy didn't say much. He seemed happier to listen to the other men talk. Nathaniel wondered if he was a little slow. Samuel had a way of moving that was very deliberate. Before he said anything, he visibly thought for some time. Nathaniel liked the boy, regardless.

Luke led them in a prayer. Then each man took out a small part of his rations. They only ate twice a day—at dawn and at night. No time to stop during good riding hours. On the first night, they all measured out a portion of food and then tore into it like ravenous animals. Now they ate slowly, chewing until there was nothing left to chew on, savouring each mouthful.

"Are we getting closer?" Luke said when everyone had finished their meal. He looked at the fire, but the question was undoubtedly for Bellis. Nathaniel watched the fire too. He saw the small body of Simon Peekman at its centre, the flames caressing the boy. He wanted to look away, but forced himself to stare at what had happened—what he had been a part of. And would be again.

"I'd say so," Bellis said, eventually. He spat into the fire. It hissed at him in response.

"But we could be quicker?"

Bellis sighed. "It's not about being 'quicker.'"

"No? Every hour we waste is an insult to the Good Lord," Luke said. "Two abominations are loose because of Barkley men and women. Unforgivable."

"Two?" Nathaniel said.

"Yes, *two*. I saw the demon creature that was the father. Are you calling me a liar?"

Nathaniel shrugged. "You saw what you saw."

"And that means the girl carries the taint. Two creatures. They must be put to flame; both of them. We were all present for the burning of Jared and Simon Peekman."

"The shaggies go as quickly as they go," Bellis said. "Push them harder and soon enough they get slower."

Nathaniel didn't want any further part in the conversation, so he went to check on the shaggies. The moon was fat in the sky. Away from the fire, the sound of scrapers and other insects filled the night. He checked the other shaggies first, making sure they were hitched right. Not that he thought the animals might bolt. These were good shaggies. But anything could spook a shaggie out here. Buster nuzzled him.

"I know what you're after," Nathaniel said. He took a handful of oats from a saddlebag. Buster's tongue was thick and wet. The opposite of how Nathaniel felt. He wished he was back at home, with Rachel, worrying about dry-stone walls and cutting back trees. He shivered. "You won't be cold out here, will you, boy?" He patted the shaggie's flanks and went back to the fire. Luke was reading aloud from the Good Book.

"'. . . came a traveller unto the rich man, and he spared to take of his own flock and of his own herd, to dress for the wayfaring man that was come unto him; but took the poor man's . . .'"

Bellis was snoring. Samuel listened to every word.

Nathaniel settled down into his blankets. The drone of the acolyte and the spitting of the fire gave him bad dreams.

The following morning, he woke to the sound of Bellis kicking dirt over the fire. Nathaniel was the last one awake. It was the same at home. The sun hadn't disentangled itself from the horizon yet. He ate his meagre breakfast of salted meat in his blankets. The cold had crept into his bones. He was too numb to shiver. He chewed so his teeth wouldn't chatter.

He seemed the only one to be suffering from rising early. It would have been normal for Samuel, the son of a farmer. For that kind of family the day started at first light and often before. Luke had probably lit candles, read ten verses, and dusted the whole church by dawn. Bellis only slept a few hours a night; though you couldn't wake him when he was under.

"Your sloth costs us time," Luke said. "It is disgusting."

"So eager to set new fires? To cut new throats?"

Luke knelt down beside him. "In the name of the Good Lord I'd cut your throat and set a fire beneath you. If He willed it." For a moment Luke took on the grim and molten countenance of the Pastor in full sermon. Nathaniel looked away from his gaze.

He finished his breakfast then got up and stretched. A little way off, Luke was clumsily mounting. What was such a man capable of? For Luke, the normal bravado and confidence of the young must have been twisted and become bound in the Good Book. It could have been a single moment—a scuffle in the playing patch, a sinful conversation between adults he overheard, or one of the Pastor's services. He would have stopped playing like the other children; become awkward and shy and quick to anger. The acolyte finally settled in the saddle. He stared down at Nathaniel with unmasked contempt.

One whole side of Nathaniel's body ached from sleeping on the ground. It was particularly bad in his shoulder and knee. He tried to walk it off, which helped, but the dull ache was still there. He packed his gear, double-checking the urns were safely strapped in.

It was another clear day. Back in the saddle, he soon warmed up. Buster was like a furnace between his thighs. He was thankful for his hat, keeping the sun from his face, but it did make his forehead sweat some. He was fanning himself when Samuel happened to pull alongside him.

"Hot today," Nathaniel said. Samuel nodded. This was the first time Nathaniel had been able to talk to the boy alone. With the shaggies picking their own way through the scrub it was hard for any of them to be close enough for a conversation. Nathaniel cut straight to it. "Why did you come with us, Samuel?"

"Ma told me to: 'One of the family needs to be there.'"

"Why do you think she said that?"

Samuel thought for a while. He looked younger then, little more than a boy. A large, muscular boy. "He is my brother. Was. And she is my niece. It's like Luke and the Pastor said. We're saving their souls. That's important." He looked at Nathaniel then, uncertain and wanting confirmation.

"It sure is," Nathaniel said.

Samuel would do whatever he was told—if it sounded holy enough. That was not good. Luke could whip him into a Leyist frenzy. Bellis might be able to stop the boy, but Nathaniel knew he himself couldn't. Not without his rifle. Shooting one McDermott to save another.

They settled back into the rhythm of the plodding shaggies. Nathaniel felt like a crust of bread bobbing on a river current. Up and down, down and up. Instead of water splashing his face it was dust. Buzzing, flying insects plagued man and shaggie alike—though Buster didn't seem to mind. He swished his thick tail and that was that. Nathaniel started the afternoon shooing them away. By early evening he had neither the energy nor the inclination. It was a losing battle.

"Look." Bellis was pointing at a group of shapes on the horizon. In the dusk light they were hard to make out, but looked like buildings. But they were deep into the Redlands. Who could possibly live here?

The group stopped. They all dismounted and led their shaggies to the same spot.

"It's a town," Luke said. He sounded excited; he could smell the pyre wood burning.

Bellis unrolled a map of Pierre County onto the ground. "It's not on here."

Luke peered at it through his misty glasses. "Where are we?" the acolyte said.

"Roughly here, I would say." Bellis made a generous circle-motion.

"There's nothing for a hundred miles."

Samuel looked nervously at each of them. Strange towns in the wilderness. Nathaniel patted his arm, as he would a skittish shaggie.

Bellis took a slug from his water-skin. "Either we go around it or through it. We're still heading in the right direction."

"What makes you so sure?" Nathaniel said. Bellis reached into his pocket. He pulled out a small piece of black cloth. It was the same kind that the women of Barkley wore. But it was just a scrap. "Where did you find that? It could have come from anywhere."

Bellis shook his head.

"I say we go through the town," Luke said. "Maybe the girl and the Walkin' are hiding there." So far he hadn't used their names once.

"There's no lights," Nathaniel said. Back in Barkley lamps would be lit now.

"Makes no difference if it's abandoned. If there's people— that could be a problem," Bellis said.

"Someone might have seen them!" Luke said. "We have to look. And it is fitting that Satan would hide his minions in an unmarked town. Be ready to strike back at the devil."

"We have to look," Samuel echoed.

They remounted and headed towards the town.

It was clear the town was abandoned. The buildings rarely had windows or doors; shells of their former selves. They were made of some kind of grey stone. It looked lifeless and weak. They came to what seemed like a central street. The hairs on the back of Nathaniel's neck stood up at the way the air moved in this place, how it whistled through the empty houses. The building-fronts reminded him of the face of a man before a pyre was lit. The soul had departed from this town. But the Good Lord had forgotten to burn it.

Luke got off his shaggie and ran into the first house.

"Luke," Bellis hissed, but the acolyte was already gone. The Law-Man reached for his rifle. He was trying to watch every-where at once. Samuel joined Luke in the house. He was no less eager.

"Should we?" Nathaniel said. Bellis shook his head.

The other two appeared in the doorway.

"Not here," Samuel said. Luke ran to the next house. He directed Samuel to take a different building. They seemed to leap-frog each other, whilst Bellis and Nathaniel plodded along on their shaggies. Nathaniel wasn't getting off Buster. Not for anything. He wanted to be able to leave this place and quickly.

Five, six, seven houses were searched with no result. Luke was like a red-wink trailing the scent of chooks. His eyes gleamed in the dying light.

There was a gunshot. First, Nathaniel heard it echoing between the vacant buildings. Then Buster reared. A sound like a plate smashing. Nathaniel fought to keep his shaggie under control. He fought to stay in the saddle. Bellis was also having trouble. He had the reins to the others' shaggies. Luke and Samuel came cautiously to the entrance of the houses they were in. Eventually they managed to get the animals under control.

"That's far enough," a man called. "I'm already reloaded."

All of them tried to find the source of the voice. The way sound travelled in this ruined warren, it was impossible. Nathaniel twisted to see what had happened. Buster didn't seem hurt. The shaggie stamped and snorted but there was nothing to suggest he'd been hit. Pieces of an urn lay scattered on the track.

3 : 4

"Who's there?" Bellis shouted.

"You need to leave." A face appeared a fair way off, in the top window of a building that was missing its roof. It was the only movement in this place and they all saw it instantly.

"He looks real pale," Samuel said. Luke strained to see without leaving the safety of the doorway.

"Life does that," the man replied. He had some hearing.

"Is it the creature?" Luke hissed.

"We're looking for someone," Bellis called.

"So I see."

"Is there anyone else in this town?"

"No."

"They might have passed through. A man and a little girl. Maybe two days ago?"

The pale face was silent for some time. Nathaniel started to wonder if the man had heard.

"Maybe."

"Did you see them?"

"In a way. They're gone."

"Which way?" Bellis said.

"Not sure."

"Bellis, we should go," Nathaniel whispered. "That face isn't just pale. It's dead."

"I know."

They were lucky the acolyte was near blind. No doubt the zealot would have charged down the whole street chanting prayers and wielding his crucifix. Right into lead shot.

"Get on your shaggies," Bellis said.

"We can't trust this man. There are things he isn't telling us," Luke said. "We should try to interrogate him."

"Do what?" Nathaniel said.

"We could make him say more. We have knives to heat, and—"

"They're not here," Bellis said.

Nathaniel stared, his mouth agape, as Luke reluctantly mounted. The acolyte had wanted to torture a man. And what could he have possibly said? Confirmed they were heading in the right direction? Said they were a day or two behind? That a description of Thomas McDermott was similar to what he had seen? None of that was worth causing pain; even if a Walkin' could feel pain. But Luke had calmly suggested hot knives for what he thought was a man. Would J. S. Barkley have taken the same action?

They rode out of the ruined town. Luke kept looking back.

"Sorry about your pot," the Walkin' called after them.

Nathaniel was glad to leave. Luke had shaken him and he'd never been in a place that felt so cold. He couldn't imagine that that might happen to Barkley one day, whatever wrongs had caused it. Barkley was stronger. They had their faith. But that was not without its costs and that worried him.

Half a mile from the town Nathaniel stopped. He brushed off the urn fragments that still clung to his saddlebag. Buster had a few little cuts on his rump, but nothing deep and the blood was already thickening.

"It won't be right without an urn," Luke said.

"Then we should go back to Barkley," he said.

"No!"

Bellis shook his head; the Law-Man agreeing with Luke. "We can carry ashes in something else," Bellis said. Nathaniel hoped it wouldn't come to that.

"A Walkin' isn't *right*. A little girl Walkin' isn't *right*," Luke said. "And you want to turn back?"

Nathaniel stared at the young man. What did Luke know of it? He hadn't married yet. Hadn't had a child. The Good Book didn't cover those kinds of feelings.

They rode until they couldn't see the town. No one spoke as they ate. Luke read more verses aloud. Only Samuel listened.

It was getting dark. Sarah had come into the kitchen to fetch a glass of water. She had gotten as far as taking a glass out of the cupboard. That was hours ago. Her mouth was dry and sticky. She was sitting at the kitchen table. In the twilight it was easy to forget. Mary was still in the shop, pretending to work hard so she could stay up a little longer. Thomas was coming back from the fields. His hands would smell of soil and leave dust on her cheek.

She had to get out. She had barely moved in the last few days. Her body felt tired with lack of use—her muscles slack and wet. Moving from one empty room to another every couple of hours. It didn't matter where in the house she sat, it was the same story.

As she opened the back door, she felt the coolness of the night air. The hairs on her arms stood up. There was a cardigan on the table but she left it behind. The house was stuffy and still—it was good to be out in the cold. She glanced down at her dress. It was spotless, though she'd been wearing it for days. The cloth felt heavy with her.

There was no one else in the alleyway. People hadn't closed their back shutters. Perhaps they never did. They had nothing to be afraid of. Nothing that could creep into their homes and change everything. Or maybe, like Sarah, they didn't have the energy to try to stop it. Either way, she had more than enough light from their windows. Twice she saw the silhouette of someone and hurried before she was spotted. She didn't know where she was going. It didn't matter. She sucked hard at the air, filling every corner of her lungs with long, shuddering breaths. Without realising it, she was crying. She didn't bother to wipe the tears from her cheeks.

She walked until it was fully dark. When she had to cross one of the bigger streets, she did so without looking anywhere but ahead. She took long, masculine strides and ignored any shapes at the edge of her vision. Reaching the alleys again was a relief—she had felt exposed on the streets. Anyone could have come up and talked to her. Asked how she was. Whether or not she was coping. And she would have to lie.

The only soul she met in the alleys was a mouser. He was big and grey. He trotted up to Sarah as if they were old friends. She stood still as he rubbed his cheeks against her shins. His tail was like a farmer's crook, ready to pull her back into line. All she could think about was yanking the mouser's tail. She didn't know why, but she wanted to hurt him. She didn't trust herself to stroke him. Eventually, he caught the scent of something more interesting than Sarah. His tail dropped and he stalked off—old friend forgotten. She was glad when the mouser went. His wordless affection was too much.

She came out onto Main. She had no idea how late it was or how long she'd been walking. The shop was across the street. Someone was standing at the door, waiting for her.

They were in the shadows; there was no way of telling who it was. Thomas, Mary, even Bellis—she hoped for a lot of people it couldn't be. And how many friends did she have left in town? Talk of Walkin' hadn't helped, no matter how hard she denied it. Jared Peekman was still fresh in Barkley's memory. Who was at her door this late? Waiting patiently; knowing she would come back.

She considered sneaking around to the back door. But they wouldn't go away. Barkley wouldn't go away. Instead, she headed straight towards her home. She kept her pace even and tried to calm her face. The coolness of dry tears made her rub her cheeks. Her eyes were likely red and puffy, but there was nothing she could do about that.

"Hello, Sarah." Pastor Gray stepped out of the shadows. The lamplight gave life to his mess of red curls. She could almost hear his hair crackle and hiss and spit. He clasped his hands behind his back. He was between her and the shop door.

"Can I help you, Pastor?" She tried to edge round him, closer to the door, but it was impossible. He wasn't a large man, but he seemed to fill the board-walk.

"I hope so."

"Do you need more candles?" she said. Please, let him need candles.

"No. Not candles. We've had plenty of things to burn recently, haven't we?"

"Plenty," she said, avoiding his gaze.

"My acolyte, Luke Morris, speaks highly of you."

"Does he?"

"He is your husband's age, isn't he?" he said.

"A little younger."

"A lot younger one day."

"I don't know what you mean," she said. She wanted to reach out and touch the door handle—just to touch it.

"Would you indulge an old preacher?" He held out the Good Book, his thumb wedged between the pages.

"Isn't it late for readings?"

"And walks." He pressed the book into her hands. "Chapter seven, verse fourteen if you will?"

The letters were fuzzy in the low light. She had to hold the Good Book under her nose. He stared at her. She felt him watching her face; his gaze as hot as the midday sun. She cleared her dry throat.

"'For the unbelieving husband is sanctified by the wife, and the unbelieving wife is sanctified by the husband: else were your children unclean; but now are they holy.'"

"Thank you, Sarah." He gave a slight smile as he took back the book. "I find the Good Book most illuminating when I'm struggling with a problem, or the burden of a secret, don't you?"

He didn't wait for an answer. The board-walk creaked under his footsteps.

Had she stumbled over her words? Over "unbelieving" or "children" or "unclean"? She had tried to read as steadily as she could but her hands shook as she held the pages. The Pastor liked to be as cryptic as his chapters and verses. He left behind a wake of warmth—Sarah suddenly felt the cold again. She rubbed her arms. She made sure he was no longer on Main Street before she opened the shop door and went inside.

Thomas kept the fire alive. He stirred the embers, sifting through the blackened flakes. Those that were spent, used up, sank to the bottom. The wood that remained had a little left to give. Each piece was like a sunset: staggered oranges and yellows and reds. He kept the fire small. "They will follow you." Sarah had been so sure. She had pressed his arm as she told him, pushing the words through his linen shirt, patches of scorched uniform, and into muscles that couldn't feel her touch. He sat facing their trail. It was only a matter of when.

Mary was sleeping near the fire. She frowned in her sleep. Since leaving Barkley dreams seemed to trouble her. She didn't cry out or wake up sweating. Instead, she appeared to be tackling a difficult problem. He wanted to help her. But he knew he *was* the problem.

Clouds drifted across the moon. From the hillock where they camped he liked to follow the shadows as they crossed the Redlands. They moved so quickly on the ground, whilst the clouds sauntered through the sky. He couldn't match up the shapes

either. It was true of people: the shadows they cast never fit. He had wanted to see his family. But not like this.

He moved the water-skin farther away from the fire. He had no idea if it would make a difference, but he would do anything that might prolong their supply. It felt so light to him; full of air. But how heavy did it need to be? Not knowing was frustrating. How could he make plans when he had no sense of how long the journey to Black Mountain was? He didn't even understand how much water Mary really needed. It couldn't have been all that long since his last drink—a matter of weeks—but he couldn't remember it specifically. He had forgotten the taste of water.

Mary shifted. She was biting her lip. Perhaps he should wake her, but dawn was a few hours away and she needed the rest. She had blisters, she must have blisters, but she didn't say so. A red-wink howled in the distance. It was a lonely sound for a lonely place. He could see for miles around and whilst it weighed on him, he was glad for that loneliness. He dreaded the sight of a tiny orange dot of a campfire. Sometimes he blinked and saw it. He would close his eyes and count to five. Then six. At seven he opened his eyes and saw nothing but rolling red earth and the shadows of clouds.

He wasn't afraid of red-winks. Every other animal he'd encountered ran from him. He doubted they would be any different. He remembered the shaggies he'd chased out of the stables. And the shaggie that was shot. He wished he had been hit instead. The wet thump the shaggie made when it hit the ground was still with him.

He blinked. A light. He counted. It was still there. The clouds had moved, covering the edge of the horizon in shadow. It was definitely a pinprick of orange light. Why hadn't he spotted it before? Did the moonlight drown it? Was the same light hiding Thomas and Mary's fire? He scrambled over to the embers and stamped on them. He kicked dirt and dust onto the fire.

Mary woke up.

"We have to go," he said. She helped him bury the fire. He picked up their supplies, refusing to let her carry anything.

"Are they close?" she said, gazing across the empty crags and gullies.

"Getting closer. Can you walk?"

She stifled a yawn and nodded. They left another camp; leaving as little to track as possible, he hoped. But how could he know? He was just a farmer turned soldier turned Walkin'. He knew how to handle bluetongue in a woollie, how to twist a bayonet so a man died quickly or slowly, but cover a trail? He tried as best he could.

"Your shoes," he said. She was carrying them.

"I want to walk barefoot for a while."

"They hurt, don't they?"

"A little."

"Go careful."

It wasn't long before she was falling asleep standing up. She stumbled and he caught her. Without asking he picked her up, lifting behind the knees. She smiled weakly at him and closed her eyes. Her breathing became slower. He could feel her heartbeat. It thumped all through his body. He suddenly and desperately wanted to have a heartbeat again.

Carrying her slowed him down. He had to be careful not to trip, but it was more than that. It was as if his frame and dormant muscles knew their limit. He could manage his own weight until the end of days, but any further burden tipped the balance. As a Walkin', the scales were set to isolation. How Black Mountain figured in that, he would find out eventually.

Every night he would carry Mary as she slept. He didn't want to see any more fires on the horizon.

3 : 5

Mary stirred in his arms. The sun was tearing itself free from the horizon. In the soft light her sleepy features were angelic. He must have been one of millions of fathers who had looked on their daughter and thought the same. The divine impression faded as Mary chewed and smacked her lips like a grazing wool-lie. Her mouth was that special kind of dry that followed sleep. He understood dry—he was as parched as the cracked Redlands—but this was different; Mary's body had an expectation of tasting water again. It would go on expecting it until she died. Then she might be truly dry, like him.

She opened her eyes. He smiled as she blinked and tried to focus on something in the near-dark. That her first reaction wasn't terror or repulsion meant a lot to Thomas. He could have forgiven her a momentary widening of the eyes, a turn of the head, a tightening of the cheeks. It would be natural and unstoppable. But she yawned and smiled back at him.

"I had a dream I was flying, like a blightbird," she said.

"If only I could carry you that high. You want to walk?"

"Not yet."

She rested against his chest; her eyes closed but not asleep.

"I need to pee," she said. He let her down. She rubbed her legs, encouraging blood down to her toes. Her first few steps were tottering and small. He remembered her very first steps. They were in the shop; she used the shelves to steady herself. Sarah was out back fetching something for someone. By the time she had returned, Mary had fallen back on her bottom. It seemed one of them always had to miss the important moments.

"Don't go too far," he said. She could have gone in front of him, but he understood she wanted some privacy. It seemed unlikely there would be outhouses at Black Mountain. And privacy would be strange in a place where you could see past people's skin to their insides. What could you hide? He kept an eye on Mary. She was heading up a slope, which came to an abrupt lip. From the looks of her, she was searching for a suitable bit of scrub to squat behind.

By his feet were a number of little black holes. Without realising, he'd stumbled into a patch of under-mutton burrows. He knelt down beside one, making sure he could still see Mary. If only he had wire for a trap; there was no way an under-mutton would come out with him there. No matter how still he kept. Animals knew. The under-mutton were most likely huddled as far from him as their burrows would take them. But there was no harm in hoping. Karl's dried meat wouldn't last for ever.

"The ass doesn't wonder what it's like to sit on a cart, rather than pull it," his father had once said. They were heading into Barkley on a cart loaded with corn. Pa flicked the reins to emphasise the point. Thomas was seven or eight years old, younger than Mary at any rate. He could tell his father was annoyed, but he couldn't stop the questions. How much would they get for the corn? What would they buy? Who brought the other goods to Barkley and how? In the face of every question, Pa flicked the leather again. But it wasn't an ass pulling the cart, it was a shaggie.

At the same age, Mary had pestered him with questions. He had tried to be patient, answering everything he could, but when he had no answer she kept asking. He even used the same line as his father, passing the great "ass" down to another generation of McDermotts. It was only when he became a father that Thomas began to understand his own.

He caught himself tonguing the inside of his mouth alongside the memory. It was a dry feeling: his teeth rough and wooden, his tongue like a thick, callused finger.

For some reason, he couldn't stop thinking about his father. Evenings spent on the porch, sitting at the foot of the rocking chair and watching the sun drop. Working the fields, yards apart but moving together. Hunting; quiet hours spent in the tall grass. The good times were quiet. No words between them—no words were kind. No words were kind words; Thomas rolled the sentence around in his head. It made sense whichever way he put it.

He remembered Pa standing beside the back door one autumn evening. He was smirking. Thomas didn't know what that meant, but he was scared. His father was usually stony or yelling, there was no smirk. Thomas flinched when Pa raised an arm, feeling silly and relieved when the old man opened the back door.

"Patience, son, and a little luck."

The door peeled open, as if Pa were drawing back a curtain rather than pushing solid wood. A whole row of animals hung limp on the porch, dried blood staining the whitewash. Under-mutton, red-wink cubs, braces of gambirs. The porch burnt in the setting sun. The rich stink of old world iron. The buzz of the hungry specks.

"Patience, son, and a little luck."

But he needed more than that to feed his daughter now.

Mary still hadn't found the right spot. She was standing near the edge of the slope, looking down to whatever was beyond. She turned back.

"Dad," she called. "You need to see this."

Thomas looked around as he hurried over. It was the same scrub he'd been walking through for days. Had the men caught up with them? Were they just behind this little horizon? Mary didn't sound scared and she knew the men from Barkley were something to be scared of. He'd made sure of that.

He stood next to her and looked into a wide valley. For a moment he was stunned—not sure what he was seeing.

"Down!" he said.

He pulled her to the ground. She didn't resist. They lay on their bellies.

"Did they see you?"

"I don't know," she said.

Thomas inched closer to the edge. Below, a column of men were marching through the valley. As best as he could guess it was a whole regiment. Thousands of red jackets. Thousands of men who would kill him without waiting for an order. And what they would do to Mary—that would be much worse. They were like a wound on the landscape. A long cut exposing bright red flesh. He had the same along his calf. He desperately wanted that cut to stay straight—not to branch off in their direction. He had no breath to hold, but his whole body was tense.

"Be ready to run as fast as you can," he said.

"I still have to pee."

"Do it now. I'm not looking."

Mary slithered back a little. He heard the sound of her water hitting the dusty ground. He had forgotten what that sound was like—what it meant. It was part of being alive.

He waited for as long as he could. If a soldier had spotted them there would have been movement by now. Men on lean and sleek shaggies picking their way up the valley. Ready to ride Thomas and Mary down. They had been lucky.

Thomas pushed himself backwards. He and Mary were a good twenty paces from the edge before either of them stood up.

"I think we're safe," he said.

3 : 6

Luke's back ached. He rubbed at the base of his spine, trying to shift the dull pain that sat there. He wasn't much of a rider. He had little need in Barkley: from his living quarters with Mr. and Mrs. Gregory, to church, to the Pastor's house, to any house calls he made, his life was within walking distance. It wasn't the speed of the animals—at times he could have got off and covered the ground at a more impressive pace on foot—it was the constant movement. Still, this journey, he conceded, would have been beyond him without the shaggie. He wasn't an idle man, but since taking up his role as acolyte he had not toiled at any single task for longer than an hour or two. Sweeping the church after a service was the most intensive labour of his week. The dirt and grime people brought with them to worship never ceased to amaze him.

His thighs were also suffering. He rarely had to guide the shaggie; it seemed happy enough to follow the rest of the group at a discreet distance that suited Luke. But again it was the long days spent in an unaccustomed manner that caused him pain.

None of this affected his conviction.

He scanned the horizon from dawn to dusk. At times he imagined that he saw them. Two black marks—but they quickly faded. Should those marks ever stay solid, then he would kick his shaggie into a gallop; demanding speed from the animal whose primitive spirit would be overwhelmed by his righteous cause. Animal and man would become mirror images—nostrils flared, breathing frantically, mouth open wide enough to devour the Redlands. He would bear down on the demon creature and its offspring and smite them as the Good Lord smote Egypt. Or the Midianites. Or the Philistines. In the name of the Good Lord he would cut the little girl's throat and burn her at the feet of her twisted father. Of this, he was certain. He waited desperately for the moment to come. At the top of every rise he prayed. When he entered a dip in the land he prayed.

At one such rise, the other men stopped. Luke had fallen behind; seeing them halt he urged his shaggie forward and kicked his heels into the animal's flanks. His efforts managed to produce a trot. Any more seemed beyond his steed and Luke started to worry for his zealous charge. He drew alongside Samuel and joined him in staring down into a valley.

The ground sloped gradually. It was rocky and covered in treacherous scree. Half a mile or so away it levelled out into an enormous flat plain. At first, he assumed he was watching a river meandering from east to west. The sudden reminder of water filled his mouth with saliva. He had to swallow twice. He had had a drink at dawn. The thirst of his body was insignificant.

The river was red. Luke glanced at the sky, wondering how the sun could turn water so red.

"What devilry makes this river red?" he said. The others looked at him.

"The colour of their uniforms," Bellis said. As if to illustrate his point, a tiny bubble of the river split off and started towards them. There had to be thousands of soldiers in the valley. Hundreds of thousands. Luke wiped his glasses. He still could not make out anything but colour. Those men had individual faces, hands, rifles, that he couldn't see.

"Impossible. There's not enough men in the world . . ."

"Will be less when that lot are through," Bellis said, spitting. It was an ugly habit of the Law-Man's; he used it to punctuate what he must have thought were profound statements. It did not impress Luke. Just as he was not impressed by the man's badge or his guns or his years. Respect for one's elders was based on a respect for how they had spent their lives.

"Are we really going to wait for them?" Nathaniel said. He was itching to be anywhere else. Luke didn't understand why the Gravekeeper had such an aversion to the soldiers. They were fighting the good fight—trying to rid this world of Satan's seed. If Luke hadn't joined the ranks of priesthood he would undoubtedly be wearing a red uniform himself. Wearing it with the same pride he wore the cassock. Wielding a rifle with the same force he brandished the crucifix.

"We've got no reason to run," Bellis said.

"I'm not about to become a conscript in this mad crusade."

"Blasph—"

"Neither am I," Bellis said, cutting Luke short.

"We should aid them if we can," Luke said.

"What could we possibly give that they don't already have?"

"Faith."

Nathaniel laughed. "Ride down and give a sermon?"

"If that is what they wish."

"They'd have you in a uniform and carrying a rifle before you finished your first verse," Nathaniel said.

"Would you like that? To see me drowned in those soldiers?"

Nathaniel shrugged.

They waited in silence as the soldiers picked their way carefully up the slope. They grew bigger with every step, starting as a drop of colour that split into individual crumbers, then red woollies, then men riding shaggies, then men riding hairless and muscular creatures. There were twenty soldiers. One of them held a banner aloft. It was a pure field of the same colour as their uniforms. It suggested a world without taint, a way for men to live without fear, and the strength to see it happen. Luke swelled with admiration for these men.

The soldiers stopped at fifty paces and readied their rifles.

Nathaniel edged his shaggie back. Luke also found the sight of that many guns trained on him unnerving.

A single soldier came forward. He looked older than the others. White stripes adorned his chest and shoulders. He wore a full beard that was similarly slashed with white. Luke didn't have to strain to see this man's blue eyes. Considering where the man had come from and what he wore, Luke was strangely surprised by that; as if red were a more appropriate colour for the soldier's eyes. The man took off his gloves before speaking, looking each of them over in turn.

"You fellas are a long way from church."

"We carry the Good Lord," Luke snapped, holding up his Good Book. The soldier smirked.

"Maybe you're looking for a good cause? There's room for four more on our march."

"What we're looking for is a stolen little girl," Bellis said. "I'm a Law-Man of Pierre County and have a right to roam these plains."

"A 'right' you say? I've got some boys behind me; each of them holding their own 'right.'"

"There's no need for threats. We're all singing in the same choir," Luke said.

"Ready!" the soldier said. Behind him, twenty rifles clanked in response. "That's my choir. You're either part of the Protectorate or you're an enemy. Which is it to be?"

"Our town gave you men!" Nathaniel said.

"Have you seen any Walkin'?" Luke tried to ignore the guns aimed at him—focusing on the soldier's blue eyes.

"We destroy Walkin' on sight." The man spat.

"So do we," Luke said.

"They infest the mountains in this backwards county." The soldier sneered as he spoke. "It'll take the Protectorate to clean them out."

"What about a little girl?"

"Does it look like I've seen any 'little girls'?"

"We'll stick to the trail," Bellis said.

The soldier thought for a long time. Perhaps he would give the order to shoot them. Take their shaggies and add them to the moving masses down in the valley. For a moment, Luke felt doubt. He silently prayed for the Good Lord's favour. The man pulled on his gloves.

"Good hunting then." The soldier turned his mount. He and his men carefully descended into the valley. The river of bodies continued to flow. Luke and the others didn't wait to see the soldiers swallowed back into the main current.

"They took ten men from Barkley," Nathaniel said. "It seemed like a lot then. Seeing that . . . How many men does it take to fight a war?"

None of them had an answer.

It had been late afternoon when 'Keeper Courie made it into town. The board-walks were busy with people. There was a strong wind. It picked up dust and hats. Ladies grimaced as they clung to their dresses and battled onward. Barber Barringsley was standing at his doorway. He nodded at Courie. Barringsley had no doubt heard about the meeting. Not much escaped his ears.

Nathaniel hitched his shaggie outside the Elder's office. The post was busy today. There were five strange-looking creatures hitched in a row; like shaggies but not the same. They didn't have hair on their necks or feet; their flanks were slick in the sunlight; and their legs were thin and spindly. Nathaniel took a full turn around one of them, a gelded male, which paid him no attention. He patted the haunch of the creature. It was all muscle. But there was no way this creature could pull a plough. Nathaniel took its muzzle in his hand. The teeth were the same—big square pegs. The nostrils flared a little and Nathaniel let go of the beast. He stared into its round eyes for a while. Finally, he decided it wasn't so different. Buster, his own faithful shaggie, had other ideas. He had inched as far away as possible from his shiny, hairless cousins.

Veronica Klimp, the Elder's secretary, came out onto the board-walk. She was a thin girl, too thin really. And she wasn't married. She kept her blonde braids tightly pulled back. So much so it raised her eyebrows slightly and gave her the constant appearance of mild surprise.

"They're all inside, waiting for you," she said.

"Who is?"

She led him inside. "The Elder, Pastor Gray, Law-Man Bellis, and the men from out of town."

"That explains those skinny things out there."

Veronica made no comment. Maybe she felt an affinity with all things underweight. They went in silence through the corridors of Richards's office. A soft green carpet ran from wall to wall. Dust and dirt marked the passage of boots. Nathaniel wondered how many times a day Veronica had to brush these halls. She stopped at a large set of doors. She knocked once and then entered.

"Gravekeeper Courie," she announced. He shuffled into the room. Such an introduction made him feel a little awkward. Luckily, no one in the room seemed overly interested in his arrival. Instead, everyone was looking at a map. It covered the substantial table, where the other representatives of Barkley were sitting. Three young men in red jackets and trousers stood to one side, trying hard to hide their boredom.

"Ah, Nathaniel, come in, come in," the Elder said. He waved Nathaniel into a seat. "Carry on, Lieutenant."

A man roughly the same age as Nathaniel stroked his sizeable moustache. His chin was bare as a baby's backside. It was hard not to stare. "Well, there's little more to say. We're still pushing on the eastern front. Making good ground, too. General Turner won the battle at Bridgewood, so we're moving west at speed."

"Fascinating. All these happenings, so far from our little town," the Elder said.

"It's not as far as you think," the Lieutenant said. "Pierre County is becoming more and more important."

"It's already important to us," Bellis said.

"I'm sorry, I realise I was late, but just what is this all about?" Nathaniel asked.

The Elder turned to him. "These officers are from the Southern Protectorate Army. They're recruiting."

Nathaniel laughed. He quickly stopped when no one joined him. "You're serious?"

"Most definitely," the Lieutenant said. "Every town and village in this land is affected by the war."

"There's a war?"

The Lieutenant narrowed his eyes. He seemed to be deciding if Nathaniel was joking. "I was under the impression that Barkley, out of all the communities in Pierre County, was most aligned to the Protectorate's goals."

"And what are those?" the Pastor said. Nathaniel had never known the man to be silent for so long.

"In summary: the total eradication of the Walkin' menace."

The Pastor nodded in approval.

"But as you can see," the Elder said, "we don't have any Walkin' in Barkley. We're very careful about that."

"That's beside the point."

"Is it?"

"You have a duty to your country." The Lieutenant was struggling to keep his voice level. "To your race. The Protectorate is asking for ten men able to bear arms. That's all."

"Doesn't this seem backwards?" Nathaniel said. "Sending men off to kill each other so we can get rid of men that have already died?"

"I'm not here to debate. We can take the men by force if necessary. I'd rather not."

The table was quiet. Many of the Barkley men were staring at their laps, as if an answer might be waiting there. The three young soldiers shifted uneasily, each had a hand resting on a pistol butt. "By force if necessary." Nathaniel pictured scores of red jackets flooding into Barkley on their skinny shaggies, rifles and pistols making their case to wives and mothers and children.

"Ten men," the Elder said eventually.

3 : 7

Thomas saw a group of blightbirds circling. They were one, maybe two miles away. He couldn't tell how many birds there were. They stayed high in the cloudless sky, but he knew they were watching the ground. Waiting for a meal. He glanced at Mary. It wouldn't be long before she felt that kind of hunger—strong enough to travel miles just to pick over bones. For now, she was coping. Her blisters had burst and the loose skin worn away. Her feet had aged over these few days—they had lost their soft innocence. A lot of Mary had changed.

She noticed the birds. "One of them might be your blind friend," she said. He had forgotten about One Eye Blind, the blightbird that haunted him on those first days of the Walk. He wasn't eager to see his "friend."

"Whatever is over there, we should avoid it."

"There's smoke," she said. "We might be able to help." The smoke was faint in the heat haze, a lazy plume of dark grey that barely registered on the backdrop of the Redlands.

Mary was right: someone could be hurt but alive. The blightbirds were still in the air. A traveller in need of their aid—what little they could give. They had no food or water to share. But it could be dangerous. He would not risk Mary, not for anyone.

"We go halfway. Then I find out what's happened. Alone."

She nodded.

At what he judged was close enough, he told her to stop. She inched farther forward and then readied herself to sit down.

"No, you have to stay standing; so I can see you," he said.

Every ten or so paces he looked back. His daughter became gradually smaller, her face became a blur, until finally she was just a black line little bigger than a grain of rice. He was not happy with how far away she was. He almost turned back. The smoke was thicker now.

As he drew closer a familiar smell assaulted him. He reeled, putting his hand to his nose. The sweetness of burnt skin. It was a pyre pit. Smaller than the one he had climbed out of. He stood on the edge and counted five bodies. They had clearly been tumbled in; their arms and legs had fallen haphazardly, like dancers stopped in motion. The flames were taking their time devouring the remains. Thomas knelt, trying to avoid the plume of smoke. He saw the faces. Three women and two men. Walkin'.

He wasn't sure how, but he knew. There was a decay in the pit that seemed older. And now he realised, the smell was slightly different. Drier. It was closer to wood burning than a piece of meat. He noticed then the wounds on each corpse's head. They had been shot before being thrown into the pit. Someone was being very careful—more careful than they had been with Thomas.

Around the pyre pit he saw the marks of hooves. As many as twenty, twenty-five animals had been here. It was impossible to single out any individual set of tracks. Would so many men leave Barkley to follow him and Mary? It didn't seem likely. Besides, a pyre pit wasn't J. S. Barkley's way. Above ground, stacks of wood, and one person per pyre. But they would be in a hurry.

He checked on Mary again. She had not moved, as far as he could tell. Then he gazed in every direction. If this was the work of the men following them, they could be ahead of Thomas. They might have lost the trail, looped in front. Thomas had been so busy watching behind them, he hadn't considered pursuit from any other direction. He cursed himself for a fool.

Next to the pyre were the remains of what looked like a small cart. It had been tipped on its side and a wheel ripped off. The contents were scattered on the ground. Brushes, pots of paint—some open and bleeding, others sealed—books, and bolts of cloth. The cloth was all the same colour, a green-tinted white. If there had been a shaggie pulling the cart, it was gone. The wheel and side of the cart were now burning at the bottom of the pit. There were bottles of liquid. Thomas rushed over and opened one. He sniffed hard, hoping for water. A bottle or two that might keep his daughter going for a few more days. It was acrid and bitter. He threw the bottle away; the sound of it breaking was small consolation.

He fetched Mary. He could have insisted they circle at a distance, but piquing Mary's curiosity had its own dangers. She could be very stubborn. And she needed to see the pit. This was the world he had brought her into. She had to know how it worked; she wasn't a child any more, at least not a child he could protect.

She stood at the edge of the pit in silence, her arms crossed. The heads and seeds of bone-grass clung to her. She tried to make sense of the shapes in the pit—the arms and legs and heads. She didn't know why, but their tangle made the whole scene worse. It wasn't long ago she had seen Karl Williams hanging on a tree and that had made her curious more than anything else. But this was different.

"Why did they die?" she said. She was squinting against the smoke.

"Because of what they were."

"What *you* are. What *I* might be."

She inspected the cart. With her toe, she rolled a bottle. The liquid inside was slow to move, it was so thick. Oil or honey maybe. Seeing it, her mouth flooded. She didn't know how that was possible—she was so thirsty and now her body was wasting water. She picked up a book. The cover was battered. She read the title three times and it still didn't make sense.

"We can't take any books," Thomas said.

She hadn't asked to. Once, they would have held an undeniable allure for her. Books used to be the most important thing in her life—the one and only book and the frustration that it caused. Those kinds of things were small now. Even smaller beside the pit. Taking the books would be like grave-robbing.

A blightbird landed on the cart. Both Thomas and Mary jumped. It came down in a mess of feathers. Its claws gripped the broken wood. Blightbirds looked graceful in the air. Face to face they were like long-limbed young men at a festival dance. This one's head bobbed on its long neck, shoulders hunched. It turned to regard her with its rain-cloud eye and cawed.

Mary ran at it. She waved her arms and screamed. The blightbird took flight in an ungainly shuffle of wings. She started walking away from the pit. She didn't look back for him. She was almost running she went so quickly—she found some energy somewhere. They needed to be away from the pit. It was like a heathen crystal ball, showing them a gruesome possibility.

That morning passed without a word from either of them. At midday they stopped. It was difficult to find shade when the sun was at its peak, but the ground was becoming craggy again. They found a hollow and Mary sat with her back leant against the cool rock. She reached for the wrapped meat. She pulled apart the waxy paper deliberately. It was her ritual. Every time she opened the package she prayed there would be more meat rather than less. So far the Good Lord hadn't heard her. This time there was one mouthful left. Was it His way of punishing her? She chewed the meat and ignored her growling stomach.

When she was finished, she wrapped up the paper again. She didn't want her father to worry.

"There were a lot of shaggies," she said. He nodded. "Were they looking for us?"

"I don't know. I doubt it."

"Was it the army?" She made it sound like a curse word.

"They want every Walkin' gone. Somewhere, there are people who disagree," he said.

"You were in the army."

He stood up. "Have some water. We need to go soon."

They didn't speak again that day. That night Thomas didn't make a fire. She soon closed her eyes, exhausted. Falling asleep she was vaguely aware she was being carried. She sniffed hard, trying to dislodge the memory of the burning Walkin'.

3 : 8

Sarah was stacking bolts of cloth when Caleb knocked on the door. It was open, but she had forgotten to flip the sign. She sighed, thinking of all the people who might have been in. Today was the first day she was supposed to be open since Mary was taken.

She opened the door and the bell chimed.

"Sorry to be a bother, Sarah. But the boat's here."

Of course, it had been a month—maybe more. She hadn't prepared for the trading.

"If you like, I could go alone. With yours," he said. He was a big man and he sweated a lot—even in spring.

"Thank you, Caleb. That would be very kind."

Sarah went to the back of the shop. He followed her. She felt overly conscious of him; aware of his large shape blocking an aisle. He smelt sharp and musky; how a man should smell. She left him in the shop and went through the house to the garden. There was washing on the line. Washing she put out yesterday. It was slick with dew and cold to the touch. She picked up an empty crate and took it back inside. She filled it with candles.

Tallow, none of the wax—they would be wasted on the traders. Caleb made a show of browsing the shelves.

"There's a crate of shaggie shoes outside, if you wouldn't mind?" she said.

"Of course." He blustered behind the counter. When he came back he made huffing and puffing noises. Sarah tried to smile. She heard him talk to his shaggie: "Now, Sampson. I hope you're feelin' strong."

Caleb put the crate down on the cart bed. Sarah followed with the candles. There were stacks of hay and a couple of cases already in there. Last year must have been a good harvest if he still had hay to trade. This late he'd get a good price.

"Shaggie shoes, eh?" Caleb said, wiping his brow.

"Yes. Smithy said he'll have plenty more for the summer."

"Good, good. Sampson here does like his new shoes. He's ever so fashionable." Caleb was trying. In the kindest way he knew how. "What should I be aiming for?" he said.

"Sugar and salt. And oranges." There was something else she was supposed to remember. If only she could write these things down. Sarah stood with Sampson, patting the grey shaggie. She felt his heart thumping beneath his big flanks. She had to stop stroking him. "And a cooking pot. For Mrs. Freeman. Not too large. She's only cooking for one."

Caleb tipped his hat and flicked the reins. With the back loaded it must have been a heavy burden, but the shaggie didn't seem to notice. He went at the same pace he always did. Sarah had never seen him run. She doubted he could.

Sarah went back inside and locked the shop door. Word would have got around that she was closed. She wasn't sure she could manage to talk about little things. To pretend to care about other people's troubles, or the price of vegetables. Instead, she cleaned.

She wrapped her hair in a cloth. She swept the shop, the kitchen, and the hallways. She even did the stairs, though she hated it. Every step was a battle. The broom barely touched the corners.

She looked up from the bottom and felt dizzy; the stairs looming above her. Two empty bedrooms. She didn't sweep upstairs. In the kitchen, she wiped down every surface twice. The fireplace still smelt of burnt woollie fat. She had barely eaten these last few days. She wasn't hungry. She opened the kitchen door to let some air in.

By the afternoon, the sun had passed behind the buildings. The garden was in shadow. She stood in the back doorway. The frame had a large kink in it, just above her shoulder. It was smooth. She ran a finger along the wood. Bellis had fired his gun here, the shot crashing into the frame and splintering the wood. The next day, he had apologised several times. Apologised for hitting the frame and not the man. She was grateful Bellis missed, but couldn't tell him.

She felt the washing, which was dry. She had forgotten to bring out a basket. A trading crate would do. She folded each piece of clothing carefully. The pegs fell to the ground. She left them there.

On the landing, she put down the crate. Two closed doors in front of her. She went into the master bedroom. She sat down on the bed, trying to ignore the layer of dust that covered the room. But she started sneezing. It wouldn't stop until her eyes and nose were running. She was sitting in exactly the same spot that Thomas had been. There was no sense of him. She couldn't smell him in the way she could still smell Caleb in the shop. Couldn't feel him there. And where was he now? Trying to run away with their daughter. She had seen the men leave Barkley on shaggies. How long before they caught up? And what would Mary do? She would be so scared. Sarah blew her nose.

She took her clothes out of the crate. She used the top two drawers in the cabinet. Their handles were the only ones not covered in dust. Then she hurried out of the room and closed the door.

In Mary's room she piled the clothes on the bed. She stared at them for a long time. She picked up a little blouse. She tried and tried, but all she could smell was soap. The washing basket had been full—and full things became empty. She cursed herself for not thinking; for doing things as if it were just another day. She threw the blouse on the floor and left the room.

The knock woke her. She was slumped over the kitchen table. Her hand had gone numb. On her way to the door she flexed her fingers, willing them to life.

It was Caleb. He was standing with his hat in his hands.

"Back so soon?" she said. He looked confused. She squinted out at the night sky, wondering when it had got so dark.

"I hope I traded well." He motioned to the crates at his feet.

"I'm sure you did. Thank you again, Caleb."

He helped her with the goods. The cooking pot was solid and small. She opened the sugar and the salt. There was plenty of each.

"You must have bargained hard," she said.

"Always good to go for a bit of theatre."

Sarah nodded. She didn't open the orange crate. He hurried out the shop and climbed up to the seat of his cart.

"Did you do well?" she said. There was a tall box in the back. It was a strange shape. Perhaps a scythe or some long farm tool.

"With a couple of sheaves of hay and some soggy vegetables? Not bad."

She put it from her mind. Caleb's business was his own.

"Will you be open tomorrow?" he said.

Sarah glanced down Main. Caleb wasn't just asking for himself, but for the whole town. And he'd tell them whatever she said. It would have to happen some time. Or she could pay someone else to do it. She could imagine what her father would have said about that, let alone people like Ma McDermott or the clucking mothers as they took their children to school. Her choice was leave or carry on. And there was washing to put away.

"Yes, I'll be open."

"Can you do something for me?" Caleb said. "Will you come to my house one evening this week?"

"What for?" she said.

"Company."

It was raining. Luke's blankets were soaked. The fire had been reduced to a wet mound of ash. It wasn't heavy rain—the kind that might have woken them. Instead, it was a persistent drizzle that managed to seep right through clothes with surprising ease. He checked his copy of the Good Book. The cover was damp, but the pages had been spared. When they packed away their blankets, he hid the book as deep in his saddlebags as he could. Nobody said a word as they broke camp. The mood seemed as colourless as the day. The clouds that covered the sky were a uniform grey; none of the impressive or ominous black thunder-heads Luke associated with rain.

The shaggies were equally as unhappy with the rain. Luke hadn't thought it possible, but they seemed to amble even more slowly across the Redlands. He expected the ground to turn to mud or quagmire almost instantly; but it just drank the water. There was less dust, which was a blessing, though there were definitely more insects today. The Lord giveth . . .

Samuel sauntered his shaggie alongside. "No raincoat?"

Luke hadn't noticed the others were all wearing oiled coats. His cassock was heavy. He could wring out the sleeves and fill a water-skin or two.

"I didn't think it rained in the Redlands," Luke said.

"We're getting near the mountains." Samuel nodded to the horizon, where rounded triangles edged towards the sky. From so far away they looked small, like a child's toy. They were still a welcome sight. Luke had grown tired of the flat, barren, and seemingly endless Redlands. They had little to offer a man beyond solitude; and that was not an option. "You can have my coat."

The offer was kind. But it was Luke's fault for not being prepared. For being hasty. He had packed a lot less food than the others. He was fortunate his Lent fasting had prepared him for meagre meals. And besides, he was already drenched.

"Thank you, Samuel, but the Lord gives us rain. I will not deny Him."

Samuel suddenly looked uncomfortable in his coat.

"You listen when I read from the Good Book," Luke said.

"Of course. Ma makes sure I never miss a sermon."

Luke smiled. He had a congregation of one; it was a start. "I'm glad to have such a devout man by my side. You will be a great aid in the battle against the devil's spawn."

"They are my family."

"Were," Luke said.

"Were my family."

The Law-Man and the Gravekeeper rode in front of Luke. They were little more than twenty paces ahead, but he could barely see them. They were talking, most likely in hushed tones. They did that often, thinking Luke didn't notice. But he did. He noticed a lot of things about those two. They schemed brazenly in front of him, Nathaniel whispering deceit and cowardice into Bellis's bendable ear. But Luke was vigilant. He had to make sure Bellis would do the right thing, when the time came.

He watched the rain drip from their hats. Luke's own head was bare, his hair flattened. His glasses were almost unusable. He had to wipe at them constantly and peer between rivulets. His face was slick. Rain seemed to gather at the clumps of hair on his cheeks and jaw. He hated not being able to shave. An unmarried man should have an unmarried face. It itched. When he scratched, a small wave of water rushed down his wrist. It was cold. All for want of a hat.

As well as mountains, the distance held a strangely joyous sight: grass. From so far away, it was simply a change in colour. From the parched ground that gave the Redlands its name to a washed-out, yellow-stained green. It was bone-grass. He didn't relish the thought of a prolonged trek through the stuff. It stuck to everything.

He had a sudden flash of memory—a woollie with bone-grass in its mouth. The single blade was broken, just below the head. He couldn't remember where he'd seen the woollie, but it was so vivid. He should have been able to recall the touch of its fluffy coat or the sound of its soft bleating. Instead, he could only picture the bone-grass. He was no farmer—when had he been close enough to a woollie to touch it?

They still had a handful of miles to cover before they'd be out of the Redlands proper. Luke wouldn't miss the clinging dust, or the hard ground when it came to sleeping. He wouldn't miss the cold night wind or the wide open views that made a man feel worthless. The humility was important, but it sapped a soul of purpose. He had the Good Lord's work to do. All the things he wouldn't miss he would be reacquainted with on the return journey. There was that to look forward to.

The rain continued throughout the afternoon. Even if they had a mind to talk the downpour discouraged it. There was a church's distance between each of them.

Bellis's shaggie reared up.

He was riding through a small gully, a few feet below the rest of them. He fell from the saddle. The shaggie whinnied—a shrill, metallic sound. There was a deep growling bark that juddered like a chair scraping across a wooden floor. Luke couldn't see Bellis. He tried to steer his mount that way, but the shaggie's ears were flat and it was determined on the other direction. The others were similarly struggling. They dismounted and ran to the gully.

3 : 9

Bellis was on his back. A red-wink crouched, just striking distance away. It was big. Its shoulders were bunched, its muzzle lowered and snarling. Teeth flashed—they were large enough for rain to drip from them. Or maybe it was spittle. The animal was a mix of greys and browns, its thick fur flattened in the rain. Luke touched his own hair. The red-wink barked. Luke flinched.

"Don't shoot it," Bellis yelled. Luke glanced over, noticing Nathaniel's rifle for the first time. The Gravekeeper had the stock braced against his shoulder. He lowered it, but looked ready to whip it back into place and fire in the same motion. Bellis edged sideways. The red-wink lunged, snapping at his foot but missing. Bellis stayed still. There was another sound—a yapping. It came from behind Bellis.

"Fire, Nathaniel," Luke said.

"But, what if—"

"No!" Bellis said.

"Shoot."

The Gravekeeper hesitated.

Luke took the rifle. Nathaniel offered no resistance, too surprised. Luke fired. He didn't think. He barely breathed as he aimed and pulled the trigger. The red-wink yelped and staggered. He had hit it high on the shoulder. It tried to stand, shuffling unevenly, until it fell to the ground. Its last breath was like a sigh, loud enough to be heard over the rain.

Bellis stood awkwardly. When he reached the group he snatched the rifle from Luke. It was so heavy in his hands, Luke almost dropped it at the Law-Man's feet.

"It was just protecting its young," Bellis said, handing the rifle back to Nathaniel.

Luke started to shake. He had never fired a gun before. The feeling of it ghosted from his hands all along his arms. He might have missed, or worse. He could have killed Bellis. Luke had no idea why he had taken the rifle. It was a compulsion. The Good Lord moved through him—guiding his hands and his aim. There was nothing else to account for it. His shot was miraculous. He was truly an agent of the Good Lord.

The Law-Man rubbed his back. He was stooping badly.

"Can you ride?" Nathaniel said.

"I'll have to."

"You look hurt, Bellis. We can't carry on with you like that."

"We must," Luke said. "The Good Lord wills it."

Bellis grimaced. "We're getting closer. I'll be fine."

"Then we should at least rest for a while."

"And let them get away? Is that it, Nathaniel?" Luke said.

Bellis shook his head.

Nathaniel and Samuel dragged the red-wink away from the gully. The shaggies didn't like it, but eventually the carcass was hauled up and secured. They wouldn't waste fresh meat, Bellis assured Luke. But he wouldn't eat the red-wink. He might not eat for the rest of his life, safe in the knowledge the Good Lord watched over him.

"I always figured red-winks were red," Samuel said.

"The Redlands," Nathaniel replied, his arms wide in a circle. "A harsh place." He cast a wary glance at Luke.

They rode off to the sound of young throats keening for their mother.

Sarah left the shop, stopping on the board-walk to look up at the stars. The sky was clear and cold. She pulled her wool hat over her ears and hugged her coat closer. The walk to Caleb's would warm her, get her blood flowing. She left behind the lamps and candles of Main and headed out of town.

She wondered if Mary was warm tonight. Sarah focused on her feet, making sure she didn't trip on the rough track. The sky had clouded over by the time she arrived at Caleb's. The big house stood watchful, presiding over the fields. The wind washed through the bone-grass. The clouds promised rain.

She knocked on the door. Caleb lived with his wife, Susanna, but no children. It was a shame, but the way of things. They accepted this absence in their lives and the majority of the town followed their example. They lived solely on the ground floor, which had two spare bedrooms. Susanna kept the whole place clean and tidy. Behind the house were Caleb's stables. He hired help for the farming.

Susanna opened the door.

"Sarah, so nice to see you," she said. She was a heavy-set woman, but not unpleasantly so, and her smile was warm and sincere. She was taller than Sarah and Caleb.

"Mrs. Williams." She took off her hat and wiped her feet.

Susanna's shoes clacked against the polished wood floor. "You'll forgive the mess," she said, smiling back at Sarah. The hallway was immaculate. Two coats hung on a stand. A walking stick leant against the wall. A large mirror was the only item on the dresser. She didn't look in it.

Susanna reached the big stairs and stopped. "He's upstairs, on the back balcony."

Sarah hesitated.

"Upstairs?"

"He's taken to the view. Are you hungry?"

"No, thank you. I'm just fine."

"Well, he's got some bits to chew on. Though I don't approve of the wine," Susanna said.

"Wine?"

"It's a right on the landing, down the corridor, second bedroom on the left. It's a double, with big doors. They'll be open."

Sarah climbed the stairs. In all the years she had known Caleb, she couldn't recall ever going upstairs. Long rugs covered the landing and corridor. They were soft with strange swirling patterns. If that weren't shocking enough, there were paintings on the walls. Paintings. Men and women posing in foreign-looking landscapes. The surfaces were rough, the paint obscenely bulging off the paper.

There was a naked woman. Sarah looked away, but was drawn back to the picture. This woman was sprawled on a luxurious chair, every bit of her on display. She looked out with an expression of utter contempt. Her black hair spiralled ridiculously straight up. Somehow, she was judging Sarah. She hurried past.

Caleb was sitting in a rocking chair, his large frame at ease. A low table and another chair were beside him.

"You could be in big trouble, Caleb."

"We're all in trouble, Sarah. Stop preaching and sit down."

On the table was a board with cheese and biscuits, and a plain bottle of dark red liquid. She'd thought Susanna was making fun of her.

"Paintings, Caleb? *Paintings*? How? Why?"

"Why not?" The farmer poured her a glass of wine before she could say no.

"Because they're forbidden."

"I didn't realise you'd brought your braids, dear girl," Caleb said.

"What if the Elder found out?"

"He knows. Christ, he has more than I do."

Sarah stared in disbelief. She drank some wine. It burnt, stung, and soothed all at the same time. She felt a little dizzy. She couldn't remember the last time she'd had wine—possibly at her wedding. Caleb rocked gently back and forth. The balcony looked out over the stables and onto the fields that rose up behind the house. The smell of shaggies was thick and sweet. It was dark, the clouds blocking the night sky. Sarah wrapped her coat tighter.

"I picked them up from the river traders over the years," Caleb said.

"What about the Pastor?" She sounded like a child, but she didn't care. She couldn't believe her friend.

"That zealot? Of course he doesn't know."

"He might find out."

"His nose is so jammed in the Good Book he can't see past the cover," Caleb said.

"He sees more than you think. Why risk it?"

"Are you going to talk about paintings all night? What pleasures do we have, Sarah? Our wives or husbands? Our work? I'll take a little extra to that; to hell with the consequences."

"To hell," Sarah said.

Caleb sipped his wine.

"You're one to be righteous," he said quietly.

Sarah didn't answer.

"They say your sight goes when you get to my age. But a young woman like you? I expect you can see in the dark better than under-mutton. Even if frightened."

Sarah's breath caught in her throat. She picked up her glass and drained it.

"He was the best farm hand I ever had, that Thomas."

Sarah filled her glass.

"Though I doubt he'd manage the traps these days. Death makes the fingers stiff."

"Enough!"

The chirp of grinders seemed to pulse, coming in waves. Tears were gathering at the edge of her eyes.

"I knew it was Thomas that took Mary, from that very first day. It was all over you. It still is," Caleb said.

"What was I supposed to do?"

"Some would say the same as the Peekmans. But not me. I like my paintings." Caleb raised his glass in his fat fingers. "You see, we're all in trouble."

She had known she couldn't fool everyone. But enough people believed her—most likely because they didn't want to think of another Barkley boy as a Walkin'. Both of them were quiet for a while.

"The Pastor is making noises about where Mary should be buried—if she's found," Caleb said. "The McDermott plot or your family's? I can try to help."

Sarah didn't answer for a long time. Caleb was asking her to think on things she had been avoiding. But what did it matter? Thomas would keep Mary safe. This was just another part of the lie. "McDermott," she said.

"Her Pa ain't there."

"No."

"I reckon there's no reason she should be."

"She's not dead," she snapped.

Caleb looked at her. "No, they're not."

Sarah thudded her way down the stairs. Her head felt fuzzy. The wine scorched through her veins, burning a trail across her forehead. She clutched the banister. Susanna was waiting at the bottom.

"Are you all right, Sarah?"

"Fine, thank you," she said.

"Was Caleb . . . all right? He's been spending a lot of time up there. Thinking, he says."

"Oh, yes, he's been thinking."

"I'm worried about him," Susanna said.

"So am I." That was the wrong answer; Susanna frowned. "He'll be fine," Sarah added lamely.

Bidding Susanna farewell, she stepped out into the night. She felt the light pat of rain on her back. The further she went the heavier it got.

She trudged down the tracks, stumbling in and out of puddles. Caleb had changed. He never used to think things over; he'd joke and smile instead. Caleb would keep her secret, as she would keep Caleb's. And learning that the Elder had paintings. It had been a strange evening.

She came to the graveyard. The small patch of ground Nathaniel Courie tended, earning him reverence from all those who couldn't face the job.

"Gravekeeper Courie," she said, spreading her arms in a grand gesture. He was somewhere out there now. Looking for Mary. Wanting to bring her back here to bury. She lurched between the headstones, from one family plot to another.

She stood at Thomas's headstone. Tears mixed with the rain; warm with the cold. She sniffed hard.

"Hello, Thomas," she said. She stamped the ground with her foot. "Empty, see?"

She craned her head back.

"So where are you?"

The rain washed down her face.

3 : 10

Tell the righteous it will be well with them,
for they will enjoy the fruit of their deeds.

Isaiah

BOOK 4

4 : 1

Ahead of Luke the ground rose into a set of craggy hills. Their tips were sharp and looked rusty. The Redlands seemed to flow smoothly towards the hills and then suddenly crumple. It was an angry part of the landscape, like the crusted lines that crossed his palms.

Bellis and Nathaniel rode close together. They were talking; Bellis gestured at the hills. This part of the Redlands seemed an ideal place for an evil creature to hide; without the honesty of a wide open space. Was the Gravekeeper trying to divert them? Suggesting they skirt around the hills? He would waste their time and let the creatures escape. Luke urged his shaggie forward.

"What is it?" he said.

"You can't see?" Bellis replied.

"See what?"

"Them."

Luke strained his failing eyes. Not for the first time he cursed his mother and father for burdening him this way. But he immediately repented his vanity in the face of the fifth commandment.

"The girl and the Walkin'?" he said.

"Most likely."

Luke barked a strangled noise as he tried to control his urge to swear at the men. "Why didn't you say so? Why are we still talking?"

"They'll reach those hills before we do," Bellis said.

"And they will *burn* before we do." Luke kicked his shaggie into an ungainly gallop. The wind pulled at his cheeks. He couldn't help but grin as he raced down the slope. He was close to his purpose, his calling. He felt a raw holiness bubbling in his blood. His heart matched the beat of the shaggie's hooves. Some part of him was aware of the other men following, though not at the same speed. He ignored their faithless lumbering.

Two taints on the landscape—he could see them now. Gradually, they became bigger. He gripped the reins until his scabs loosened and began to bleed again. He drank in the rich smell; he remembered it pouring from Simon Peekman to fill the church. He would have it again with Mary McDermott in his arms. It was the scent of the living. It was what separated man from evil.

Luke raised a hand to the sky. He implored the Good Lord to see him, to see his good work. And then it took him. He convulsed. His thighs clamped down on the saddle, but the rest of his body shook. All noises ceased to be; he could only hear his own voice. He spoke in tongues. Loud, guttural syllables; words he did not know. Ancient words.

The two shapes ballooned into gigantic devils. Their wings folded to the size and shape of mountains. Their hands and feet were taloned. Both faces were the same: Thomas McDermott. One cheek was missing—an eye floated by some dark arts. His skin was pale and in places it curled like burnt paper.

An enormous hand reached for Luke. He held out his crucifix, confident this would hold back the devil, as he continued in tongues. The talons closed around him and everything was black.

Mary heard the noise first. She looked back. The riders were behind them. A mile; two at most. Thomas saw them too.

"Run!" he said. He took her hand.

But Mary was too tired and too hungry. She walked as quickly as she could with her father urging her on. Her legs buckled. She clung to him so she could stay on her feet.

Those were men from Barkley; men who wanted her to burn. Would she know them? There weren't many people in town she *didn't* know. She imagined different faces leering and sneering at her, bubbling up out of the flames. Mr. Adams with his bald head and crooked teeth. Pastor Gray, his hair and beard part of the fire itself. Grandpa McDermott frowning. Gravekeeper Courie with his workers busy around his veiled head. All of them changed by the pyre. Her pyre.

In the days before she had been careful about where she stepped—trying to avoid stones that hurt her feet. Her shoes felt thin and they rubbed in so many places they seemed more trouble than they were worth. She wanted to sit down. Or, even better, lie down in a bed. Night after night she had sat on her bed and wished she were somewhere else, someone else.

Her father squeezed her hand. They were almost in the hills. She looked back one last time. The riders were closer—she was sure of it.

Luke opened his eyes. The hazy faces of Bellis, Nathaniel, and Samuel were leant over him. Even Bellis managed to look worried. The back of Luke's head pounded. He found a bump just below his crown. When he took away his hand there was blood on his finger tips.

"What happened?" he said.

"You came off your shaggie," Bellis said.

"Where are my glasses?"

Samuel had been cradling something. He opened his hands to show Luke. The glasses were broken in the middle and missing one arm. Luke took the pieces carefully.

"Did they get away?"

Bellis nodded. "They know we're here."

They helped Luke stand. The sun was far across the sky. He had wasted hours by falling; that hurt more than his head. The creatures could be anywhere in the warren of hills.

"We should let the acolyte rest," Nathaniel said.

Luke glared in the direction of the Gravekeeper's voice. "More delay, Nathaniel? A blind man could see through your devil schemes."

"He seems well enough," Bellis said.

Luke's shaggie seemed to bear him no ill will. The animal accepted him back into the saddle with barely a flick of its tail. Perhaps saints learnt their patience from shaggies. He made sure to stay close to the others—he was afraid of losing them in the blanket red-grey that started ten paces from his nose. They set a slow pace.

Luke used the time to repair his glasses. The arm was gone, lost in the Redlands. He used one of the leather thongs from his crucifix to tie the broken halves together. The mended glasses sat heavily on his nose and regularly slipped, but he could see again. They were no more than half a mile from the hills.

"I saw the devils," Luke said to Samuel. "They were bigger than those hills and had your brother's face. Both of them."

"Mary had a pretty face." He thought for a long moment. "We'll do what is needed."

"That's right, Samuel. It will be a glorious day. They will burn and enter into His kingdom, amen."

"Amen." Samuel led his shaggie away.

They entered through a narrow gorge. It felt like a corridor in a big, old building—like the enormous ruined house in Miracle. Rough stone walls criss-crossed like a maze. She didn't know where her father was leading her. She wondered if he knew. For some reason that seemed more important in the hills. She hadn't known where they were going the whole time, not really, but she hadn't cared. It was enough to be with him. Now, though, they might get lost.

"Where are we going?" she said.

"We're going to hide."

"Will they find us?"

He stopped. "Not if I can help it. I promised your mother nothing would happen to you."

They both heard the shaggies at the same time. A dull thud that might have been relaxing if it hadn't been so terrible. The noise grew louder. It echoed through the rocks, feeling as inevitable as the sunset. You couldn't outrun it.

"Up," Thomas said. He pointed to a part of the rocky wall that had crumbled. She went first. It was just like climbing by the Col River. Feet were the most important thing—if you were sure of your feet the rest was easy. She held her breath every time she put her foot on a new piece of rock. The bluff was as big as a house in Barkley, but she had climbed that high before. Games when boys chased her; she wasn't sure why they did, but that wasn't important. Rocks came loose in her hands. One tumbled down and hit her father. She said she was sorry, but he didn't hear.

Finally, she came to a ledge. She pulled herself over the edge and lay on the stone. Her breath came in fast and shallow spasms. Her stomach cramped. Stars danced at the corners of her vision. She closed her eyes, but they didn't go away. Thomas arrived beside her. He put his arm around her, holding her tightly. He was strangely still; she felt like every part of her was pounding. He peeked down at the path below. She shuffled up to see.

The riders were just rounding a corner. She saw the Law-Man before Thomas pulled her back. He put his finger to his lips. Mary tried hard not to make a sound, not to even breathe, but her body was like a parade drum. How could the Law-Man not hear? She buried herself in her father's arms, trying to smother her noise.

She listened to the rhythm of the shaggies. They seemed to take for ever. She didn't understand. Before, they had been impossibly quick—flying across the land like a hungry blight-bird. Thomas stroked her hair as they waited. His shirt itched her forehead.

The clop-clop of the shaggies grew fainter. Thomas inched forward. Mary rolled over and saw a line of crumbers making their way across the ledge. A lot of crumbers, heading away from them.

"They're gone," Thomas said. "We'll stay up high, okay?"

The going was slower than walking. Climbing from ledge to ledge made different parts of her ache. They stopped often, just to listen. When they heard the shaggies they kept very still and very quiet, until they couldn't hear them any more.

They rode single file, Bellis leading, Nathaniel at the rear. The ground was littered with loose rocks. On either side, high walls of stone seemed to lean in. Luke felt himself stooping in his saddle, glancing up every few seconds. All manner of crea-tures could be hiding in this place—not just the two they had chased in. The silence echoed around them, tangible enough to resist the noise of the shaggies' hooves. He felt as much as heard it. He ducked at the sound of a rock bouncing down a stony slope somewhere in the distance. He could not see it. There was so much here he could not see. After the open expanse of the Redlands it was almost too much to bear. His skin crawled with the sensation of being touched completely from all sides: a soft embrace of rock.

"We have entered our tomb," Nathaniel said, loud enough for them all to hear. For once, Luke agreed with the Grave-keeper. The hills drained Luke's energy. It was almost as if the stone walls blocked his connection to the Good Lord. At times the walls were so high they covered all but a little strip of the heavens. Despite the men around him, Luke was alone. Then the sun began to set.

Eventually, they came out of the gorge into an open area. Luke let out a breath he hadn't realised he was holding. His ribs ached. The space was no bigger than the church in Barkley, but the sense of it was a relief. Four other corridors branched off it, like the points of a compass.

"We'll make camp here," Bellis said.

"But they are here, somewhere. We should continue," Luke said, though he wasn't sure how much farther he could go.

"We might not find such a good spot all night."

They led the shaggies to one corner. There was nothing to hitch them to, but the animals seemed content to stand by their dropped reins. Luke opened his bag of oats—still half empty from his Lent fasting—and fed his shaggie. He had overheard Nathaniel talking to "Buster." Luke hadn't named his mount and why should he? It was an animal. Names were for people. The men laid their blankets down in a circle in the middle of the space.

"No chance of finding wood for a fire," Bellis said. Luke shivered at the mention of warmth. It was a clear sky and he could already feel the cold ground beneath his blanket.

"We have wood," Nathaniel said.

"No!" Luke said.

"I'm not freezing to death."

"That wood has a sacred purpose."

"And how are we to do that dead?" Nathaniel said. Luke didn't think it was cold enough to die, but Nathaniel and Bellis were older than he was.

The Gravekeeper made to get up, but Luke was faster. He scrambled over to the shaggies and pulled out a log from one of the packs. He swung it above his head. He could smell the rose scenting. The bark was rough against his scabs.

"I'll take this to your head before I let you make a fire with it," he said. Nathaniel stood up slowly. He kept his distance.

Luke was poised like a husht ready to strike. He shuffled towards Nathaniel. The Gravekeeper moved back.

"You don't want to hit me, Luke."

"This wood is needed! They must burn on it."

"Put it down," Bellis said. His rifle was aimed at Luke.

"You wouldn't," Luke said.

"Put it down."

He glanced from Bellis to Nathaniel. They were fools. Their faith failed them.

"There will be other wood," Nathaniel said, as if he had no notion of his blasphemy.

Luke dropped the log. What could he do? He was surrounded by those who claimed to believe, but acted otherwise.

Samuel, who had watched them in silence, came over to Luke.

"Your hands are hurt," Samuel said, taking them in his own.

"There isn't any pain."

"Are you okay?"

"The Pastor will hear of this," Luke said.

They used four stout logs for the fire. They were supposed to be the top layer of a pyre—wood blessed and scented for the passage to the afterlife. To try to appease the Good Lord, Luke led them in a prayer. As the fire was lit, the smell of roses was strong. Luke remembered every pyre he had ever seen. But the image of Simon Peekman, lying at the feet of his Walkin' father, was the strongest. The Walkin' couldn't cry, it wasn't possible, but it had seemed to nonetheless. It made Luke wonder if crying was more than tears. The small boy's face was like a cherub's—soft, round cheeks and skin the sun had barely touched. Luke tried to ignore the angry red mark around his neck. Where *he* had touched.

"We should take turns on watch," Bellis said. Luke nodded in approval. Now they had spotted the devils, who knew what kind of danger they were in? And the Walkin' were indeed creatures of the night.

"I'll go first," Luke said.

"You won't. You need rest."

"I do not. The Good Lord gives me strength."

"Strength to set a pyre for a child," Nathaniel said.

"To do what has to be done," Luke snapped. "What's the matter, 'Keeper? Now we've found them does your meagre faith abandon you?"

"I *will* save my brother," Samuel said. They all looked at the young man. He so rarely said a word when they all spoke; it somehow added weight to already heavy words.

"I'll take first watch," Bellis said. It was no longer open to debate.

Luke slumped back into his blankets. It took him a long time to get to sleep. His head throbbed. The blood had dried and was already starting to form a scab. It felt like a thick piece of paper that he couldn't quite turn over. No matter how he shifted, he couldn't get comfortable. Even lying on his side made his scalp itch. Samuel started snoring. It was a purr that grew and sputtered into a loud snort, and then back to a purr. Luke counted the seconds between each snort. Samuel was strangely consistent.

A cloud passed over the moon, plunging the church-sized space into darkness. The rose-scented feeble fire did nothing to hold off the black. The taloned hand. It came for him again. Luke clutched his crucifix, now missing its thong. Silently, he prayed for strength and forgiveness. The two seemed entwined.

He fell asleep watching Bellis's face; the lines and creases reflected in the firelight.

Thomas laid Mary down. He tried to clear away the loose rocks, but the ground made a poor mattress. She stirred but didn't wake up. They had been hurrying ever since they entered the hills. He was confident they could lose the men in this place. Now, he wanted to find them.

He put the wrapped parcel of meat and the water-skin beside Mary. They both felt dangerously empty. He bound them as best he could. He didn't want any curious red-wink or other scavenger to find his daughter alone. He didn't want to leave her, either. But he had little choice. The men wouldn't give up—they'd followed them this far. Thomas had to do something and it was better he do it alone.

He had climbed as best he could with Mary in his arms. She was now on a wide ledge, overlooking a series of slim gullies and gorges. She was invisible to anyone below. The blightbirds would have a good view of her. He hoped she looked alive and dangerous to their keen eyes.

Coming through the hills he had tried his best to memorise every twist and turn. Even before the Walk he had had a good sense of direction. In chasing games with his brothers and sisters he was the best at getting from one side of town to the other—to be quick but not seen. But he needed some help in this strange place. He picked up a stone. At every branch or turning he marked the walls with a cross. He forced himself to go carefully, stopping often to listen. The rock was silent. He tried to step as quietly as he could, but to his ears he was louder than a shaggie. How could he possibly sneak up on the riders? They had to sleep eventually. Where he could he kept to higher ground. Their shaggies couldn't manage that kind of terrain. He ducked into shadows gratefully. He didn't have long. The night was already old.

He was in the shadow of one of the peaks when he lost his footing. What was solid rock suddenly crumbled beneath him. The sky tilted madly as he fell. The stars shot across his vision like white raindrops. His arms flailed at the air. Then he rolled and hit stone. Rocks ranging from the size of his fist to as big as his head rolled with him. The noise was colossal. He hit the slope on his shoulder and continued to roll down towards a thin corridor ten feet deep. He landed in a heap; scree coating him in dust and stone flakes.

4 : 2

Thomas got up and waited for the voices—the shouts of alarm or rage. He had risked everything coming out here and he'd been clumsy. But the night returned to silence. He pushed himself up and noticed his hand looked odd. Two fingers were splayed at an angle. He tried to move them and only one weakly responded. He stood. The bone of his little finger had snapped. It was being held on by his patchy skin; he could see the break through a hole—a jagged black line. With a child-like fascination, he slowly ripped off his little finger. The skin eased apart fibre by fibre like splitting dough. He felt nothing. It was useless, but he wanted to keep it. He put it in the pocket of his trousers. His ring finger seemed slow and he couldn't quite make a fist with it.

The maze continued for some way. He made his scratches every so often. When a gap came in the stone wall he climbed. His hand felt different, clutching at rock with what seemed like all of his fingers. He tried to move the finger that wasn't there any more. When he reached the top, he saw the glow of a fire. He had been dreading that sight for the past six days.

Constantly looking back, hoping the horizon would stay dark. And now he was actively seeking out their fire.

He crept towards it. He tested every step, making sure the rock was solid, and treading as lightly as possible. Soon he was close enough to hear the fire hissing and popping. He saw the men who were chasing him and his daughter. The men he knew from as early as he could remember. Law-Man Bellis. Grave-keeper Courie. Luke Morris.

And his own brother, Samuel.

Samuel. They had brought his brother to hunt him down. What twisted sense of justice drove Elder Richards to that? The others he had expected. They were obvious choices, necessary to what they felt had to be done. What part could Samuel possibly play? He was a sweet, simple-minded young man, too shy to be married yet. And he was here to kill his brother and his niece. It was clearly the Pastor's doing. Samuel was a strong believer.

The men were resting in their blankets—a luxury he hadn't been able to give Mary—except for Gravekeeper Courie. He was squatting next to the fire. His head rested on his chin. His eyes were closed. Thomas had done his share of sentry duty in the Protectorate. Staying awake was the hardest part.

He had the power to kill these men from his past. By the time they knew what was happening he'd have crushed two skulls. Their rifles would be useless, their fire not nearly big enough. Thinking of his little girl, sleeping on hard rock, he could almost bring himself to do it. But he knew Bellis, Nathaniel, Luke, and Samuel. Two were married. He grew up with the other two. It wouldn't be right to kill them. But he had to protect Mary.

Something snorted in the shadows. The shaggies. He couldn't see them—they must be some way from the fire.

Thomas inched around the ledge. He watched Nathaniel, ready for when the Gravekeeper should come to. Thomas's foot brushed against a pebble. It tumbled, each bounce like a horn blast from an Easter parade. Nathaniel didn't move. They were clearly exhausted. Six days in the saddle had taken their toll.

He could see the shaggies. They had wandered into one of the narrow corridors, likely searching for food. He gazed down at the animals. His family had used shaggies for almost everything—ploughing, seeding, ranging with the woollies, even driving to church. Now all he seemed to do was scare them. He had to, but he was sorry for it. They would have packets of food and drink in their bulging saddlebags. Food Mary badly needed. If only he could get close enough to take some.

The nearest shaggie lifted its head. It went rigid. The muscles on its rump twinged. Thomas was almost on top of them now. He jumped down. As one, the shaggies bolted. He chased them down the winding gorge. The shaggies jostled each other in their panic. As they came to a fork in the path, they split up. Thomas followed the biggest group. He would spread them across these hills. From behind, he could hear faint voices: the men were awake. He ran as fast as his legs would take him. He wanted to pick up speed, but his body didn't work that way. Another branch and the shaggies continued to go in different directions. They saw no safety in numbers and they were right in a way. Thomas was now following a single shaggie, and slowly falling behind. If they'd been on open ground, he would have lost the animal a long time ago. But the shaggie struggled with the sharp corners. Finally, Thomas stopped. The shaggie would keep going, the memory of the terror remaining fresh in its mind. Thomas found a spot to climb and tried to keep to the higher ground.

The men would spend the night looking for their mounts. He hoped their interrupted sleep would make them slow. They might get lost themselves.

Now all Thomas had to do was get back to Mary. He tried to orientate himself, but the peaks and crags all looked the same. From his vantage point he spotted a shaggie. It had stopped a hundred paces from him and was looking back down a gorge, ready to run again if it had to. Thomas wanted to chase it farther, but he needed to find Mary. He checked every stone wall for a cross. The sun was rising before he found one.

* * *

Mary was still asleep when Thomas returned. It had taken him an
hour or so to find her. He was glad she'd had this opportunity to
rest. He had pushed her hard, with no real food, over the last few
days—not hard enough considering they had almost been caught.
If it wasn't for the hills, Bellis and his men would have overtaken
them. Sarah had said they would burn him and Mary together. He
couldn't believe Bellis or Samuel or even 'Keeper Courie would do
that. But that's what they'd done to Jared and his boy.

He checked on the food and water. It was all still there. He
couldn't see any sign of animals or anything that might be interested in their supplies. To make sure, he undid the cap of the
water-skin. He peered inside, trying to see the water or its reflection. He could smell its dampness. He carefully unwrapped the
food. There was nothing there. He didn't know of any animal
that could wrap.

"Mary," he sighed. How long had she lied to him? How long
had she been starving herself?

He looked down at his sleeping daughter. She was beautiful.
For once she seemed calm in her sleep; her usual frown was
gone. He tried to rub away some of the dirt and grime that
framed her face. He went to lick his finger and got nothing but
a leather-dry tongue. Mary had rolled a few feet in the night.
She was further from the ledge's edge than he remembered,
which was a relief.

Gathering up their things, he waited for as long as he possibly could before waking her. It would take some time for the
men to find their shaggies, but it was time Thomas and Mary
badly needed. He shook Mary's shoulder. She didn't wake up.

He shook harder.

"Mary."

She rolled onto her back. A white speck of foamy dribble was
at the corner of her lips. He dropped the supplies.

4 : 3

"Mary!" He was shaking her with both his hands. Her neck lolled limply. He searched for a pulse, pressing his fingers hard against her wrist. It was weak. He spotted two black marks on her ankle. A husht bite. The surrounding skin was red raw. There was a hole in the ground. Her leg had been covering it. She'd rolled over the husht's lair and it had bitten her.

He knelt down by her ankle, placing his foot firmly over the hole. He sucked drily at the bite. Warm blood sprang into his mouth. There was something else too, slick and wasting, like lamp oil spilt on water. He didn't bother to spit. Blood ran down his throat. It lined his stomach and then began seeping out of his wounds, as if *he* were bleeding. He was back on the battlefield, the bayonet draining him. He began to shiver, but he ignored it. He kept sucking at the bite until he couldn't feel anything dark mixed with the blood. There was no way to tell how long the venom had been in her body. He thought back to all the time he had wasted: losing his footing; chasing the shaggies; creeping around the men's camp. He should have been here. In trying to keep Mary safe, he had let this happen.

He didn't wipe the blood from his mouth. He saw movement and looked up. Something was over by the rocky fringe of the ledge; he couldn't see into the shadows. He glanced down at the hole his foot was covering—the husht wanted to go home. Scrambling forward, he reached out. He felt the sudden urge to pluck out its fangs. His hand brushed against a cold and supple skin. He tried to close his fist around it, but his broken fingers could only make a claw. The husht slipped through and was gone. He picked up rocks and tossed them aside, hunting. But the more he moved the deeper he knew the husht went. His hope of revenge was well buried.

He picked Mary up. She still seemed so calm. Was she lighter in his arms? He carefully carried her down to the floor of the gorge. He turned to the rising sun. East. Always east.

Thomas emerged from the hills by mid-afternoon, Mary still asleep in his arms. Her breath was light against his chest. She had to wake up soon.

He had got lost in the hills many times. He tried to keep to the same direction, but the stony corridors twisted and turned. Twice he came to a dead end and had to retrace his steps. There was no space between the rocks. He hadn't felt it before but now they pressed in on him. At times the way became so narrow he had to turn sideways, and Mary's shoulder still brushed against the stone. At least some of the passageways would be impossible for shaggies.

The Redlands gradually faded behind him. The scrub turned to plains of knee-high bone-grass. The tops of the grass clung to his trousers, dry but somehow sticky. Mary's dipped toes ran a line through the plains, as if it were the Col River. Memories of family picnics at its banks came to him. Sarah laughed more—or maybe he just remembered it that way. She had told him to keep Mary safe. She couldn't do that herself any more, not since he went back to Barkley. He had failed. Mary might be dying in his arms and he could do nothing about it. His daughter might start the Walk at thirteen years of age. Even though he was an exile from Barkley, he couldn't leave behind the teachings he grew up with. It was how he naturally looked at things—his instincts—and a little girl Walkin' was a great wrong. It didn't matter what had happened to him. It wasn't what he wanted for her. The significance of the husht was not lost on him. The Pastor used to call the Walkin' "Satan's seed," and "the devil's taint." Long sermons every Sunday that said the same things in different words. The devil was speeding Mary's way into his fiery embrace.

Thomas wasn't the strongest believer in Barkley—especially now—but even he could not deny the signs. He was facing the Good Lord's wrath. Every step he took towards Black Mountain was a defiance. He would be held to account on the day of his judgement. But the Good Lord was punishing him through Mary. His daughter was all he had left. He had caused so much trouble. Not for the first time, he wished he had burnt properly in the pyre pit.

Mountains grew on the horizon. At first, he did not recognise them for what they were. He had come so many miles that he had started to doubt Black Mountain existed. He had trusted the word of two Walkin'. Ghouls who stood beside a pit of dead men waiting for any sign of movement. They promised sanctuary. He had gambled on that promise.

The peaks of the Black Hills frayed like torn cloth. Thomas had no idea where the Walkin' community was. He stood at the edge of the forest and peered in. But even in daylight, the trees that covered the Black Hills justified the name and it was impossible to see much more than ten paces. Towering, the tree trunks were bare for the first twenty feet or so. Then, a circle of spiny branches, a gap, and then another circle, a gap, a circle, carrying on and on. The needles were the colour of his shadow. The forest was quiet, but that was likely his fault. He was surprised by how much that hurt, how lonely it made him feel. He had always loved the family's animals. It was a love he'd taken for granted.

There was no air amongst the trees. Humid and suffocating: a wonderfully uncomfortable feeling. It was a relief to feel anything after the arid Redlands. The pyre pit had made holes in his body and now the surrounding flesh was swelling up. The exposed muscles on his arms and legs bulged. Water was trying to find a place in his body. Old haunts, the corridors and passages where it used to be essential, had changed. Water was no longer needed.

Mary was having a worse time of it. She was sweating and shaking in his arms. Her lips were moving soundlessly. He stopped and laid her on the ground. He mopped her brow and watched her fight the fever. He didn't know how much time he had bought by scaring the shaggies.

There was something else. Each minute or so he glanced up and expected to see someone between the trees. He couldn't stop himself; he looked in every direction. There was no one there that he could see. But he could feel them. Watching him. It weighed on him, stooping his shoulders as he sat next to Mary. So much so, he wanted to lie down beside her and hope the feeling washed right over him. Instead, he stood up and challenged the watching eyes.

Row after row of trees stretched out in every direction. Thin trunks and needle-coated ground. The Redlands and now the Black Hills—he was getting used to seemingly endless horizons. He could lose Bellis and his men in the forest. Or he could simply become lost. He had no idea where to start looking. A whole community was bound to make its mark: a clearing of trees; roads or paths; and houses. A normal community.

Mary was looking worse. She was pale and slick with sweat. She was weak when the husht bit her—not enough food or water for days. She might die before they even reached Black Mountain. If that were the case, he could only hope his blood was as tainted as the men from Barkley believed. Was it all his fault? Had he been treating her as if she were a Walkin' already? Forgetting food. Ignoring water. He should have known the meat wouldn't last as long as Mary pretended. Did he really wish his daughter was like him?

4 : 4

It took them all day to round up the shaggies. They had to search together, in case they lost each other in the hills. The morning was cold and it didn't get any warmer as the day went on. The rocks seemed to steal the sun's heat. More than at any other time on the trail Nathaniel wished he was home. The men said only what was absolutely necessary. Nathaniel could tell the others shared his feeling. It was in the way they walked: shoulders rounded, eyes focused on the ground. He heard their sighs like the stirrings of a breeze.

The shaggies seemed neither pleased nor upset to see them. They found the animals, each alone but unharmed—grazing on the tough roots that sprouted between the rocks. Buster nuzzled his palm, looking for oats.

"What scared you off then?" Nathaniel said. He stroked the shaggie's mane. "You'd tell me if you could."

Buster was the first shaggie they recovered. The others had spread out across the hills. When the last shaggie was spotted the sun was setting. It was Samuel's. He and Nathaniel had left Bellis with the other animals at a fork in the path. Luke looked as if he might follow, but was too tired. It was a rare moment for Nathaniel to be alone with the farmer's son.

"I sure miss my bed," he said. Samuel nodded. "You still live with your ma and pa?"

"Yes."

"But there's a girl?"

Samuel's cheeks turned red. "Anna Jackson."

Nathaniel tried to picture Anna—the Jacksons' youngest daughter. There was a skinny daughter, a larger one, and the last was taller than Samuel by almost a foot. He hoped Anna was the skinny one, for Samuel's sake. They had plenty of years together before she'd need to put on weight around the hips.

"It must be nice for your ma and pa having some of you living at home," he said.

"There's me and Hannah."

"Are you and your sister close?"

"All of us are. Were," Samuel said. He motioned to the shaggie. "When I was little, I opened the gate to the lower field. I thought the shaggies would bolt; make a run to be free. They didn't move. I left the gate open all night and they were still there in the morning." He patted the side of the placid animal. "When Pa found out, I couldn't admit I did it. He beat all of us with his belt. I can remember Thomas's face as the belt came down—he grinned right at me. He knew, but didn't say anything. That's how it was with us."

"You might see that face again," Nathaniel said.

Samuel picked up the reins of his shaggie. "I don't think so."

Nathaniel was more tired that night than any before. They didn't go back to the space they'd camped in the previous night. He doubted they could find it even if they'd wanted to. Instead, they stumbled into a dead end the shape of a bulb. They put the shaggies at the far end. If something—or someone—spooked the animals again the men would know about it. Trampled by a scared shaggie; it would be a suitable end to the journey.

More pyre wood was put to flame. Nathaniel was sick to the pit of his stomach at the smell of roses. But he appreciated the warmth. They ate the last of the red-wink meat. Luke still refused to eat the animal he had killed. The acolyte survived on a shaggie's diet. The image of Luke's face buried between rocks, snuffling for roots, made Nathaniel smile to himself.

"We should set watch," Bellis said.

"What for? Much good it did last night," Luke said. Subtlety was clearly not required as a holy man. Perhaps it would detract from a man's ability to preach.

"I'm sorry I fell asleep." And he was. It meant more days in this wilderness. He wanted his bed and the warm body of his wife.

"Sorry isn't enough. Another mark against you; the Pastor will hear them all."

"If you're itching to say something, say it."

"You've done everything you could to make this journey end in failure," Luke said.

"I think you shook a few things loose when you bumped your head."

"First when the urn broke, then at the den of the red-wink, and then falling asleep on watch. You've wanted to turn back the whole time. Always trying to delay us."

"For some of us this is more than a jolly ride to the tune of the Good Book."

"You are a faithless man, Nathaniel!"

"You're just an ignorant boy."

"Quiet," Bellis ordered.

They said no more that night. Luke read the Good Book in silence. The others watched the fire, listening to it crack and spit. Nathaniel made sure Luke was fast asleep before bedding down.

Thomas watched Mary sleep until the heat of the day was well past. She thrashed out often, arms and legs jerking. He clutched at them, making sure she didn't hurt herself, and whispered soft sounds. The rest of the time she shivered. He took off his shirt and laid it over her. She shivered and sweated at the same time. He was no medicine man; what was he supposed to do? All he could do was wait and make sure nothing else happened to her. It was a kind of torture.

In the moments she was quiet, he went to the edge of the trees and looked back at the Redlands. Samuel, Gravekeeper Courie, Law-Man Bellis and the acolyte. Four men who would look so small. But they were worse than an entire regiment of the Protectorate.

It was early evening when she came to. Her eyelids fluttered. He was next to her with the water-skin in hand. She lifted her head enough to drink and then fell asleep again. It became their rhythm—brief moments when he gave her water followed by an hour or so of sleep. They passed the night this way. He didn't move an inch the whole time. The feeling they weren't alone didn't go away. At dawn she managed to sit up.

"Hello, my darlin'," he said. She smiled weakly.

"What happened?"

"You were bitten by a husht." He showed her the marks on her ankle. She had big black bags under her eyes. She needed a proper night's sleep and soon. He hoped Black Mountain had some beds, but he couldn't think why they would. He had no idea how far away the community at Black Mountain was. He asked her if she was able to walk a little. She nodded and handed him back his shirt. He helped her up. They made their way slowly, Mary using his arm as a support. The trees appeared to grow taller with each stride.

They had to rest regularly. She needed food after her fever to get back her strength. But they had none. He didn't mention her lies. When she pretended to eat from the waxy parcel, he turned away. Mary had new blisters on her heels. She wanted to pop the little bubbles, but he told her that would make it worse. She was quick to accept the advice of her elders; she got that from him—definitely not from her mother. Barkley shoes were not made for hiking through the Redlands or mountains.

"All these trees," she said, when they stopped again, and she rubbed her toes. "Think of what you could build." She was out of breath and took great gulps of air between each word.

"I like them as trees."

"I bet the Walkin' live in a huge city. Big buildings made of wood." She put her shoes back on. She paused, one shoe half on, as if listening. But the forest was so still, so quiet. A forest was not supposed to be like this. Animals, insects, all sorts of life should be making noise and moving and growing. "I feel like I'm playing catch-my-neighbour, but I don't know who with," she said.

"It's been there since we came into the forest. It could be the trees or the quiet or . . ."

Mary nodded. The ground began to rise. He had no idea how much more Mary could take and he didn't want to ask. The sun was getting weak. The light would disappear soon. Thomas watched her drink, ready to scold her if she spilt any. But she didn't.

"Dad, look," she said. Thomas shielded his eyes. He couldn't see anything but trees. Were his eyes that bad?

"What is it?"

"Two people. They're coming towards us."

Thomas squinted up the slope. He could just about make out two little lines. "What are they wearing?"

"They look red."

"Both of them?"

"Yes."

He saw them now. They were running, but a run that swung only one arm; the other clutched a rifle.

"We have to go," he said.

"What? Why?"

He pulled Mary to her feet. "They're soldiers. Not Walkin.'"

"But their uniform is red, like yours."

"And they tried to burn me once, remember?"

Mary didn't need any more persuading. She shuffled along the hillside as fast as she could. Thomas didn't look back to see if the soldiers followed. He hoped they would be too lazy or busy to chase them. Or too frightened of the thick trees in the fading light.

Mary was already slowing down. He wasn't surprised. She had walked farther in nine days than she had in her entire life, leaving aside the husht bite. When she stopped, she almost toppled over. He picked her up. He dashed behind a tree, his daughter cradled in his arms. He had carried her away from danger before and he would do it again. He heard men's voices. They were arguing.

"We're supposed to report back if we see anyone."

"Did you see blue uniforms?"

"And who knows what's in here? I'm being bitten, I swear it!"

"Shut up, will you?"

They were coming closer. He could make a run for it. With all the trees and the surprise the soldiers would barely get a shot off. But if they did and hit Mary—

Slowly, he let his daughter down.

"Stay here, tight against this tree," he whispered. She nodded. She was trying to breathe quietly. He smiled at her. "It will be okay."

Thomas peered around the trunk of the tree. He saw one of the soldiers clearly: the one who was complaining. He was overweight and carried his rifle badly. He was red in the face from the run. He wouldn't hit a barn door. The other man he saw skulking from tree to tree. Thomas waited. The fat one was close now. He had lost sight of the other. One more step.

Thomas rushed him. The man was so scared he dropped his gun. Thomas shouldered into him, knocking him down. The warm air of his breath poured out against Thomas's neck. Carrying on, Thomas dived behind a tree. The crack of gunfire followed him. Bark exploded. The fat soldier was wheezing—struggling to suck air into his lungs. The other man had to reload. Thomas went for the fallen rifle. He was almost there. He could feel the wooden stock in his hand. The heavy trigger.

The second soldier came at him, swinging his rifle like a club. Reloading wasn't the idea. The rifle caught him in the ribs. Bones cracked. He clamped his arm down over the gun. The soldier struggled to pull it clear. Panic started to set in; Thomas saw it on the man's face. That blow could have felled a tree.

"Simmons, get up!" the man yelled. Simmons continued to wheeze.

From beneath Thomas's shirt, a small ball of lead shot rolled out and hit the ground. Sarah's shot. It thumped loudly against the soil. Both of them watched it happen. Then the man grew more frantic. He realised fully what Thomas was. Part of him must have known, when Thomas barely budged when he was hit, but didn't want to admit it. Didn't want to lose all hope of leaving this forest alive. Thomas kept hold of the rifle. He wouldn't tire or grow weak.

A scream stopped them both. It was Mary. A figure in a pale robe ran out from behind a tree. It was carrying Mary. His daughter was fighting: flailing her arms and kicking her legs. But it made no difference.

4 : 5

Thomas pushed where he had been pulling. The soldier fell backwards. Thomas ran after Mary. The pale robe flashed between the trees. It was like chasing under-mutton through long grass.

He heard whistles. Ten, maybe twenty different high-pitched blasts. They chorused, a disjointed and harsh birdsong. He kept running. Below him on the hill, near the edge of the forest, men streamed through the trees. Men wearing a deep blue made darker by the shade of the pines. Shadows standing upright. They seemed to move slowly, at a steady rhythm. Every one of them held a rifle at the ready.

The robed figure was still in front of him. He was being led across a battle line. He tried to put as many tree trunks as possible between him and the rifles. Soon they would be in range. How many balls of lead would they waste on him? One lucky shot was all that was needed. But they didn't shoot.

Above him came more whistles and more men. The bright colour of the Protectorate seeped between the trees like spilt blood. They were eager. They ran down the slope. The air became full of lead shot and smoke and splintered bark. Rifles sounded like cannons beneath the branches. Behind their roar was the faint noise of men dying. There was little more than a hundred paces of rough ground between them. Thomas ran that ground. He ducked as low as he could. He tried to ignore the skirmish around him and hoped it would do the same.

He tore through the trees. He used his hands as much as his legs: to steady himself on the rough bark and then to propel him forward. There were fewer soldiers on either side of him now. He hesitated and searched for a flash of white. Bark exploded inches above his ruined hand. He jumped behind the trunk. He remembered doing the same in Barkley—dodging gunfire. Except this time there was no shaggie to hide behind. He peered around the tree. There was nothing.

A yell made him turn back. It was a battle cry. A man in red was charging him, rifle lowered. The bayonet was dull in the tree's shadow. He had always known them as shiny and in such great numbers that they were the tips of waves. There was no time to move. The blade went straight through him and into the tree. The soldier was little more than a boy—eighteen at most. He had light blond hair and soft cheeks. His face was pulled into a snarl that seemed rehearsed, like a red-wink cub at play. Both of them looked down to Thomas's chest. The boy's face dropped as he saw the lack of blood. Thomas punched the soldier on his shallow chin. He hit the ground hard. Thomas wrenched clear the rifle. He now had two bayonet holes, almost symmetrical on his stomach. He thought about taking the gun. He might be able to stop whoever had stolen Mary. But he couldn't bring himself to unman the boy-soldier.

Thomas had lost ground, but he spotted the pale cloth once more, like moonlight on the Col River before clouds took it away. He kept the glimpses of the robe right in front of him. He wasn't gaining. But he wouldn't tire. This was something Thomas could do indefinitely. He would chase his daughter until the end of days. Could whoever had taken her say the same? If it was a Walkin' then yes. He hoped Mary wasn't caught in a cold, dead embrace.

He was almost beyond the battle now. Its noise was faint, like a hymn sung behind closed doors. The landscape changed. The ground began to undulate. He skidded down slopes, fallen pine needles slippery as ice. The bottoms of these gullies were muddy; his feet made squelching noises. When the ground rose, he tried as hard as he could to run faster, but there was no change in his pace. This was the speed Thomas ran at. As he struggled with the rise he lost sight of them.

"Mary!" he cried from the top.

"Dad?"

Thomas followed the sound. He had stopped for only a moment. But it was a moment he might not get back. He ran on. He felt like crying when he saw the robe again, now a little further on, but he couldn't. He wouldn't cry for as long as he still lived.

"Dad, help!"

"I'm coming."

How could he have been this stupid? He took his daughter, his only child, away from her home and led her into the wilderness. He risked the Redlands, with its waterless bluffs and spiteful sun, and as if that weren't enough, he sought out a Walkin' town. A home for the dead. A battlefield would have been just as safe; and now she had seen that.

He pushed off another tree. Old bark crumbled in his hand. He had made the selfish choice. Again. Was he always this selfish? He tried to remember a lifetime ago. But what was sharing food or a plough when compared to the future of his child? He wanted Mary to know he cared. That he did not abandon her. And he wanted to know Mary. But seeing her snatched away . . . He had been selfish. If he could, he would ask the Good Lord for forgiveness. He came close to praying as he ran, but the Good Lord's ears would not hear him. He was a creature of the devil. And Thomas didn't know how to pray to the devil.

He was closer now. Maybe it wasn't a Walkin'. Maybe they were getting tired.

"I'm coming," he said, over and over. He would make it right. Fix his mistakes. He would never put his family in danger again.

The ground rose once more. He saw the robed figure in full at the top of the hill. Mary had stopped fighting. Then he lost them.

"Mary!" he screamed. There was no answer. He cast around. He saw no robe, only trees. The bottom of the gully was a mire. Then he spotted the footprints. He followed through the boggy mud, crusted with decaying needles.

"Dad." Mary was faint, but he was going in the right direction. The trees began to thin. The ground became firmer. He was worried he would lose the trail.

He stopped. He was standing on the edge of a clearing. In the middle, Mary was lying on the ground, seemingly asleep. A naked woman stood over her.

"Hello, Thomas."

4 : 6

He stepped into the clearing. He felt again the heavy sensation of being watched by many eyes; it weighed on his shoulders.

"What have you done to my daughter?"

"Nothing. She is exhausted from your journey. And the husht bite," the Walkin' said. "We have time to talk before she wakes."

"Who are you?"

"Mary didn't recognise me either. But I knew her right away. She has changed; not as much as you, though." The woman smiled. Her skin was a watery silver. Blue veins criss-crossed her arms. Her stomach was bloated in a slack and withered way. Her hair was long and black, tumbling in ringlets, but dull. He suddenly felt conscious of his burnt and withered face.

"Lydia Courie," he said. "I saw you burn on a pyre."

"You saw what you expected. What the gravekeeper showed you." Her robe was under Mary. "I haven't seen a young girl in decades. Even in her fever she looks beautiful. You should not have brought her here."

"I was told this was a sanctuary."

"For you," she said.

"She had to leave Barkley; they would have killed her. I had to keep her safe!"

"What is 'safe'? It sounds as if you're chasing a dream, Thomas. Your daughter was not safe in Barkley. Or the Redlands. Where would she be safe?" She sat next to Mary and stroked her hair.

"Stop touching her."

Lydia looked up at him. "Be careful, Thomas. This forest looks after its own; it's dangerous for outsiders. Even Walkin.'"

"Is this Black Mountain?" He looked around—his own question seemed foolish with no obvious buildings or streets. The trees made an odd rustling sound, like long-tails scratching in the attic, though there wasn't a breeze.

"No. Black Mountain is a long way from where you are."

"What do you mean?" He decided to sit; it didn't feel right to stand above a naked woman. It was somehow threatening.

"Both armies come into these hills looking for a Walkin' town. They expect it to be like Barkley or wherever they're from. They never find a thing." Lydia went back to stroking Mary's hair, despite what he'd said. His daughter stirred, but didn't wake. "Mary couldn't find Black Mountain, even if she looked her whole life. You wouldn't either, as long as she's with you."

"I don't understand."

"We know."

Thomas cast around, trying to find who Lydia meant by "we." Seeing no one he asked her.

"Black Mountain is more than a place. It is a commune in every sense."

"Are we being watched?" he said, still feeling those eyes on him.

"Always." She closed her eyes. "There are others from Barkley in the forest. Nathaniel, Bellis, Luke, and Samuel. They have stopped. They are feeding their shaggies and arguing about which direction to take. Two of them have rifles—though they are old and worn." She looked at him. "It is good to see old friends."

"Impossible."

"The Walkin' here are very close and very old," she said, as if that were explanation enough.

"You're trying to trick me."

"Why would I do that?" she said.

He couldn't think of a reason. But he wasn't thinking right at all—from the moment he stepped into the clearing.

"Don't you miss Nathaniel? Barkley?" he said.

"I could never go back. What would I do? See the man I loved grow old and die. All those men and women I once called friends. None of them would Walk with me and, given the choice, none of them would want to."

Nathaniel had never been the same since Lydia's death. Now Thomas knew why. It wasn't just the normal grief, though that would be enough. Nathaniel knew she was still somewhere in the world.

"If we're not supposed to be here, why did you take Mary?" he said.

"We saw the battle coming. You were in the middle. It was decided she was worth saving."

"But I wasn't."

"You saved yourself," she said. "As we knew you would."

Mary stirred. Thomas helped her to sit up a little. She drank from the water-skin and fell back onto the robe.

"I will find her some food," Lydia said. "But, Thomas, do not leave the clearing." She stood and wandered off naked between the trees.

He brushed the hair from Mary's forehead. "What are we going to do, my darlin'?" he said. Black Mountain, wherever it was, whatever it was, might be a home for him, but apparently not for his daughter.

Lydia returned carrying roots and a handful of berries. They waited in silence for Mary to wake fully. Thomas had much to think on and much he didn't understand. Lydia seemed happy enough to watch Mary.

Mary ate the berries first. They looked sour, but she made quick work of them. The roots she had to chew and chew, her jaw working hard until it started making sounds like footsteps on a wooden floor. She didn't say a word while she ate; didn't question where she was or what had happened. Food was her world. When she finished, Lydia stood up. She went over to the edge of the clearing. Thomas followed.

"You see these flowers?" she said, kneeling down. "They only grow in this part of the forest. It's difficult to find them in daylight; they like the moon."

"One story says they are ghosts-in-waiting. That when a soul begins the Walk, a flower grows. When the soul rests finally, the flower drops its petals." She gazed at the patches of flowers that pooled like milk. "I say sorry when I pick them. There's a flower somewhere for you. But not for Mary."

"What now?" Thomas said.

"There is only one way out of this forest for you and Mary. It has been decided. I will take you."

4 : 7

When an event changes the world, it is fair to say the world is the first to know about it. Before the event is given a name, before it has been recorded and talked about and then lost in the archives of history, the world has already moved on.

Imagine a child throwing a stone into a still pond. On point of impact the world has changed. But the child is unaware the act has had any effect until it sees the ripples of water. Where the stone fell, the world has moved on.

Imagine, then, that the world is actually the life of a single man or woman. An ancient poet once said: 'No man is an island.' I happen to agree. One man is every island. They are a world. An event changes them, and in that instant they feel the effects and move on. Each other human feels the ripple.

One begins the Walk. An event. A change. He or she accepts what has happened. Across their world loved ones, friends, enemies, all register those ripples to varying degrees.

How do I know this to be true? Am I privy to some long-lost arcana? Do I have magical or mechanik power? Or have I simply Walked for three hundred years, with open eyes and ready ears?

—a transcribed extract from candidate Cirr's opening speech, in the Black Mountain Common Consensus of Winters 2886

Luke heard many gunshots. The sound danced between the trees. Somehow he had a general impression of where the fighting was, but the echoes seemed to come from everywhere at once. Bellis called them to a stop. The shaggies pawed at the ground and nodded their heads violently. Were the animals picking up on their riders' nervousness, or was it the other way around? Bellis and Courie readied their rifles. Looking at Nathaniel's rifle, Luke could still feel the ghost of it against his shoulder from when he shot the red-wink. The sudden heaviness of the metal barrel that only registered after he had fired; a lot of things only registered afterwards. That was how men used guns.

"Could be the army," Bellis said.

Luke righted his glasses. "They said these mountains were infested with Walkin.' Would the Walkin' use guns?" He had imagined the creatures of the night with talons and claws, rending and tearing at innocent souls.

"I don't know," Bellis said. He started them moving again, slower now. His rifle balanced at the top of his saddle.

The air between the trees was hot and wet. Trickles of sweat ran down Luke's ribs. His palms were slick. At first he thought his scabs were bleeding—that he had become used to. Instead, the sweat stung where he had cut himself. It made holding the leather reins uncomfortable. He felt uncomfortable all over. He was surprised to find himself wishing he were back in the Redlands, with enough air and space to breathe. This wet heat smothered him. His cassock smelt damp and salty. He shivered at the thought of a bath.

He missed seeing Sarah. It seemed as though decades had passed since he had watched her through the window. Soft skin in the steam. Her blonde hair let loose. He prayed for forgiveness for his lusty thoughts. But with her husband finally put to rest, and their infernal spawn with him, Sarah would need another man. She couldn't manage by herself. And Luke would be there. Luke, who had personally seen to the salvation of her husband's and daughter's souls. The rewards she would lavish on him . . . He shifted on his saddle, suddenly aware of his rising manhood. He recited his prayers until he regained his composure.

These trees would provide plenty of pyre wood. He wondered if the dampness in the air might affect how they burnt. It lacked the scented blessing, but perhaps there would be a natural replacement to cover the smell of burning flesh. Blessed pyre wood was too good for the creature that had forsaken his faith and stolen his own daughter. Perhaps it was better they had used it to warm the bodies of righteous men.

More gunshots. Luke had to fight to keep his shaggie under control. He supposed the animals were as unaccustomed to the forest as he was. The way the trees limited his vision more than his affliction did—it would be unnerving to a primitive beast of burden. He patted its neck as he had seen Nathaniel do.

Thomas McDermott came into view. It was as if he had been hiding behind a tree and then suddenly stepped out not more than ten paces in front of them. He was holding his daughter's hand. There was another with them, wearing a pale robe. The shaggies all stopped—heedless of their riders. The animals' ears flattened on their heads. The McDermott creature stood similarly frozen. Luke had hoped for this moment for so many days, he didn't believe it was real. Had he wished McDermott into being?

Bellis raised his rifle. Nathaniel slowly followed his example.

The creature put himself between the guns and the little girl. He threw an accusing look at his robed companion. "What have you done? They will kill her!"

"This is the way it has to be, Thomas. Mary belongs with her own kind."

"They will shoot you too."

"No, they won't. We have watched them for some time."

The two creatures were arguing. It was more than Luke could contain.

"Minions of Satan! Hell has boiled over onto this earth. Shoot them, Bellis. Shoot them all!"

4 : 8

Luke's outburst seemed to go unheard. The Walkin' were focused entirely on the two men holding guns. Neither 'Keeper nor Law-Man fired. Nathaniel glanced over at Bellis, his old friend.

"There's no more running," Bellis said.

"Bellis!" Luke said.

"We're not here to kill—"

"Thomas? Is it you?"

"Hello, Samuel. I'm sorry you had to be here."

Samuel shook his head once and then lowered his gaze. He had tears at the edge of his eyes.

The Walkin' looked at Bellis. "Why couldn't you let us be?"

"You made this happen when you took Mary," Bellis said.

"Leave her to be killed? Is that what you would have done, Bellis? Nathaniel?"

The Gravekeeper didn't answer. He wasn't looking at the creature, but at the woman in the robe.

"Lydia?" he said.

"Nathaniel. You're looking well," the Walkin' said.

Nathaniel got off his shaggie. He left his rifle on the saddle. So often he had dreamed about her. Thought of her when his mind should have been on Rachel. Remembered her dark ringlets when his hand touched a blonde ponytail. "What . . . Why are you here?"

"I live here, now."

"You could have chosen anywhere in the world. You were so close. All these years," he said. Nathaniel embraced Lydia.

"I'm sorry."

"*I'm* sorry. I let this happen."

"Don't be. I am happy. More than ever," she said.

"'Happy'!" Luke snapped. "The servants of the devil do not know what happiness is." Again, they ignored the acolyte.

"She doesn't have to die, Nathaniel. You know this," Lydia said.

"The husht's tongue," Luke screamed. "It is divine *law*. The word of the Good Lord. Why are we listening to demons?"

"A moment alone, Bellis?" Nathaniel said. The Law-Man nodded.

Nathaniel led Lydia away from the scene. He could hear Luke's objections behind him.

"You say you're happy. I'm still sorry."

"It's okay. I've watched you in the forest."

She was still beautiful. Her long dark hair, just as he remembered it. He wanted to touch her face. To kiss her. But he couldn't. He took her hand in his. That was enough.

"I've thought about seeing you for so long," Lydia said. "About what I would say. It's as hard as I imagined it would be. Can you make me a promise? Promise not to open it until you are back in Barkley?"

"Open what?"

She pressed a letter into his hands.

Nathaniel returned alone. The Gravekeeper seemed on the edge of tears. Had he been turned? Enslaved? Luke struggled with the need to save a soul and his aversion to the Walkin'.

The way Nathaniel had casually hugged her. Her hands on his bare arms.

Nathaniel stood by himself, watching the forest. Luke sneered at the man. He had clearly lost his senses.

"Thomas, you just come with us," Bellis said.

"No. Do it now!" Luke said.

"This forest is busy. Come on, get moving." The Law-Man motioned with his rifle.

The creature and his spawn started out ahead of them. Bellis kept his rifle aimed, but Nathaniel didn't pick his up again.

"What is wrong with you?" Luke asked him. "Are you bewitched? I can perform an exorcism."

"That was my first wife."

Luke was stunned. He had no memory of Nathaniel with a woman other than Rachel. And why was she now a Walkin'? She should have burnt like everyone who died in Barkley. He was the *Gravekeeper*. It was his job. Nathaniel dropped to the back of their group.

Samuel was still silently crying for his brother. The little girl looked back at them. She hadn't said a word. She was pale, her cheeks drained of colour, and her hair lank and lifeless. Had she already turned? There was something wrong in the way she looked at them, as if she were older than she really was. It was the same acceptance of life and events Luke had seen in the elderly; people who had seen enough. He shuddered under her stoic gaze and was glad when she turned away again. The earth would sigh with relief when it was cleansed of two such abominations.

The forest was quiet. The sound of gunfire was far enough behind them now to be drowned out by the soft thumps of shaggie hooves. No one spoke. Luke was ready in case the Walkin' tried to escape. He sat up in his saddle, his heels almost touching the flanks of his mount. His toes itched with the need to fulfil his divine charge, to save these souls, but he tried to stay calm. He had become over-excited before; it had delayed this moment and given him a bump below his crown. He rode next to Bellis, as close as he dared get to the creatures.

"That's far enough," Bellis said. They stopped in a small clearing. The trees were thinning here; they were close to the edge of the forest.

Luke began to chant in a high-pitched voice. "'With the indignation of His anger. And the flame of a devouring fire. He has made it deep and large. Its pyre is fire with much wood. The breath of the LORD, like a stream—'"

Bellis slapped him. Luke felt his cheek. The skin was hot and tingled. He glared at Bellis, who stared plainly back.

They got off the shaggies. Nathaniel took their reins, still avoiding the sight of the abominations. Nathaniel lacked the strength and courage of true faith. Luke pitied the old man.

"Bellis. Listen, now. Do what you will with me. But let my daughter go." The Walkin' held out his hands, entreating them. Bile rose in Luke's throat. He swallowed hard—he would not ruin everything in a moment of physical weakness.

"On your knees, Thomas," Bellis said.

The Walkin' complied. The little girl threw herself on him.

"Don't hurt him!" she cried. Her face became puffy and tears rained down her cheeks.

"She's just a little girl, Bellis. Samuel, she's your niece, for Christ's sake! You can't do this," the creature said.

Nathaniel went over to her. "It's okay, Mary. Everything is going to be okay." He loosened her grip and picked her up. She fought, but he ignored her small fists.

Bellis took his position behind the creature's head. He cocked his rifle. Luke held up his hands—crucifix in one, the Good Book in the other.

"'The breath of the LORD, like a stream of brimstone kindles it,'" he sang.

"No!" Samuel shouted. He strode purposefully towards Bellis. "He's my brother. It should be me that does it."

"Keep her safe, Samuel," the creature pleaded. "You saw her every Sabbath. She ate at the family table."

Bellis was still for a while. Samuel stood his ground. The Law-Man stepped away from the Walkin'.

"Take Nathaniel's rifle. Nice and slowly now, Samuel." Bellis moved to a spot where he could cover both the McDermotts. Did he think Samuel might turn on them? He was young, but devout. Luke had talked to him about the Good Book many times on their journey. Luke was sure Samuel could be trusted to do the right thing.

Samuel took the gun from Nathaniel's saddle. It seemed small in the boy's large hands. The girl continued to struggle.

"I love you, Mary," the creature said. Luke felt the bile in his stomach. He wanted to spit at this nightmare, this false life, that claimed to know of "love." Samuel stood in the same manner Bellis had.

Luke raised the Good Book once more. "'For the life of the flesh is in the blood: it is the blood that maketh an atonement for the soul.'"

The shot thundered.

4 : 9

Thomas opened his eyes. Mary had turned away, her face buried in 'Keeper Courie's stomach. He could feel the metal of the rifle's barrel on the back of his head. It was cold. He didn't dare move. He didn't understand why he was still alive, but these few moments could be a gift; he wanted to spend them watching his daughter. He expected a darkness to come. After that, he had no idea.

Luke Morris fell to the ground. The young man's knees buckled. His descent seemed weightless and accepting—until he hit the ground. Above his right eye was a dark red hole. He was still smiling, his mouth open, ready to continue reading from the Good Book. Gradually, his smile slackened.

"It's okay, Samuel," Bellis said. The metal remained against the back of Thomas's head.

"I don't—"

"Let him go."

His brother stepped back. Thomas sagged; the barrel a great burden he had been holding.

"Dad!" Mary ran to him. He hugged her, reeling from the warmth of her body. Her cheeks were wet against the side of his face. Behind him, he heard Samuel drop the rifle. Mary started to laugh. It was a manic, pinched sound. Nathaniel checked Luke over.

"Bellis. You killed him," Nathaniel said.

"We're taking Mary back home; without you, Thomas. We never saw a Walkin' the whole time. We found her with a man. In the struggle, he killed Luke."

"What are you talking about? You just shot Luke Morris," Nathaniel said.

"No. I didn't."

"You're asking us to lie?"

"I'm telling you. It's the only way for Mary."

Nathaniel looked at the girl. Thomas had kept quiet through the whole exchange. This was the best he could hope for: his daughter safe. It was all he had ever wanted.

"Why, Bellis?" Thomas said.

The Law-Man spat. "I don't kill children."

4 : 10

The LORD said, "What have you done?
Listen! Your brother's blood
cries out to me from the ground."

Genesis

EPILOGUE

Dear Nathaniel,

Some of the words written here may be painful and you may not wish to hear them. But they are long overdue. There is much I owe you.

I know you must work as hard as ever, Nathaniel. It is not an easy job and I know from our life together there is much burden to shoulder. I hear you have married Rachel Ginsly. She was a kind woman when I knew her. I wish you both happiness.

My life now is one of contentment. You may feel guilt over the choice you made, but do not feel it on my behalf. I have found a community that values me. I do not, and never will, blame you for anything.

The time we had together, though it may not have seemed so, was the happiest of my first life. It has given me countless fond memories. I carry those memories with me, wherever I go. Whilst they give me strength, they do not hold me back from enjoying my time now. Please, Nathaniel, find joy in the moments you have.

I loved you in a different life. Let me go.

Lydia

He read the letter three times. He glanced around the grave-yard. The wind shook the willows, but there was calm amongst the headstones.

He stood up and folded the letter into his pocket. He'd only just arrived at the cemetery, but he went home.

Rachel wasn't there. He walked over to the cooking pot. He lit some kindling and held the letter to it. A ring of black ate its way towards his hand; an orange tongue licking over the words. He dropped the last of the letter into the pot.

He carried it out into the garden. Careful of the breeze, he tipped the ashes into the empty urn on the porch.

Along with the ash he poured in every touch, every kiss, every heated word and every act of kindness.

The urn had been made for Mary.

He would bury Lydia.

ACKNOWLEDGEMENTS

Thanks to the staff of the departments of English & Creative Writing at Aberystwyth and Bath Spa universities, for all their support and advice. Particular thanks to Matthew Francis and Tricia Wastvedt who have both shown infinite patience when presented with pages. To my editor and agent; I've tested how far the "because they're paid to" logic stretches on many occasions.

Special thanks to Katherine Stansfield for reading everything I write, Keith Boulton for his SF insight, and Ian Redman at Jupiter for initially seeing something in the Walkin'.

ABOUT THE TYPE

Typeset in Swift EF, 11/15 pt.

Named for an acrobatic city bird native to Holland, Swift was designed by Gerard Unger in 1985 to meet the need for a typeface that could remain crisp and clear after coming off the high-speed newspaper presses of the day. For its original distribution as a PostScript font, it was leased to German foundry Elsner+Flake.

Typeset by Scribe Inc., Philadelphia, Pennsylvania.